P9-DVV-491

THERE WILL BE A ROAD

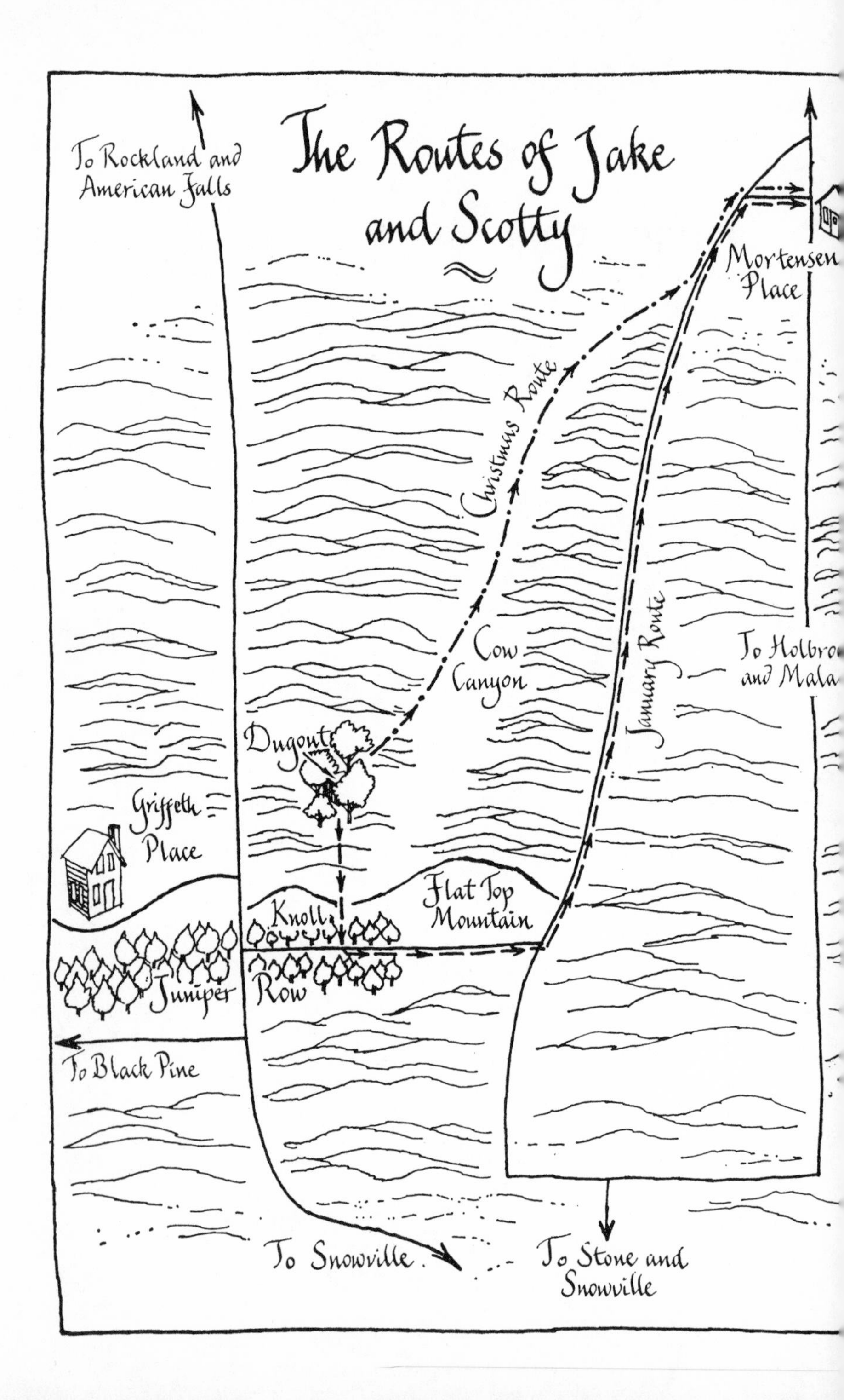
The Routes of Jake and Scotty
To Rockland and American Falls
Mortensen Place
Christmas Route
January Route
Cow Canyon
To Holbro
and Mala
Dugout
Griffeth Place
Knoll
Flat Top Mountain
Juniper Row
To Black Pine
To Snowville
To Stone and Snowville

THERE WILL BE A ROAD

DWIGHT JENSEN

DOUBLEDAY & COMPANY, INC.
GARDEN CITY, NEW YORK 1978

All of the characters in this book are fictitious; any resemblance to actual persons, living or dead, is purely coincidental.

ISBN: 0-385-14003-7
Library of Congress Catalog Card Number 77-90810

Printed in the United States of America
First Edition

To my father,
Glenden Jacob Jensen

THERE WILL BE A ROAD

CHAPTER ONE

An old truck labored its way up a grade and arrived at the crest of the highest ridge in the valley. The valley was ten or twelve miles from east to west. The road that ran from horizon to horizon mounted and descended a series of rolling ridges. It was a brown valley of dead November grass, lying under a dark gray sky. Spots of bare white earth broke the brownness here and there. Clumps and patches of blue-green junipers grew on the ridges. One long thicket of these stunted trees, a thicket perhaps eight or ten miles long and a quarter of a mile wide, paralleled the road most of the way across the valley. The road, though, stayed a few hundred yards south of the trees. A very tall juniper tree might be twice as high as a man.

The driver—everyone called him Bud—bent forward over his steering wheel. He surveyed the rolling valley with a frown and a squint. The truck had climbed the ridge in a whining second gear. Now it began to regain speed. Bud stepped on the clutch and shifted to third.

The man in the middle, Scotty, was older than the other two, but still not very old. He dozed, jerking upright and awake when the truck lurched or when he bumped into one of his companions. Each time he woke he looked about, settled back, closed his eyes, and began to doze again.

The man on the right was young, slender, with skin already roughened and reddened by weather. He wore a plaid cloth cap and a worn jacket over his work clothes. His blue eyes scanned the valley. His name was Jake.

The driver asked, "Where do we go?"

Jack said, "Stay to the right. This road goes on down the hill and cuts through Juniper Row."

"Ya. I know that."

"Couple miles north of that is a turn. I'll show you where."

The driver fixed his attention for the moment on a point far off on the landscape. Finally he asked, "What's that?"

"Where?"

"North of Juniper Row a quarter mile or so. Maybe two miles off."

"Looks like a load of hay."

"He must of hauled it up from Snowville."

"Where's he taking it?"

"Don't look to me like he's taking it no place. He's stopped."

"I mean when he goes again."

"There's a few places up that way to the west. Five or six families and a little school spread out in that next valley. I imagine he's one of them."

The truck was picking up speed as it cruised down the gentle slope to the low part of the valley. Jake looked out the window at a big clump of juniper they were passing. The rise on which the juniper stood gave way to a downward slope covered with sagebrush and dead bunch grass.

Jake said, "There goes a rabbit."

"There's lotsa rabbits here."

"Rabbits ain't bad to eat in the fall."

"If there's nothing else."

"We used to eat a lot of rabbits. Snowshoes in the winter, some jack rabbits in the fall. As many as I could snare, or shoot with a .22." Jake scanned the rolling land around him. They were no longer high. Their view was limited. "Well, I shouldn't say 'used to.' We still eat them if anybody has time to go after them. It seems I don't never have the time no more."

Bud said, "You might catch a few up here."

"I think I'll set some snares. A few rabbits will make that pig last longer."

The road leveled out and ran between barbed-wire fences. The wire, four strands, was strung between rough posts cut from the juniper that grew on the slopes and ridges. Jake studied the fence as it hurried by.

The truck slowed. The driver said, "Here's the Snowville road."

"Turn right."

They turned from the hard dirt to a wider, graveled road. The driver hunched forward, stared up at the gray cold sky. "I bet it snows tonight."

"No," Jake said. "It won't snow."

"It's going to be rough on you if it snows right away."

They drove into the belt of juniper and the dark day grew darker in the shadows. They rode in silence for half a minute or more and then came out the other side, climbing an easy slope toward another ridge.

Bud said, "Think I oughta wake Scotty up?" He took a hand from the wheel and jabbed an elbow into the ribs of the man in the middle. "Wake up, Scotty."

Scotty slowly opened his eyes. "Wake up why?"

"You're missing the scenery."

"I've already seen it." Scotty closed his eyes again.

Bud said, "You ain't going to get no posts cut out here."

"Why not?"

"You'll be too busy waking up Scotty so he won't starve to death."

Scotty, his eyes closed, said, "I ain't never slept through a meal in my life."

"If Jake was cooking rabbit for supper, I think I'd sleep through it."

Jake said, "Slow down. Take that right turn up there. The road's pretty bad. Take it easy."

Bud shifted down to low and made the turn. The old truck eased itself onto a rutted, bumpy dirt road that would have oozed mud after a heavy rain. Sometimes in low, sometimes in second, he steered the truck along the ruts. The flatbed of the truck swayed and lurched. Now and again the three men in the cab were jerked around by the bumps.

Bud said, "You say this road's pretty bad?"

"Ya."

"I'm glad you told me. I'd hardly notice otherwise."

They pulled over a rise of ground, descended into a wash, and the driver put the truck into compound to ease it across the ripples of frozen mud in the bottom of the wash and take it up the far side.

"How much further is it?" Bud asked.

"See how this road curves around and goes up that little hill? Stop on top of that hill."

They were back in low, careening and lurching. Bud said, "How can Scotty sleep on a road like this?"

Jake said, "Just like a baby in a cradle."

One lone juniper and a few sparse sagebrush grew on the top of the knoll where they stopped. Doors on both sides of the cab opened. Jake climbed quickly down from his side. He walked in a little circle, taking the kinks out of his legs and looking up at the gray sky and the rows of ridges all around. The driver climbed down from his side of the cab. A moment later, Scotty followed Jake out and slammed the door behind him. The tinny sound of the door banging shut hung in the cold air. Scotty stood with his hands in his jacket pockets, looking across the sagebrush toward the Snowville road.

Jake walked up to the bed of the truck. He began to untie the knot by which a rope was fastened to the front corner of the flatbed. The rope stretched across the bed, lashing down a pile of bags and bundles that were tucked up against the back of the cab. Bud began untying the ropes on the other side of the truck.

Bud asked, "Is this where you're gonna camp? This wind will blow across this hump like sixty and take you both off with it."

"No," Jake said. "See that canyon behind you? Not the one at the foot of Flat Top Mountain. The next one north."

The driver turned around to look at the canyons. "Ya." He turned back and resumed his work.

"There's a good camping place up that canyon about two miles from here."

Scotty turned around from contemplating the valley. "Two miles? You didn't tell me about no two miles."

Bud said, "How you gonna get this stuff up there?"

"Carry it."

"*Carry* it?"

"I don't think it's gonna grow legs and walk."

"Scotty, I think Jake just found a way to wake you up."

Scotty came up to the truck and began untying one of the ropes. "That's okay. I'll take the hundred pounds of potatoes in one hand and the half a pig in the other and load the flour on my back. Jake can carry the rest."

"That's too much for me," Jake said. "You better carry the guns and the bedrolls, too."

"Stick 'em in my pocket," agreed Scotty.

Scotty began coiling up the loose rope. Jake pressed his palms down on the flatbed and hoisted himself smoothly onto the truck. He began picking up the bags and bundles on the truck and handing them off to Bud, who carried them a few steps from the truck and put them down around the one small cedar on the knoll. A hundred-pound bag of potatoes. Fifty pounds of flour. Half a hog, wrapped in white flour sacking. Two thick bedrolls. A flour sack that rattled and thunked with its cargo of pots and pans, tin plates and cups, and jars and cans of condiments. A sack of beans. A case of canned peas. Four axes. A .22, a hunting rifle, and a shotgun. A gunny sack heavy with ax heads, ammunition, whetstones, and a few tools. A white canvas tent folded into a bundle. A small camp stove. A shovel.

"That's everything," Jake said.

The driver put down the tent and looked back at the truck. "Are you sure? I ain't seen you unload the rocking chair or the plow so far."

"I'll bring them in the next load," Jake said. He leaped off the truck, picked up the camp stove from the edge of the flatbed, and carried it over to the little tree.

"What shall I do with this rope?" Scotty asked.

"Take it with," Jake said.

"He's gonna use it to snare jack rabbits," Bud said.

"Easier to just lasso them," Scotty said.

Bud stood with his gloved fists on his hips, looking down at the heap of supplies and equipment that clustered around the small tree. Then he looked up toward the distant canyon that was to be the destination for all this. He shook his head a couple of times, sighed, and let his hands drop to his sides. He turned and walked toward the truck.

"The wind's starting to blow," he said.

Jake followed him to the truck, taking the leather glove off his right hand as he walked. Jake dug the hand into the pocket of his pants. He came out with three silver dollars. He said, "Bud."

Bud stopped, turned around. "Ya?"

"Here's three bucks for your gas and your trouble."

Bud looked at the money without taking it. "You sure you can afford that?"

"Ya. Better'n you can afford not to take it."

"You have some money left?"

"There's no place to spend money up here. But I left some at home. You don't need to worry none."

"Okay." Bud put out his hand, accepted the money, put it into his own pocket. "I guess I oughta stay and help you pack this stuff up there," he said.

"No, you got things to do. You done all you promised. Thanks a lot."

"Ya. I better get back. I should cut some wood yet today."

Jake laughed, just a one-syllable laugh. "So should we."

"Good luck."

"Thanks."

Bud got into the cab of his truck. The door whanged shut. Scotty had been walking slowly to the front of the truck. Now, at a nod of the head from Bud, he bent and began to turn the crank. The engine caught almost at once. Scotty fastened the crank back in place and stepped out of the way. Bud raised his right hand in a little farewell gesture. The truck began to move. It went forward, turned to the right, stopped, backed up while turning to the left, made another right turn and drove forward, coming back past Jake and Scotty. Bud did not look toward them. They stood side by side, watching Bud drive down the knoll and out onto the flatter ground. The truck bumped and lurched as he eased it toward the graveled road. When the truck had gone about halfway, Jake turned and walked over to their pile of gear. Scotty followed closely. They stood side by side, looking down at their equipment.

"We need the tent," Jake said. "We need the blankets. We need the dishes. We better take the guns. We better take the meat."

Scotty asked, "What time is it?"

Jake looked up toward the sky, squinting. He looked back down. "Can't see the sun. About eleven-thirty or so, I'd guess."

"If you're going to be the boss of this outfit, you ought to have a watch."

"Well, it's mealtime when somebody gets the cooking done, and it's quitting time when it gets dark. Why else do we need a watch?"

"A man can't argue with that," Scotty said.

Jake looked long at the pile of supplies and equipment. "Maybe it wasn't smart of me to butcher that pig. If the weather turns warm, it's gonna spoil."

Scotty said, "You'd stand in the desert and worry about drowning, wouldn't you."

Another silence, then Jake said, "Well . . ." He bent over, picked up the hunting rifle. There was a canvas sling attached to it. He slung the weapon over his shoulder. He picked up one of the thick bedrolls. It had been tied with clothesline rope and the same rope wrapped in rags had been arranged so that the bundle could be slung from a person's shoulders. Jake fitted it over his arms.

Scotty was also fitting his bedroll to his back. Jake squatted, picked up the long length of the pig, and stood again, boosting it onto his shoulder. It hung there awkwardly in its white wrapping. Jake looked around at the rest of the stuff, then squatted again, carefully balancing the pig, and picked up the white canvas package of the tent. He lifted it by the ropes that tied it.

"You better bring an ax," he said, "and that flour sack with the dishes in."

Scotty picked up both with one hand. With the other he slung the fifty pounds of flour over one shoulder. "We better not leave this here," he said. "If it rains, it's gonna ruin it."

Jake led out, walking down the eastern slope of the knoll. Scotty looked around at the equipment again.

"I hate to leave those guns here," he said.

"They'll be okay."

Scotty looked again. He put down the things in his hands. He tucked the .22 and the shotgun as far under the little tree as he could get them. He put the sack of potatoes where it would help hide them. He leaned some other things against the potatoes. Then he picked up his load again and followed Jake.

The downhill slope leveled out for a ways, then became an uphill slope. It grew steeper as Jake led the way toward the ridge. Halfway up, Scotty stopped and exhaled a great gust of air.

"Wouldn't it be as easy to walk up the canyon?" he said.

Jake stopped, turned around, drew two deep breaths before answering. "It's easier to walk on top of the ridge. Anyhow, we've got to climb most of the way now or later. Might as well do it while we're fresh." He turned and resumed the climb. Scotty kept up.

The last twenty yards were steep. Each man picked his wav step by step, getting the upper foot firmly and carefully planted before putting his weight on it and raising the other foot to a new stepping place. They leaned forward under their loads and both breathed heavily. But when they gained the crest of the ridge they walked on for several yards before Jake stopped and knelt and let his load slide down his arms to the ground. Scotty put his things down a few feet away.

Both men stood, stretched their arms, wiggled arms and shoulders to relax them. Jake turned and looked back the way they had come.

They were higher than the knoll. They could see their little cluster of gear around the small tree. Between them and the knoll, and beyond it and on all sides, lay the brown terrain with its gray-green sage, its blue-green junipers, and the cold gray day over all.

Jake said, "That truck's still there."

"What truck?"

"See?" He pointed. "A little north of Juniper Row. That's where they were when we first seen them."

"Don't look like they've moved."

"I think they're stuck." Jake stared across the valley at the spot that was the truck. "I guess we better go help them."

"That's an hour's walk across there."

"Naw, it's a couple of miles."

"They'll be gone when we get there."

"I doubt it. I think they're stuck. They might need help."

CHAPTER TWO

The walk took maybe half an hour, maybe less. With nothing to carry, they moved rapidly across the terrain. They followed the contours of the land, making no effort to do the climbing and descending that a beeline would have cost.

The truck was still there. They did not see it from the time they left the high ground until they crested a little rise and saw it a couple of hundred yards ahead of them. To their left they could see the dirt road it had followed once it turned off the gravel. They inclined toward the road. The sagebrush here was thicker than it had been east of the gravel road and the walking was not as easy. They made the last hundred yards of the approach on the road.

At first they saw only one figure. It was crouched under one edge of the truck, working with a shovel. Presently another figure emerged into the open on the other side of the truck and stood looking toward them across the sagebrush. That person must have called to the one with the shovel, for the one with the shovel stood up beside the truck and also looked toward them. As they drew closer they saw that the person with the shovel was a man well into middle age; the other was a woman about the same age. They walked toward the man. No one said anything until they were eight or ten feet apart and the young men stopped. Jake said, "Howdy."

"Hello."

"Looks like you've got trouble."

"You might say that."

It was easy to identify the trouble. The man had gone somewhere —probably to Snowville—and loaded his truck with hay. On this dirt road it should have been safe going, even though rough, because the ground was hard. But the road led through a dry creek bed. It had not always been dry; water had run here last summer or spring. Some had formed a pool. The pool had frozen. The man, instead of avoiding it as he crossed the creek bed, had allowed his right rear tire to drive across it. The truck had broken the ice, and beneath the ice was water and mud. It was not only that the truck was stuck. The side of the creek made an abrupt rise just beyond the mudhole. The frame of the truck rested on the ground.

Jake walked down into the creek bed and squatted so he could see under the truck. He put a hand on the truck bed to help him keep his balance and leaned forward under the truck for a better look. The drive shaft was close to the ground. The man had been digging at the creek bank, trying to get the frame loose from the dirt.

Scotty said, "You got pretty far to the right."

"I was trying to miss a big rock on the other side."

"Might almost of paid to move the rock."

Jake stood up and walked around the truck. The left front tire was an inch or so off the ground. He came around to the back.

The woman was inspecting him as closely as he was inspecting the truck. The man stood leaning on his shovel. Scotty turned his head away from the truck and spat on the ground, then stood with his fingertips in his hip pockets and watched Jake.

Jake finished his survey and walked back across the creek bed. He stood near Scotty and studied the problem before him.

The woman said, "Where you boys from?"

"Holbrook," Jake said.

"How'd you get way over here?"

"Walked," Scotty said.

"All the way from Holbrook? That must be twenty miles."

"About eighteen as the crow flies," Jake said. "Twenty-five or so by road."

"What you doing way out in these parts?"

Jake, ignoring the question, stepped back down into the creek bed and walked toward the farmer. Scotty said, "We're hunting rabbits."

"Hunting rabbits? Where's your guns?"

"We don't shoot 'em. We just run 'em down and catch 'em by the tails."

Jake said, "We better get that load off or you'll be here forever. You got any forks?"

"Couple stuck in the hay." The farmer pointed toward the tines of the two pitchforks that jutted from the load and pointed toward the cloudy sky. The handles of the forks had been poked down into the hay against the front of the truck bed, just behind the passenger side of the cab.

"Scotty," Jake said, "let's unload her."

Jake stepped onto the running board of the truck and grabbed the rack with one hand so he could pull himself up. In that position, one foot on the running board and one hand on the rack, he came face to face with a girl.

She was sitting in the truck cab on the passenger side, looking out the window. As Jake saw her she began to roll down the window, looking at him with a slight smile.

"Hello," he said.

"Hello."

"I was just gonna climb up on the truck."

"Go ahead."

Jake put his other hand on top of the cab and raised the foot from the ground to the base of the fender. He pushed off from the rack, scrambled up the fender to the hood, stepped onto the cab, and grabbed the pitchforks by the tines. He jabbed the tines of one fork into the hay. The other he used as a balancing pole as he climbed from the cab onto the load of hay. Once he fell to his knees, got up again, and found his balance on top of the load.

Scotty stood on the ground looking up at the girl in the truck. She wore a warm blue scarf around her hair and ears, and looked at him impassively.

"Are you holding the ladder?" he asked.

"Sure," she said. "Climb on up."

He followed Jake, seizing the other pitchfork as he stepped onto the hay.

Each man dug his fork into the hay and pulled out a forkful. Scotty flung his through the air so it landed a few feet from the fender on the passenger side of the truck. Jake stood braced against the heavy forkload that jutted into the air over the edge of the truck. He looked down at the woman, who stood near the driver's door looking at him.

"You're standing where I want to throw," he said.

"Oh!" She scurried to get out of the way, hurrying to the road and standing in front of the truck. Jake threw his hay onto the ground where she had been.

They worked steadily, without talking. When the load was down even with the top of the rack the old man said, "I could take over for one of you. I ain't got no more forks."

"We're okay," Scotty said.

The piles of hay on either side of the truck grew. Early in the unloading the girl had slipped out the passenger door and, watching her chance between forkfuls, had run up past the truck. She stood beside the woman in the road. The man stood off to the right, leaning on his shovel.

Jake ran the points of the tines of his fork along the bed of the rack, scraping up the last wisps of hay. He tossed the last forkful onto the pile that now stood as high as the rack on the driver's side of the truck. He tossed the fork after it and it landed upright, its tines digging into the side of the pile of hay. Scotty pitched his fork into the other pile. They walked to the back of the truck, climbed over the rack, and dropped into the dry creek bed.

The left front tire had come down and now rested on the road. The frame on the right side still pressed into the dirt. The right rear tire still hung in the pool of water. Chips and thin slivers of muddy ice floated in the pool.

The man walked down the ditch bank carrying his shovel before him. He used the tip of the shovel to scoop away some of the ice. Then he planted the tip on the ground and resumed his leaning position. He was stocky. He wore shabby but warm clothing, good gloves, a cap with earflaps that hung loose and only approximately covered his ears. Scotty looked at him, then removed his own cap, pulled the earflaps down from inside it, and put it back on, covering his ears with the liner.

The women walked around the other side of the truck slowly, almost cautiously, the girl following the older woman by a few steps. They stood on the edge of the creek bed and watched, each with her arms folded across her chest. The girl wore waist overalls and a heavy blue coat. The woman, as stocky as her husband, was in brown—scuffed brown sturdy shoes, dark brown coat, brown wool stockings, a brown skirt that hung lower than her coat, and a brownish-orange scarf tied beneath her chin. Her face, too, was brown and lined.

"What are you going to do?" she finally asked.

"Get you unstuck," Jake said. He put the tip of his tongue between his teeth and lips and squinted at the tire that hung in the mudhole.

"What's your names?" she asked.

Jake did not reply. He seemed not to hear her. Scotty said, "His name's Jake Mortensen."

"What's yours?"

"Scotty Tubbs."

Jake said, "Let's see that big rock you was trying to miss."

The man led them to the driver's side of the truck and tapped the rock with his shovel point. He moved out of the way. The rock was about the size of a car tire and shaped like a Brazil nut.

"You take that end," Jake said.

He and Scotty squatted, fumbled with the rock until each had a firm handhold.

"Ready. Hyo!"

They lifted it and, stooped over and shuffling, Jake walking backward, they lugged it around behind the truck.

"Your end wants to go north," Jake said, with effort. He stood in one place and pivoted as Scotty moved around him.

"On three. One—two—three!"

On each count they made a tiny swing toward the truck, and on three the rock was thrown and pushed into the muddy pool behind the stuck tire. It landed sharp-edge-down and came to rest just beneath the surface of the water.

"You got a claw bar in your toolbox?" Jake asked the man.

"Ya." He went up to the front of the truck and brought it back. As Jake took it, he also took the shovel from the man.

Jake put the shovel into the water, point-down, bowl toward the tire. He used the claw bar as a lever, its fulcrum resting on the spade and its lower end under the rock.

"Hold the shovel," he told Scotty. Crouching beneath the truck bed, he tugged on the claw bar and moved the rock a little closer to the back wheel. He crawled back out and he and Scotty handed the tools back to the man.

"Stand over here," Jake instructed Scotty. "If it looks like I'm gonna scrape the ground with something, stop me." He looked over at the girl, who had walked around to the other side of the truck to watch. "Stand right where you are," he told her. "If he wants me to stop, he'll yell and you wave your arms or something."

"Okay."

Jake walked slowly around the back of the truck, looking at the rock and the tire and the roadway, then climbed into the driver's seat. He looked out the passenger window at the girl, who stood ready, her hands in the air as if a holdup man were accosting her, her eyes fixed on Scotty. Jake switched on the ignition, stepped on the starter, worked the choke. The engine started.

He crammed the wheels sharply to the left. Then he pushed on the clutch, put the truck into reverse, eased down gently on the gas, and let the clutch out smoothly.

The truck strained backward, hung, then he heard the tire spinning in the mud. He stepped on the clutch and the truck rocked forward. At once, he let the clutch out again and the truck rocked backward. The tire found purchase on the rock. There was a bump as it dropped from the rock into the edge of the pool and then climbed out to dry ground.

Jake stepped on the clutch with one foot, the brake with the other, and held the truck in place. His hands pulled the wheel through one turn after another until the front tires were jammed far to the right. Again he drove backward.

Then he stopped, straightened the wheels, put the truck into forward gear. The right rear tire dipped slightly as it crossed a corner of the puddle, grabbed for a moment at the rock, then was on the dry edge of the hole. Jake turned to the right and the truck climbed up out of the creek bed. He brought it to a stop between the piles of hay and turned off the ignition.

Jake got out. He picked up the pitchfork and began pitching the hay back onto the truck.

On the other side, Scotty also started to work. He said to the girl, "Maybe you better get up there and tromp."

"Okay."

She climbed up the back tire and over the sides of the rack and kept moving around the load, trying to pack it down, kicking hay as best she could from high spots to low spots, slipping to her knees at times on the slippery load.

The man said to Scotty, "I can go ahead and load that back on."

"Oh, we might as well."

When the load was a couple of feet above the top rails of the rack, Scotty climbed up over the cab and used his fork to build the load evenly at the top. Jake finished pitching on the last hay from his side and then from Scotty's and then, watching to see that Scotty and the girl were out of the way, tossed his fork up and onto the load. Scotty took it and his own fork and jabbed them back down into the hay against the front of the rack, leaving them tines-up as Jake had found them.

"I'll give you a hand down," Scotty said to the girl.

He held her gloved hand in his as she lowered herself to the top of the cab. He released her hand and she climbed the rest of the way down. Scotty slid down the load to the cab and followed her to the ground.

Jake was standing near the passenger side, waiting for him. The woman walked up to Jake. "How old are you?" she asked.

"Eighteen."

"You're just a sprout."

The man said. "Eighteen?" He looked Jake up and down. The young man was six feet tall, well built. "Eighteen. You'll be a big help to your ma when you get your growth."

The woman had turned to Scotty. "How old are you?"

"Twenty-three."

"Are you married to his sister or something?"

"I'm not married to anybody."

"What are you doing in these parts?"

Jake said, "We're going to spend the winter cutting cedar posts."

"What for?"

"Twenty, thirty cents apiece. Whatever we can get for them."

The man said, "How much do I owe you?"

"Nothing."

"Oughta pay you something."

"That's okay." Jake started to walk back toward the dry creek. Scotty followed.

The woman said, "Just a minute." They stopped. "If we can't pay you, you should let us give you something. We got a box of groceries in the truck. Anything you boys need?"

Scotty said, "We got about everthing we can carry."

"Where'd you leave it?"

Jake said, "Back across the road."

"Where you sleeping?"

"We got a camp up there."

The man was walking around toward the driver's side of the truck. The girl, who had been looking at them in silence, began to walk toward the other door. The woman said, "Why don't you come to supper?"

Jake said, "It's getting pretty late. We better get up to the camp before dark."

"Tomorrow's Sunday. Come have Sunday dinner with us."

"I don't think we better. We have a lot to do tomorrow." He turned and started away again, but she had not given up.

"Come on Thanksgiving. You'd like to have a nice Thanksgiving dinner, wouldn't you? We have plenty."

Jake stopped and turned back. "Where do you live?"

The man said, "Follow this road about six miles. It goes over that ridge yonder and down into another valley a lot like this one. You'll see a old cabin all busted up and falling down. There'll be a road to the right just the other side of that cabin. Take that road and in about a mile you'll come to our place."

"It's easy to find," the woman said. "It's a painted house."

"Okay. We'll come Thanksgiving."

The man said, "I could drive up this far and meet you."

"We're not sure when we'll be coming down. We don't have a watch."

The woman said, "Come early and visit."

"Okay."

The man said, "I don't think we give our names. I'm Max Griffeth. That's my wife, Lois. That's our girl, Maxine."

The girl nodded an acknowledgment to them and got into the truck. The man hesitated a moment, as if thinking there might be more to say, then he got into the truck.

"We'll see you Thanksgiving," the woman said. She climbed in after her daughter. The truck started and pulled slowly away.

Scotty said, "She's kind of a nosy old battle-ax."

"Well, there's a lot she needs to know."

"There's only one thing she needs to know, and she ain't found that out yet. But she will."

"What's that?"

"I am not gonna marry her daughter."

CHAPTER THREE

It was almost dark along the ridge. Neither man could see the details of the ground on the trail. They could see only the trail itself, finding its way through sagebrush and bunch grass, skirting the edges of little patches of juniper.

"Watch out," Jake said. "I nearly stepped in a badger hole."

He was breathing heavily, but his breathing could not be heard above the stiff wind that was blowing from behind them. The wind had made the air, already chill, much colder. But each man could feel perspiration on his face and neither was cold beneath his clothing.

There was a fork in the black trail. Jake took the right-hand branch. The way led off the ridge, not straight down but along a pathway that was almost level and let the canyon floor come up to meet them. They walked past a large clump of juniper and some unusually high sagebrush and then they were in gloomy dark. The wind was somewhat abated, cut by the ridges that protected them on either side and by the juniper trees growing in the canyon.

They walked slowly now but evenly, Jake leading and picking his way carefully. The trail passed one more clump of juniper and they could dimly see a patch of ground that was almost level. Jake stopped, knelt, let the pig slide from his shoulder, left the rest of his load on the ground beside it. He stood, clenched his fists, flexed his muscles, stretched, exhaled strongly, and turned back to Scotty. "We'll camp here."

Scotty put down his load. Jake picked up the bundle that was the tent and carried it a few steps away and plopped it down. In the darkness he and Scotty bent over it, finding and untying the knots in the ropes, spreading the canvas on the ground, dividing up the stakes and ropes. Each took an ax and went along one side of the tent, driving stakes into the ground. Scotty placed the poles to support the front and back. Together they lifted the canvas, pulled the ropes taut, and tied the ropes to the stakes. There was some fumbling in the dark but the tent went up quickly.

Jake began moving stuff into the tent. He untied and unrolled his own bedroll—Scotty's he dropped on the other side of the tent. Inside the blankets was tied a little bundle of clothing. Jake lay that in a corner of the tent. Near it he put the hunting rifle and his ax.

Scotty had taken the other ax and gone in search of firewood. Now and then a "thunk" arose above the sound of the wind as he chopped at a sagebrush or a dead and fallen juniper. He came back twice with armloads of wood.

Jake used his feet and hands to kick and scrape a clear space where a fire could be built on the side of the tent away from the wind, with no danger of setting fire to twigs and dead grass and ground cover.

While Scotty finished getting wood, and laid and started the fire, Jake opened the sack of pots and pans and found a skillet. He unwrapped the pig and cut slices, huddling over the carcass and striking matches to see where to cut. He filled the skillet with thick slices of meat and set it aside with a piece of sacking over it to keep out the dirt. He sliced some bacon to have it ready for breakfast. When he was through he wrapped up the carcass and the bacon. He left the meat inside the tent, at the end farthest from the tent flap.

Scotty put the skillet on the fire so the meat could cook. He put green logs on top of the fire and balanced the skillet on them. If the logs caught fire or rolled out of position, he brought more logs and adjusted them. He worked by firelight. He dug into the sack of kitchen tools and found a sack of coffee.

"Is there any water?" he asked.

"There's a spring over there," Jake said. He picked up a kettle and went to get water.

Aspens grew close around the spring. Their whiteness made it lighter there, but Jake had to feel his way to the little pool of water around the spring. The water bubbled up in a natural artesian well. In daytime one could see that the pool was recessed in rocks and was maybe a foot deep. Jake dipped the kettle full of water and returned to the fire.

"It's getting cold," he said as he put down the water and squatted near the fire.

"That's because we stopped walking. Trouble with pork is it takes so long to cook."

"So does rabbit."

"Rabbit can take forever and be fine with me."

Scotty rearranged the skillet and set about brewing coffee. Jake explored the flour sack and found tin plates and cups and put them near the fire. He took half a loaf of bread from the sack, broke it in half, broke one half in half. He put one of the smaller pieces on each tin plate. The bigger chunk he wrapped in its paper again and returned to the flour sack.

"I'll bake some bread tomorrow," Jake said.

"If you can dig a hole to bake it in."

"Oh, I don't think the ground's froze. Not here in the canyon. We're kind of protected in here."

"That's a comfort to know." Scotty made a show of pulling his jacket tighter around the throat.

"The spring wasn't froze." Jake looked off into the darkness for a moment. "I hope the ground ain't froze."

Scotty said, "Why do they always say that hell is a place where there's always a fire burning? That don't seem like such a bad kind of place to me. If I was to set up a hell, I'd make it a lot like this canyon, only not so many trees to block the wind."

"When we get set up here we'll be snug."

"If the ground ain't froze."

Jake said, "I'll tell you what it's gonna be like. It's gonna be a place where ever day you have to pitch June grass in a windstorm."

"That guy today had some pretty good hay."

"It's early yet. He probably had his pick. This winter the guys is gonna be taking their sleds to Snowville and paying dear for what they can get."

"He must of not had much of a hay crop if he has to buy this early."

"He might be buying now to save later."

Scotty said, "I need a fork."

Jake got back into the flour sack and found forks and spoons and knives. He handed a fork to Scotty and arranged the rest of the utensils on the tin plates. Scotty turned the meat over and put the skillet back on the fire.

"We can try the coffee," Scotty said. He used his gloves as hot pads and poured coffee from the blue enamel pot into the cups that Jake held. He replaced the pot a little farther from the flame and held out his hand for his cup. When he touched the cup he got burned and jerked his hand back, then took the cup with his glove as a protection.

"You've got two choices up here. Freeze or burn," he said.

They huddled near the fire and sipped the hot coffee. Scotty squatted on his heels. Jake sat cross-legged on a small log he had salvaged from the firewood. The pork was sizzling in its own grease. The wood in the fire popped and burned. They could feel the heat reddening their faces; they could feel the wind chilling their backs. The fire was a splash of red in a circle of black, and they blended partly with the red, partly with the black. Jake's shadow flickered on the white canvas of the tent. Scotty studied that for a moment.

Then he said, "We didn't bring up that lantern, did we?"

"No. It's inside the stove. We'll get it tomorrow."

"I was thinking we could eat in the tent if we had any light."

"I got some candles in my pocket. But it'll be colder in the tent than it is out here."

"There won't be the wind."

"We can go in if you want."

Scotty sipped his coffee and looked into the flames. "Oh," he said, "we might as well stay by the fire." He put his cup on the ground, picked up the coffeepot, and poured the cup full again. Still holding the pot, he looked over at Jake. "Want some more?"

"Sure." Jake held out his cup and Scotty filled it. In a pensive mood Jake started quoting from his favorite poem "Gunga Din."

Jake launched into it. He raised his voice a little in pitch and turned his vowels into an approximation of an English accent and recited Kipling's lines with feeling and vigor:

> " '. . . *Though I've belted you and flayed you,*
> *By the livin' God that made you*
> *You're a better man than I am, Gunga Din.*' "

"I think this is ready," Scotty said. Jake passed the plates, and Scotty filled them with meat. Jake put his on the ground and went back to the flour sack. From it he took a clean tin can.

"Pour the grease in this," he said. "We'll need it when we make hot cakes or fry potatoes." Scotty tilted the skillet and poured the grease into the can and gave the can back to Jake. Jake fastened a piece of cloth over the top as a cover.

They scrunched up near the fire, holding their plates in their laps, cutting their meat, chewing and swallowing without much talking.

Once, Jake put down his plate and poured water into a pan. He put the pan on the fire. When they had finished eating, he took the pan off the fire and dropped a bar of soap into it. He added cold water until he could stand to put his hand into the water. There was a dishrag in the flour sack. When all the dishes except the coffee cups had been washed he emptied the pan, rinsed it and the dishes in cold water, and left the clean dishes upside down in the empty pan to dry. He put the pan inside the tent.

Scotty had poured more coffee and set the pot aside. The fire was dying. While it lasted they hovered over it, drank coffee, talked some, looked into the darkness some.

"That wasn't bad meat," Scotty said.

"No."

"There's some of this country I think is going to survive when the end of the world comes."

"Oh?"

"If the world ends in fire like it's supposed to, there's a lot of places around here that ain't gonna burn."

"It'll all burn."

"That's what my Sunday-school teacher told us. She scared the dickens out of some kids. Not me, though."

"You don't mind burning, huh?"

"I just told her I wasn't going to die in the fire. I was just as sure as sure could be. I remember saying to her, 'The fire won't get me. I'll get out.' And she'd say, 'If you're on earth, Scotty, you'll perish with everone else. But you'll be resurrected if you're good.' And I'd say, 'Oh, no. I won't burn. I'll get away.' And she'd ask, 'How are you going to get away when everthing's in flames?' And I'd say, 'There'll be a road for me. They'll open up a path for me.' I was sure I could find a cool place in all that heat." He looked about him in the darkness. "I think I've found my cool place."

Jake said, "I been told that maybe the earth will freeze over instead of burn up."

"I'd rather it burned up. I wouldn't want to freeze to death." He shivered. "I'd hate to freeze to death. There was an old guy used to live by us that froze to death when I was a little kid. I had nightmares about that. Some folks went over to his house 'cause they wasn't sure he had nothing to eat, and come to find out he didn't have no firewood nor nothing. He was huddled up under his blankets froze to death. I hope that don't happen to me."

Jake said quietly, "I helped kill a guy with ice once."

Scotty stared at him over his coffee cup. "You what?"

Jake stared at the ground and, in a small, reluctant voice, said, "We didn't mean no harm. It was one Halloween night and there was this old guy that was always mean to us. So a bunch of us went to his house and made a lot of noise around the toilet. When he come out to keep us from tipping it over, we grabbed him and tied him up and blindfolded him and carried him back in his house." He paused for a moment and stared into the flames. Scotty, scarcely breathing, leaned forward to hear better. "We—uh"—Jake cleared his throat and began again—"we took off his shirt and told him we was going to cut him open. We was just teasing. We run a icicle down his belly and he thought it was a knife. Then we poured warm water on him and he thought it was blood and he bled to death."

"Oh, you knothead." Scotty stood up, laughing. He tossed the last of his coffee out onto the ground. "I'm not gonna listen to no more of your stories. I'm going to bed."

Jake stood up as Scotty began to walk around the fire toward the tent flap. "Do you think this fire will be okay?"

"I don't see how it can get away. There's nothing else to burn."

"Except the tent. I'd hate to burn down the tent."

"Oh, it'll be okay. Kick a little dirt on it if you want." Scotty went into the tent.

Jake looked down at the red-hot coals. There were occasional licks of flame. A not completely burned piece of wood popped, making ash flare up and fall back. Dark shapes formed in the red coals.

He turned away, leaving the fire to die by itself. He crouched, pushed through the tent flap, then turned and, feeling in the darkness, tied the flap shut against the wind.

He felt his way through the darkness to his blankets and knelt beside them. From his coat pocket he took out a short candle, a jar lid, and a box of matches. He struck a match and lit the candle. He put the jar lid on the ground, upside down, a few feet from where their heads would be when they slept. Scotty was sitting on his blankets, pulling off his high-topped shoes.

Jake held the candle tilted acutely over the jar lid. The flame ate at the candle, melted wax that dripped into the jar lid. When there was a little pool of the soft wax, Jake set the candle upright in the lid, pressing the base of the candle into the wax to make it stand firmly. The little flame threw a steady light to all corners of the small tent. Scotty, in his long underwear, crawled under his blankets and pulled and tugged and grunted and shifted until he was comfortably settled.

Jake undressed down to his long-handled underwear, folding his clothing and piling it on top of his shoes near the foot of his bed. Before he got into his bedroll he reached beneath the blankets and explored until his hand found a book that had been rolled up in the bedroll. He got into bed, turned over onto his stomach, and began to read by candlelight.

"Whatcha got there?"

"Book of poems."

"I thought you knowed all the poems there was."

"My folks give me this book for my birthday. Most of them I haven't read."

"Read me one."

"Okay:

> 'I *wanted the gold, and I sought it.*
> *I scrabbled and mucked like a slave.*
> *Was it famine or scurvy—I fought it.*
> *I hurled my youth into a grave. . . .*' "

CHAPTER FOUR

It took them two trips the next day to bring up the rest of their belongings.

When they had them all up by the tent, Scotty opened a can of peas and a can of corned beef and heated them for dinner. Jake took the shovel and walked along the north wall of the canyon, examining the ground, sometimes digging out a spadeful of earth. When he came back to eat dinner, he pointed up the canyon to where he had been.

"We didn't go quite far enough. See that patch of brush?"

"Ya."

"Just past it I think is a good place for the dugout."

"Okay. Here. Fill these cups with water."

"There was ice on the spring this morning."

"Well, it's a nice day now." Scotty looked up at the sky, as cloudless today as it had been overcast yesterday. "It might warm up some this afternoon."

After dinner, Jake shoveled the fire aside, putting it out, and where it had been he dug a hole. Then Scotty took the shovel, walked up near the patch of brush, and dug a hole there. He dropped the empty cans from dinner into it and brought the shovel back.

Jake had assembled his pans and condiments and was mixing sourdough bread. Scotty opened the sack of potatoes.

"It looks like you sewed this sack," Scotty said.

"Ya, I did. How did you know?"

"I don't know. It's just the way you do it." He took out a bunch of potatoes and began washing them in the dishpan of cold water. He put the clean ones into another pan.

"Next year I'm gonna haul wheat instead of sew sacks."

"If you get your truck."

"Yeah."

"I reckon I'll drive Smith's horses again. That's a pretty good job."

"Jim Black always liked working for Smith."

"Smith liked having Jim work for him. He can sure sew sacks."

"I've saw him sew eight hundred in one day."

"That's a lot of sacks."

"He can jig a sack so full of wheat it can bust the seams."

"Why would you want to do that?"

"To show you can."

"How many of these potatoes should I wash?"

"Oh, just fill that pan. What we don't eat for supper we can slice up and fry for breakfast."

"Do you know Bill Evans?"

"I don't think so."

"Willard Evans's boy."

"I've saw a big kid over at Willard's. About my age."

"That's him. Clem Buttars hired him to tie sacks with the threshing crew last year, and it just about done him in."

"Couldn't lift the sacks? I've saw big guys that couldn't lift the sacks. There's a trick to it."

"Nobody ever knowed if he could lift the sacks." Scotty set the pan of clean potatoes near Jake and turned to close up the sack. "He couldn't tie 'em. His hands was too tender. He hadn't done nothing to toughen 'em up. What work he done, he done with gloves on."

"I've knowed guys to soak their hands in brine ever night for a while before they tied sacks. I done it once myself."

"He didn't. Before noon his hands was all raw and bleeding. Well, first he tried to tie with gloves on, and of course you can't. So it was really painful for him, and by dinnertime you know how a woman can tie a knot in a thread using just the two fingers and the thumb of one hand? Well, by dinnertime he was doing that. He never showed up in the afternoon." Scotty lugged the potatoes over to a corner of the tent and balanced the sack against the rope that held the tent to the peg. He wiped his hands dry on his pants. "Are you gonna start digging the dugout this afternoon?"

"Ya, once I get this bread mixed so's it can raise. Why don't you put a dishtowel over them potatoes so the dirt won't get on them."

Scotty found a towel and arranged it. He said, "Maybe I better cut some wood."

"Wouldn't hurt. When I get done here and get that hole lined with rocks, let's take a walk."

"Okay."

Jake carried his .22 on the walk. He walked with his hands in his coat pockets. The rifle was under his right arm, its muzzle pointing at the ground, its barrel resting across his wrist, the stock lightly levered up into his armpit. His eyes moved back and forth across the terrain in front of them, taking in all the details as they moved. Scotty walked on his left, hands in pockets, eyes down, apparently absorbed in mildly amusing thoughts. Once in a while he looked up at something that caught his eye, or at something Jake was pointing out.

They moved generally south and a little east. The land rose and fell at angles that often approached and sometimes surpassed forty-five degrees. The sagebrush was mostly small and mostly scattered, so the walking over the dead brown grass was easy and casual. They came to clumps and groves and tiny forests of juniper. Each time they reached such a patch they paused to walk around and through it, studying the trees.

"Quite a few badger holes," Scotty said.

"Yep."

They came to Juniper Row. Seen at a distance, the row appeared to be a long narrow grove thick with trees. Up close, at least at this part of it, the trees were seen to be several yards apart, not as thick as in most of the other patches.

"Are we gonna cut in here?"

"I kind of hate to."

"Why?"

"I don't know. I'm just used to seeing it here, I guess. I wouldn't want to be the one to cut it all down. We'll see how much else we cut first. There's plenty of trees."

The belt of trees was four or five hundred yards across. When they had finished walking through it Jake said, "It wouldn't hurt none to cut a few in there, I guess."

They continued for another few hundred yards, mounting a gentle rise as they did and stopping at last on top of a low ridge. Before them, to the south, they saw the dirt road on which they had come from Holbrook the day before.

"I don't want to work no closer to the road than this," Jake said.

"You think somebody might steal some posts?"

"Maybe." He turned and looked eastward. "Let's go look at that patch up there."

A small forest of the trees spread along and down the north slope of the ridge and partway up the next slope. They walked through it, studying the number and size of the trees. Farther east they saw another large patch of juniper. They studied that one, too. At last they stood between the two, near one and looking toward the other.

Jake said, "We might as well spend this week on these two pieces. That's about as far from camp as we'll get. We can save the closer ones for when there's snow and it's hard to walk this far."

"Okay."

They walked back to camp, taking a more easterly route and inspecting other patches of juniper as they went.

As they emerged from one small clump of trees Jake raised the .22, swung the barrel as he followed something in his sights, and fired. He lowered the rifle and began walking rapidly in the direction he had shot.

"Did you get him?"

"Yup."

Jake picked up the rabbit from the trail where he had fallen and held him by the hind legs.

"Big one," Scotty said.

"Yeah." Jake set off walking again, carrying the rabbit.

Scotty said, "Where you taking him?"

"Back to camp."

"What for?"

"To fry him up."

"You mean you really do eat rabbit?"

"Sure."

"I thought Bud was kidding me."

"This one will taste good fried."

"You can have my share."

At the camp, Scotty cut firewood while Jake skinned and cleaned the rabbit. He cut it into pieces and arranged it in the skillet, adding a dollop of the leftover pork grease. Then he covered it and set it aside.

Jake built a fire in the rock-lined pit he had dug. When it was burning well, he picked up the shovel and walked back to the place where he had decided to build the dugout.

The ground sloped upward there at about forty-five degrees. There were many large rocks scattered about, most of them tending to be rectangular. When Jake began to dig he found more rocks. He dug around the large ones and used the shovel and his hands to pry them out. Some were so large he had to struggle to move them. For one, he had to enlist Scotty's help.

When they got that one moved aside, Jake walked back to his fire. It had burned down to coals. He placed the pan of potatoes on those coals, covered it with a cookie sheet, and covered that with dirt. On the dirt he built another fire.

He returned to the rocks, dug some more, then came back and put the fire out. He put his bread on the coals, covered the pan, and shoveled dirt onto the pan.

He built another fire and put the skillet on it so the rabbit would cook. Scotty put down his latest load of wood and walked over to him.

"If it's all the same with you, I'll get by on the potatoes," he said.

"I can fry some pork for you."

"I hate to eat more than my share of the pork."

"It don't matter none. I'll fix some for you."

"Won't it make the rabbit taste funny if you cook it in the same pan?"

"I'll use this other pan for the pork. I won't mix them."

When he had the meat started he got Scotty to help him carry the pig to a tree near the dugout. Scotty climbed into the tree and draped a rope over a high limb. Jake tied one end of the rope to the pig. They hoisted it into the air, out of reach of wild animals. They tied off the rope so they could lower the pig when they wanted to cut slices for a meal.

The bread and the potatoes and the rabbit were done at the same time; the pork stayed on the fire until Jake had the rest of the meal prepared. Scotty had moved a couple of larger logs near the fire. They sat on those, held their plates on their knees, and ate.

"You look like you like that rabbit."

"It's good."

"I guess I'm just deprived. I don't think I could handle it."

"Try some."

"No, thanks."

"I might make a snare tonight. I could probably have rabbit regular if I kept my eyes open."

"Well, it cuts down on the amount of rabbits. There's that to the good."

"They're how come I come to do this."

"Rabbits?"

"Yup." Jake wiped his hands on his pants and reached for another piece of rabbit. "One of the first jobs I got when I quit school was cutting brush and weaving them rabbit-tight fences to keep rabbits out of haystacks."

"I've seen you do that. You sort of weave the brush in and out of the barbed wire."

"Sometimes I'd see a post that was bigger than I needed for brush, but I'd cut it and take it home, and when I had a chance I'd take it in to Holbrook to the store. He always give me eighteen cents credit on it for groceries. That helped some with the grocery bill. He was always able to sell the posts and make money. This past summer I got to thinking about that, and I decided it might be a good way to spend the winter."

"Oh, we won't have no trouble selling 'em, if we can haul 'em out of here."

"I'll get 'em hauled."

The sun had gone down and the twilight was failing when they began to eat; they finished in the dark. They washed the dishes and let the fire go out. Jake put the uneaten potatoes and the rest of the bread in the tent. They went to the spring together and resupplied their drinking water. They walked to the just-started dugout but could not see well enough to work, so they went back to their tent. Jake lit the candle.

"Want to play some cribbage?" Scotty asked.

"Okay."

Scotty took out the board and the cards and some dirty, broken matchsticks that had seen hard use in previous games. Each lounged on his bedroll, playing the cards on the ground between them, near the candle.

"I don't feel sleepy," Scotty said.

"It's early yet. The days is short."

"Ya. I guess if we was smart we could have cooked supper in the dark and spent some of the daylight getting started on them posts. We could of cut quite a bunch if we hadn't took that walk."

Jake shook his head and squinted at his cards in the wavering candlelight. "I'd just as soon take a little time each Sunday to figure out what we're gonna do the rest of the week. Anyhow, I don't like to work on Sunday."

CHAPTER FIVE

They settled quickly into a routine.

Jake got up first in the morning and built a fire in the stove. Then he dressed and got water from the spring while Scotty got up and made breakfast. While it was cooking, Jake did whatever had to be done to prepare the tools for the day's work. When the coffee was hot he filled their thermos bottles. He made their lunches—cold rabbit for himself whenever there was any; for Scotty, a ham sandwich and a sandwich with homemade jam between the slices of the bread they had baked. They had a large lard bucket in which they carried the food.

"I used to carry my dinner in a lard bucket like this, only littler," Jake said, "when I went to school. A lot of times we'd spread grease on bread and I'd take that. It's kind of good when it's still hot, but I didn't like it much cold."

"I ain't never carried a dinner pail," Scotty said. "My old man told me once that a guy that starts out carrying a dinner pail is gonna be carrying a dinner pail all his life. So I decided not to start. Of course, I never went to school as much as you, neither. I got kicked out of the fourth grade for not shaving."

"I went through the eighth grade. My older sisters both went over to Malad to high school."

"I know."

So Jake, as a concession to Scotty's strict upbringing, carried the dinner bucket. They left the camp early. By the time the dawn was beginning to cast light onto the ridges they were at the juniper groves near the south road. With a sharp slap and a splitting crack the first blows of the axes echoed across the rolling land.

Jake picked a tree. One that had a long length of sturdy trunk, but not so thick that it would be unwieldy and heavy. He trimmed off any limbs that prevented his ax from reaching the trunk, and he began to chop. It did not take many blows to fell the tree. He trimmed away the limbs and cut the trunk into one—very rarely more than one—eight-foot post. He added the post to the pile he had started and picked another tree. Not far away, Scotty was doing the same. Sometimes a tree had a multiple trunk or an unusually large limb and would make more than one post.

An hour's work might net five or six or seven posts apiece. Once in a while more; sometimes tough wood held a man to two or three posts in an hour. A good day's work was forty each. Sometimes one or the other would go well over that. On Jake's best day that winter he cut seventy-five.

Whenever they thought the limbs and ends were strewn about too much, they gathered the slash and piled it up.

"Some of this a guy might sell as firewood," Jake said.

"Ya, the big ends and those real thick limbs. But it'd be a lot of trouble to haul it out of here."

"Not this close to the road."

"Maybe not."

When they figured it was noon—when, on a clear day, the sun told them it was noon—Jake drove his ax into a tree stump and gathered an armload of the slash and laid and lit a fire. Scotty drove his ax into a stump and walked to the fire. They sat on logs or stones or the ground near the fire. Scotty, looking off into the distance or surveying the cutting they had done, slowly unscrewed the cap from his thermos and poured coffee into the lid. He pushed the cork back into the thermos and sat reflecting on the view and tasting his coffee.

Jake opened the lard bucket and handed out the sandwiches. They ate in silence, then poured second cups of coffee and lounged near the fire, dozing in its warmth.

"That's not a bad morning. What did we get between us?"

"I got twenty-one."

"Twenty even. Forty-one. Say, two bits apiece. Ten and a quarter. That's not bad."

"I think we can get more for them."

"Maybe."

"Course, you gotta deduct expenses."

"Ya. But those ain't bad. We'll do okay."

Refreshed, they left the fire to burn itself out and went back to work. They often seemed to get their second wind in the afternoon and do a little better than they had in the morning. They started work near each other each morning, but as the afternoons went along they were likely as not to find themselves moving farther apart.

When the sun hung only a couple of hours or less above the western hills, Jake gathered up the remaining slash around him and piled it. He went back to the noon fire and picked up the lard bucket and his thermos. He took another drink from the thermos, then, carrying ax and bucket and both thermoses, he went to where Scotty worked. Jake handed Scotty's thermos to him.

"I'm going in now," Jake said.

"Okay." Scotty opened his thermos to take a drink, and Jake began walking back across the ridges and gullies to the camp.

When he got there he put down his ax and picked up a shovel and went to work on the dugout again. He worked on it as long as there was light enough to see. When it was dark, he went back to the tent and built the campfire. About that time, Scotty came walking in.

Scotty cooked the suppers, although if Jake found a rabbit in the snare he had set he did the skinning and cleaning and preparing of the rabbit for the skillet. They opened a can of peas every two or three days. The rest of their diet consisted of pork and rabbit and potatoes and bread at supper, pork and fried potatoes and biscuits for breakfast, water and coffee, and their noontime sandwiches.

While Scotty cooked, Jake replenished the water supply and sharpened the axes. "At Christmas," he said, "I think I better bring back some extra ax handles."

"Wouldn't hurt. We're bound to break one sooner or later."

"Well, we've got the extra axes until then."

"You know what I wish we had? I wish we had some syrup."

"For hot cakes?"

"I can make good sourdough hot cakes, but there ain't no syrup."

"We got that bottle of jam. We could use that."

"Hate to use up the jam. It's good to have that on some bread once in a while."

"Well, make some hot cakes on Sunday and we can use some of the jam."

Every other night Jake mixed up a batch of biscuits and let them sit overnight. In the morning he built the fire early and baked them for breakfast. The next day they ate the leftover biscuits cold. In midweek he mixed another batch of bread in the morning and baked it in the evening.

Jake said, "I could bring back some oatmeal at Christmas, too."

"I don't like oatmeal. I had it too much when I was a kid."

"We had it all the time when I was a kid, but I like it."

"You'd have to have milk to put on it."

"Yeah."

"Tell you what you could bring, though, is a sack of apples."

By Sunday, Jake had done about all the digging he had to do on the dugout. It burrowed almost fifteen feet into the gully and was about five feet across. The last few feet were a cave, but he wasn't sure the earthen roof would not fall in on them so he removed it. He used the shovel to level the banks about six and a half feet above the floor, and he dug earthen shelves on both sides of the dugout about four and a half feet from the floor.

Scotty made the hot cakes Sunday morning. They spread them with jam and feasted. They took their bedding out and hung it on juniper trees to air. They filled every container they had with water and set all the containers near or on the campfire so the water could heat. Then they set to work on the dugout.

They found the most nearly rectangular of the stones that littered the canyon floor and piled them up as walls, abutting them to the sloping earthen walls so that the sides of the dugout were about six and a half feet high, earthen walls in back giving way to stone walls in front. The earthen part of the walls had those shelves dug back on the sides.

"Think we ought to chink them rocks with mud?" Scotty asked.

"I don't think it would do much good. I think they'll hold."

"I hope so. I'd hate to have somebody come up here next July and find two skeletons under a pile of caved-in rock."

"I don't think nobody's gonna come up here next July."

When the last rock was in place they spent some time walking around inside their dugout, trying to imagine what it would be like when it was finished. Then they went back to their fire and hot water. They stripped and bathed, each in turn standing in the largest pan to keep his feet clean while he dried the rest of his body, then stepping carefully out and standing on his dirty clothes while he dressed in clean long underwear and an extra set of work clothes.

"I'll tell you something," Scotty said. "When the snow flies, I'm gonna give up bathing until spring thaw. It's already too cold for this."

"Then you can sleep outside," Jake said. "I'll take the dugout."

They washed their clothes with hot water and bar soap, rinsed them repeatedly, and draped them over tent and trees and stumps to dry.

Jake took the .22 and Scotty took the shotgun, and they walked eastward, up the canyon they lived in and across the ridge at its upper end. They moved another mile or so until they stood among an exceptionally heavy cluster of juniper on the highest ridge around them.

"We've got a whole winter's work right here," Scotty said.

"Well, maybe. There's a lot that's too gnarled and crooked for posts. But there's a lot that's good."

"You want to cut here this week?"

"What have we got at the other place? One day's work?"

"Maybe two. A short two."

"We'll wanta quit early Wednesday. That could be the short day. Let's say we come here tomorrow, then go south on Tuesday and Wednesday, and then come back here steady."

"Okay." Scotty's voice dropped to a whisper. "Look."

"What?"

Scotty was raising his shotgun and taking careful aim. "Sage grouse. Throw a rock at 'em."

Jake picked up a rock and threw it, and as the grouse rose, Scotty fired, then fired the other barrel. He got three of them in the two shots.

"Look at that!" This time it was Jake pointing. Scotty followed the direction of the point. Two mule deer were springing out of the juniper trees and leaping across a ridge out of sight into the next gully.

"We should of brought the rifle," Scotty said.

"We couldn't catch them now anyhow."

"Let's bring the rifle up when we cut here."

"Let's hope they come back and don't just keep a-going."

They spent the next hour hunting and brought down two more grouse and two rabbits. They ate the grouse for supper.

They sat in the tent after supper. The week had been sunny and the temperatures a little above freezing during the daytime, barely cold enough at night to freeze the spring. They had moved the pig to another tree to make sure it would stay in the shade and, once frozen, not thaw. Tonight it was noticeably colder. They had two candles burning and a small fire going in the camp stove. There was a coziness in the tent that teased them now and then toward drowsiness. Jake read his book of poems. Scotty played solitaire for a while, spreading the cards on the bottom of the big pan. Presently he put the deck aside and took a mouth organ from his pocket. He began to play—jolly songs, melancholy songs. Jake read and listened for a while. Then he put his book down and, at one familiar tune, began to sing:

"Oh bury me not on the lone prairie
Where the wild coyote will howl o'er me,
Where the rabbits run and the wind blows free.
Oh bury me not on the lone prairie."

What woke Jake was the noise of Scotty building a fire in the camp stove. Jake rolled over onto his stomach and looked up past the burning candle to his friend. Scotty was fully dressed. He knelt beside the stove arranging the wood inside it.

"Did I sleep too long?" Jake asked.

Scotty turned in surprise. "I thought you was asleep." He turned back to his work. "It's early yet."

"How come you're up?"

"I'm gonna take the rifle and go up there where we saw them deer. If I go early, I might get one."

"You gonna have any breakfast?"

"No. I'll take some of them cold biscuits. It snowed last night. I might be able to find their tracks."

"Want me to come with?"

"Naw, go ahead and sleep a little if you want, and get yourself some breakfast." Scotty struck a match to the fire, watched it a moment until it took, then put the lid on the stove and stood up, bending over inside the low tent. "I'll see you up there."

"Okay."

Jake lay there a few minutes, giving Scotty time to set out on his expedition, then he pulled himself out of his bedroll and got dressed. He went outside and stood in the fresh snow. The moon, still approaching fullness, was about to set. It gave him plenty of light to see by. The inch or so of new snow sparkled in the moonlight. The air seemed warm in spite of the snow. The morning smelled good.

He cleared the snow out of the campfire pit as well as he could and laid a fire there. While it was getting started he went back inside the tent and peeled a bunch of potatoes and fried some bacon for his breakfast. He dipped bread in the hot bacon grease and ate the bread and bacon for breakfast.

He walked up to the spring and filled the bucket and a pan with water. He washed the potatoes and put them into a kettle and added water. He took out the rabbits he had shot and cleaned and cut up yesterday and put them into the kettle with the potatoes and water.

Jake worked on the campfire until he had it well fueled and banked so it would burn all day but not flare up. He fixed the kettle over it. He stood looking at the fire, then, as a precaution, took the shovel and scooped up snow and tossed it onto the tent near the fire. A stray spark would be less likely to set the tent on fire.

He made the dinners and picked up his ax and set out to the east. The dawn was paling and the moon still shining and it was easy to follow Scotty's tracks. The sun was up and glaring him in the face before he got to the working area. He paused and listened and heard Scotty's ax biting into a tree. Jake followed the sound instead of the tracks and came upon his partner.

"Get a deer?" he asked.

Scotty left the ax stuck in the tree trunk and took one hand off the handle. "Nope. Didn't even see 'em. I seen some tracks, though. They're still around. It looks like they heard me coming and high-tailed it north of here. I followed a little ways but then I figured I wasn't gonna catch them, so I come back and went to work."

Jake came in early again that day. His fire had gone out, but the kettle still felt hot. He built the fire up again.

He began cutting juniper logs from a grove near the dugout. As each log was cut and trimmed he lifted it to the top of the dugout and laid it across the walls, forming a roof. He had four logs up by the time Scotty came in.

Scotty stood in the twilight and inspected the work, then said, "I'll cook supper."

"I've got it cooking," Jake said.

"Okay." Scotty put down his ax and thermos and gathered up a bunch of juniper boughs. He held several of them together and used them as a broom to sweep the snow out of their dugout. He tossed the boughs away. As Jake began putting the fifth log into place, Scotty walked down to the fire.

"Whatcha got cooking?"

"Stew."

"What kind of stew?"

"Just some meat and potatoes."

"What kind of meat?"

Jake said nothing for a moment, concentrating on his work.

Scotty said, "Pork?"

"No. Rabbit."

"Oh." Scotty studied the pot for a minute. "Okay. I'll just have some of the potatoes."

"Rabbit stew is real good."

"Well, you enjoy it, then."

Jake finished adjusting the log and walked through the increasing darkness to the fire. "I could fry you up a pork chop or something."

"Never mind. Potatoes is fine."

They finished cutting the grove near the road by dinnertime Wednesday. The stout straight trees were gone. There were piles of posts dotted among the younger and the gnarled trees that remained. They stood on a ridge, leaning on their axes and surveying their work.

"We cut a pretty good swath through there," Jake said.

"Yup. Them are gonna be the easy ones to get out. Too bad we can't do more cutting that close to a road."

"I can borrow a team in the spring and drag the rest of them to where we can get them with the truck."

Scotty leaned over and picked up his thermos. "Well, let's go in. Maybe we can get some done on that roof."

"I want to bath, too."

"On Wednesday?"

"I don't want to drowned out the smell of the turkey when we have dinner with them people tomorrow."

"They probably won't have turkey."

"Well, whatever they have."

"I guess I might as well take a bath, too."

CHAPTER SIX

It was overcast again on Thanksgiving morning, with a threat of more snow. Jake and Scotty slept in, and made themselves a scanty breakfast. "If they're going to invite me to dinner," Scotty said, "I'm not going to make them feel bad by going there already full and not be able to eat their grub."

The sun was already thirty degrees above the eastern ridges when they set out from their camp on the walk toward the west. They walked empty-handed. "If I take the .22," Jake said, "I might shoot something, and if I shoot something I'll have to clean it, and that ain't the way to spend a holiday." With snow on the ground they didn't think they'd need to carry water.

There were tire tracks on the main road when they crossed it. "Quite a few guys went by here," Scotty said.

"Somebody might be bringing home some hay before the snow gets deep."

"That, or just going to see their folks somewhere for Thanksgiving."

It was a long, swift, silent walk across the valley from the road to the next ridge line and an easy climb along the road to the crest of that ridge. From the ridge they looked out across another broad valley. They could pick out three farmhouses scattered about, smoke from their chimneys blending quickly with the overcast sky.

"There's some good farms down there," Scotty said. "It's better land than what our folks have."

"Papa used to sell Rawleigh goods over this way," Jake said.

"He sold all over this part of the country, didn't he?"

"Ya. This was the best time of year, I guess. People was buying for Thanksgiving and Christmas. One time he was up toward Rockland and couldn't get home for Christmas. So he sent us a present of a shoe box full of little potatoes. I was pretty young then. I remember Mama boiled them with the skins on and we eat them for Christmas dinner. They tasted so good."

"These folks might know your dad."

"Ya, they might. He ain't sold Rawleigh goods for a few years, though. He's trying to make that farm pay out."

"He's doing pretty good, ain't he? He's got all you kids to help him."

"He's got all us kids to support. The ones at home, anyway, and that's most of 'em."

"Jeff and Jerry work."

"Sometimes. They don't get much for it. You don't get much working for farmers."

"That's true."

"Jean's married and I don't think her and her husband is having too easy a time of it. Joanne's teaching school down to Stone. She brings in a little. When she gets paid."

"Don't she always get paid?"

"Oh, the school board acts like it don't care whether she gets paid or not. They didn't give her nothing for September or October, so right around my birthday Papa went with her to see the chairman of the school board. He said he'd plumb forgot to pay her, but he would, but the paperwork would take a while. So I hope she's got paid by now."

"You'd think a guy smart enough to be chairman of the school board would remember to pay the teacher."

"If he's smart enough to get elected chairman of the school board, maybe he's smart enough to save tax money by not paying her at all."

"Maybe. What was them folks' name?"

"Who?"

"Where we're going."

"Griffeth. Max and I forget her name and the girl's Maxine."

It was the one whose name they couldn't remember who saw them first. She was standing beside the front gate, wearing a long apron over her dress, standing bare-armed without coat or hat. There was some sunshine working its way through the overcast.

"Land o' Goshen," she said, "we was wondering if you two would show up. We got enough food in there to feed a threshing crew. Come on in and make yourselves to home."

She marched toward the house and the young men followed her, Scotty pausing to latch the wooden gate. There was a cluster of outbuildings a little farther along the lane that had brought them here. They could see pigs, chickens, and a few cows in fields and pens near the house.

The woman opened the door and left it open for them. "The boys is here," she shouted to the interior of the house.

Jake stepped inside and met Max Griffeth coming down the hallway with a magazine in his hand and his reading glasses on. They shook hands, and Griffeth reached past him to shake hands with Scotty.

"Shut that door and come in the front room where it's warm," Mrs. Griffeth instructed. She had pushed past her husband and led the way. He stood against the wall and let them pass. Scotty glanced up and to his right. The stairway there led into darkness on the second floor.

"You can take off your coats and stick 'em in that there closet," Griffeth said. The closet was built into the staircase.

The parlor had a freshly-swept-and-dusted look of being seldom used. The furniture was shiny and little worn. Jake, standing in the doorway that led from hall to parlor, could see into another room in which the easy chair and rocker looked worn with use. He could also see a table set for dinner in that room. He could smell food being cooked somewhere deeper in the house.

He turned and gave his attention to the parlor. Portraits of an imposing bearded man and a grim middle-aged woman hung high on the high walls. A bookcase was covered with a fancy brown velvet cloth that hung in front of the books. An intricately crocheted tablecloth covered a round oak table. There was a dark brown upholstered sofa. There was a dark brown leather davenport with arms. One of the two easy chairs matched the sofa; the other was off-white and seemed a bit out of place in the room but gave it a cheerful touch. The wallpaper was a brown design on a tan background. A fancy brown and yellow glass shade covered the light bulb, which hung from the center of the ceiling on a cord. It was a room that spoke of money, of not having to scratch for a living.

"Sit down, boys," Griffeth said. "Anywhere."

Jake looked at the assortment of chairs and had not made up his mind by the time Scotty walked past him and sat on the davenport. Jake sat beside him. Griffeth eased himself into the brown chair and placed his magazine carefully on the floor beside it. He took off his glasses, folded them, and put them into his shirt pocket. He was wearing crisp new waist overalls and a clean blue shirt.

"How was the walk?"

"They're all about the same," Scotty said.

"You getting your work done okay?"

"Yup."

Griffeth sat looking out the front window. Jake continued his survey of the room. There was a cupboard in the corner with knickknacks on its shelves. Opposite the sofa, against the wall separating them from the dining room, stood a heavy oaken sideboard with drawers in it and a mirror above it. A fancy lamp sat in the middle of it.

Scotty said, "You've got a pretty house."

Mrs. Griffeth had returned in time to hear him say that. She stood in the doorway, wiping her hands with her apron. She said, "Max's dad built it. Max was just a boy then, but he helped. Him and his brother."

Scotty asked, "Where does your brother live?"

"He's dead."

Mrs. Griffeth came into the room and sat down in the white chair. "His brother's dead, and my brother and sister, and all our folks. There's just us and Maxine. We ain't got no other relations."

Scotty said, "You can have some of mine."

"You got lots of relations?"

"Well, I thought I had until I met Jake here. He has ten kids in his family and—how many cousins you got, Jake?"

"Ain't counted 'em lately. About twenty. Twenty, I think."

Mrs. Griffeth said, "Most folks has got quite a few relations. We're just not that lucky, I guess. I had one baby stillborn, and one died a baby, and I had some miscarriages. We've just got Maxine. She's the only chick in the nest. When we die, she gets the whole farm."

"How big a farm you got?" Scotty asked.

"I've got just over sixteen hundred acres here in the valley, two hundred of it with water, the rest dry farm. Then I've got a little piece, three hundred twenty acres, up toward Black Pine. I run a few cattle on there."

"You run it by yourself, or you got some hired help?"

"He runs it himself," she said. "He never quits working."

"Oh, that ain't so. I loaf most of the time. I hire the cutting done, and I get some help in the hay, and there's a couple boys does most of the work of taking care of the stock on the upper ranch. There ain't a lot of work to that. I do some plowing and hire some done. I milk—we ain't got but two milk cows; the rest of them's for beef."

"We'll have plenty of fresh milk for your dinner," she said. "And ice cream. Max made some ice cream. Maxine's cooking the dinner. I was just out to the kitchen to see if I could help, but she don't need me. She's a real good cook."

"That milk will be good," Jake said.

As if he had not been interrupted, Griffeth said, "The girl helps quite a bit."

"Not so much since she's been teaching school," his wife said.

"Oh," said Scotty, "she's a schoolmarm, huh?"

"She's bright. She went to the Normal School and done real good. We have a little school across the valley. She teaches it."

"My sister teaches," Jake said.

"Oh? Where?"

"Down to Stone."

Griffeth said, "But mostly I just do what everday work there is by myself."

"He's been thinking of hiring somebody steady, though," Mrs. Griffeth said.

"Is that right?" said Scotty.

"Well, I've thought about it," Max said. He looked appraisingly at Scotty. "Why? You looking for a steady job?"

Scotty laughed, shifted position, shook his head. "No, sir, that's about what I'm not looking for. Nothing too steady. I like to be free to come and go."

"Why's that?" Mrs. Griffeth's inquiry was severe.

"That's just the way I am, I guess. I don't like to get tied down."

"Everbody's got to settle down."

"Maybe. My time might come."

Griffeth said, "Don't you take no steady jobs?"

"Haven't yet. I shear sheep in the spring, haul wheat and hay in the summer, plow in the fall, do what I can in the winter. I like to keep on the move."

Mrs. Griffeth said, "Don't sound like too good a life to me."

"It ain't the best, I guess. I like it."

"Seems like your belly would do a lot of rubbing against your backbone."

"I ain't missed a meal yet that I recall."

"You're lucky."

"I have a uncle figured pretty much the same way I do, but he broke the rule, and he suffered for it."

"Broke the rule?" she asked.

"I have a rule not to stay on a job longer than I want to. Be a good quitter, that's my motto. When you get tired of a job, move on. Well, my uncle always done that until he got this one job. One day he decided it was time to quit, so he went to the boss and quit. But the boss begged him to stay on just one more day, so's he'd have time to get more help. Well, my uncle didn't want to, but the boss finally talked him into working just one more day. And about a half a hour before quitting time on that extra day, some dynamite they was using went off too soon and my uncle got hurt, and he's been in a wheel chair ever since. He got paralyzed from the waist down. So I learned my lesson from that."

The woman asked, "Whatcha gonna do when you get older?"

"Just keep moving along."

"A rolling stone gathers no moss," she warned.

"No, ma'am. And a setting hen lays no eggs."

The woman stood up. "I better go back out to the kitchen a minute. Surely that girl needs a little help with that big dinner."

Max Griffeth turned to Jake. "What about you?"

Scotty said, "Oh, he's plumb different than I am. He gloms onto a job and won't let go till the money peters out."

"You looking for a steady job?"

Jake said, "I'm trying to get into some kind of business for myself."

"Like what?"

"Custom hauling."

"You got a truck?"

"I'm gonna get one."

"Is there any money in that?"

"If I keep at it there should be."

They sat in silence for a while, then the man got up. "You boys might need to wash up for dinner. Come here. I'll show you."

They followed him back into the hallway and along it to the front door. He pointed up the stairway. "Just up to the head of the stairs and to the left there's a heater with some water on it and a washbasin and some towels and washcloths and soap and whatnot. Come here." He led them out the front door and along the front porch to one side of the house. He pointed toward the back yard. "The outhouse sets out there in them there lilacs." He turned and went back into the house.

Jake and Scotty went upstairs, walking slowly and cautiously in order to make as little noise as possible on the wooden steps. The stairs ended in a wide landing walled by shelves.

"They've sure got a lot of books," Scotty said.

"Yeah. And games, it looks like." They spoke in whispers.

"There's a phonograph. And a big stack of records."

Jake stood looking about him. There was a door facing the stairs, another to the left. A hallway ran back beside the stairway and led to a window overlooking the front yard, and to another door off to one side.

Scotty peered through the doorway into the dark room that faced the stairway. "Looks like a spare room," he whispered.

"Let's wash up," Jake said.

The door to the left of the stairs opened into a spacious bedroom. Its windows opened on the east and the south, and the midday sunshine brightened the room.

"It sure smells good in here," Jake said, breathing deeply.

"This must be the girl's room," Scotty said.

"It's warm, too."

"They've got a fire burning in that heater. That's sure a fancy stove they've got down in the parlor."

"I didn't notice it."

"Look at it when we go back. Big and square with a sort of a fancy brown enamel grillwork all around it. Looks almost like a cabinet or something. It's right below this heater. They must use the same chimney."

"This is sure a pretty room."

A pink and white bedspread covered a brass double bed. At the foot of the bed stood a blond cedar chest. A white chest of drawers with a pink design painted on it matched a small white bookcase filled with books. Two rag rugs, with blues the dominant colors, lay on the floor. There was a dresser with a chair. Both were painted white. A mirror hung above the dresser. On the bed was a large, finely dressed doll.

"I have a sister that would sure like a china doll like that," Jake said.

Scotty had rolled up his sleeves. He picked up the kettle from the stove and poured steaming water into the washbasin. He replaced the kettle and began to ladle cold water from a bucket to the washbasin, testing the wash water with his finger after each dipperful to see if it was cool enough to use.

"She seems pretty well fixed for life," Scotty said.

"It might not hurt you none if you did marry her."

Scotty hung the dipper back in the bucket and picked up the soap. "She may be the only chick in the nest, but she ain't the only fish in the pond. Anyway, she ain't asked me yet." He lathered his hands with the soap, put the soap back in its dish, and began vigorously soaping his face and forearms with the lather in his hands.

When Scotty had finished, Jake washed, then poured the water into the empty bucket that stood beneath the washstand. Scotty handed him the towel and, as Jake dried himself, Scotty took out a comb and peered into the mirror and began combing his hair.

"Let me borrow your comb when you're done," Jake said.

"Okay."

Jake glanced at the floor. There were drops of water here and there on the boards. He pulled a red bandanna from a back pocket, knelt on one knee, and mopped up the fallen water.

"You'll make some woman a good housekeeper," Scotty said.

Jake stood and Scotty handed him the comb. Jake stepped in front of the mirror and began combing his hair.

"I never seen a stove on the second floor of a house before," Scotty said.

"Me neither. They're pretty rich, though."

"I wonder why she don't marry none of the boys here in the valley if she's so set on getting married."

"Maybe there ain't none."

"I met one or two from over this way."

Jake returned the comb and they went downstairs, Jake pausing for one last look around the bedroom.

Both parents were seated in the parlor when they got there. The woman said, "All spruced up, I see."

Scotty said, "Yes, ma'am. We wash our faces ever Thanksgiving whether they need it or not." He sat back down on the davenport and Jake sat beside him.

"I sure like this house," Jake said.

"Well, we're kinda proud of it."

He looked at the brown heater, in which a fire could now be heard roaring. Someone must have stoked it while they were upstairs.

"I see you burn coal," Jake said. The hod stood beside the heater.

Griffeth said, "Yeah, we haul in a couple loads or so ever summer. Saves a lot of woodcutting."

"That's nice," Jake said.

Mrs. Griffeth looked up toward the parlor doorway and said, "Oh, here she is now."

The young men looked. In the doorway stood Maxine. She wore a dark yellow dress with a collar that buttoned close around her throat. Her dress was knee-length, and she wore silk stockings and plain black patent-leather pumps. Over the dress she wore a long red apron. Her black hair reached just to the collar of her dress, and she had fixed a smooth red ribbon in her hair. The dress was short-sleeved, and the skin on her arms, throat, face, and legs was flawless. She looked toward the young men with a nervous smile and said, "Hello."

"Hello," Scotty said. He began to get up, but seemed to lose his balance and fell, turning, onto Jake. They almost bumped heads. Scotty's mouth was close to Jake's ear. Scotty whispered, "You're gawkin' at her."

CHAPTER SEVEN

With one hand on Jake's shoulder and another on Jake's knee, Scotty pushed himself upright and stood. He grinned at Maxine. "I'm clumsy," he said. "Would you like to set down here by Jake?"

Her smile seemed to lose its nervousness. "Oh, no. I'll sit over on the sofa."

Mrs. Griffeth said, "Dear, you remember the boys that helped us. Scotty Tubbs and—I don't seem to recall your name."

"Jake Mortensen."

"Oh, sure."

Maxine moved to the sofa and sat at one end of it, resting an arm on the upholstered arm of the sofa. Jake watched her as she sat, then looked at one of the pictures on the walls. Scotty remained standing near the davenport.

"Jake was just telling us about his family," Mrs. Griffeth said. "He has ten brothers and sisters."

"No, nine," Jake corrected. "There's ten altogether."

"Are you the oldest?"

"I'm the oldest boy. I've got two sisters older."

"Are they married?"

"The one is. The other teaches school."

Scotty said, "Lots of Jake's folks don't believe in getting married."

Mrs. Griffeth raised her eyebrows. "Oh? Don't your sister want to get married?"

Jake glanced up at Scotty, his mouth a straight line, then looked down at the floor. "I don't know."

She said, "Is it the sister that teaches that don't want to get married?"

Scotty said, "I said the wrong thing and give you the wrong idea.

Sometimes I get to teasing when I'd be better off to keep my mouth shut."

Maxine said, "Do you have a sister who teaches?"

"Ya."

"What's her name? Maybe I knew her at Normal School."

"Joanne. She never went to Normal School. She just got a job teaching."

Mrs. Griffeth said, "How old is she?"

"She's twenty-one. She's my oldest sister."

"That's my age," Maxine said.

"And she don't want to get married?" Mrs. Griffeth said.

Max Griffeth said, "Tell us about some more of your family. How many boys is there?"

"Five boys and five girls. The littlest was born last summer."

"It must be exciting to live in such a large family," Maxine said.

"It's hard work, mostly. Ten kids takes a lot of feeding."

"Yes, I guess they would. What does your father do?"

"He farms."

"Where's your farm?" Max Griffeth asked.

"It's the last one south of Holbrook. The last place before you get to the farms down around Stone."

"I guess I don't know him. I can't place him or that place."

Scotty said, "He might have come through here years ago with a horse and wagon selling Rawleigh goods. He used to be the Rawleigh man."

"Oh, I remember him," Maxine said. "A tall thin blond man?"

"Ya."

"I liked him. He was a nice man."

"Warn't his name Jim?" Griffeth asked.

"Yes. James Mortensen."

"Ya, I remember him."

Maxine stood up. "We shouldn't sit here too long. I have dinner on the table."

Mrs. Griffeth seemed to propel herself to her feet by waving her arms in the air in a swimming motion. "Well, why didn't you say so? We don't want it to get cold. Come on, boys. Maxine fixed up the best chicken you're ever gonna eat."

Scotty grinned. "Chicken, huh? That's going to be a disappointment to Jake. He was hoping you'd have rabbit."

"Rabbit?" asked Mrs. Griffeth. "Would you rather have rabbit for Thanksgiving?"

Maxine said, "Do you like rabbit? Well, I'm glad you said something." She swept past the young men toward the door, moving swiftly and with purpose. "I fried two rabbits while I was at it, but I didn't think you'd want them for dinner so I was going to save them for myself. I'll put them on the table."

"Rabbit?" said Mrs. Griffeth. "Maxine, you don't—"

"Now, just leave her alone," Max Griffeth said. "She's in charge of the dinner."

"But, Max—"

"Just don't say nothing about it. Leave it up to Maxine. She knows what she's doing."

"But, Max, we don't—"

"Now, just don't say nothing. You're going to make me mad. Come on in, boys, and set down to the table."

Through the doorway they could see Maxine pick up two platters of chicken from the table and carry them out of the room. Max Griffeth had his hand around his wife's arm, and he urged her toward the table. "You boys just set down on this side—Scotty, we've got you there on the right, and Jake on the left. Lois, you might as well be at this end of the table. I'll set across from the boys."

They sat down. Max Griffeth looked complacent, happy about the meal that was about to be served. Jake was smiling. The other two did not look well. It was hard to see the white tablecloth beneath the array of serving dishes that were crowded onto the table. Before each chair were a china plate with an intricate red design, clear glasses of milk and of water, and heavy pieces of silverware, with two forks at each place. A white napkin that matched the tablecloth was folded on each plate. The fragrance of the hot food was heady.

Maxine came back into the room carrying a single platter of meat. She was beaming with a delighted smile. "I love rabbit," she said. Still holding the platter, she sat at the head of the table, with her father at her right and Scotty on her left. She held the platter out toward Scotty. "Here, you be first. Take whatever piece you like."

Scotty looked expressionlessly at the pieces of meat, then picked up his fork and seemed to be pondering which one to spear. Maxine pointed at one meaty piece. "Try the thigh. They're good."

Scotty stuck his fork into it and lifted it to his plate. He sat looking at it. Maxine did not pass the platter. She said, "Oh, don't stop with just one piece."

"One's plenty for now."

She picked up her own fork. "Oh, have another." She jabbed the fork into a small piece at her end of the platter and deposited the piece on Scotty's plate. "Have the gizzard. That's the tastiest part of a rabbit."

Scotty wore a worried frown. He touched the gizzard with his fork, moved it a little. He said, "I didn't know rabbits had gizzards."

That was too much for even Mrs. Griffeth. She erupted in a hoot of laughter and turned away from the table, holding her side as she shook with laughter. "Rabbits—rabbits don't have gizzards!" she cried through her laughter.

The others were laughing, too. Scotty put down his fork and glared at them, then began to smile. He said, "Is this really chicken?" That set them off again.

Max Griffeth got himself partly under control first. He said, "She fooled you. She just took off the wings so you wouldn't recognize them and brought back the chicken."

"You could of left the wings on the plate," Jake said. "He'd of thought they was the ears!" That broke Mrs. Griffeth up again. She was wiping at her eyes with her apron and laughing.

Maxine permitted herself one last, pursed-lip giggle, wiped her own eyes with the back of her hand, and said, "It's perfectly safe chicken. Have all you want. There's plenty. I'll go get the other platter."

Mrs. Griffeth turned back to the table, her mirth subsiding. "You boys fill up your plates, now. Looks like Maxine made a right good dinner. Start them peas, Jake. Scotty, dish up some sweet potatoes as soon as you get done with the chicken. Max, start the spuds."

"What's this?" Jake asked.

"That's cranberry sauce. It goes real good with the chicken. Where's the dressing? Oh, there it is. Maxine'll start it when she gets back. Here she comes. Maxine, start the dressing. And the bread and butter. Max, have some gravy."

"Well, hold on a minute," Max said. "We ain't said the blessing yet." There was immediate quiet around the table. "Maxine."

They lowered their heads. Maxine said, "Our Father, Who art in heaven, we thank you for this food you have given us and for the blessings you have bestowed on us. We thank you for these friends who have come to share thy plenty with us. Amen."

"Amen."

"Amen."

"Amen."

"Amen. Okay, boys, dig in."

For a few minutes there was little talk. Utensils clicked against china, plates were filled to capacity, dishes were passed, food was salted and peppered, butter was spread, the first bites were taken. Maxine still wore her smile; she kept her head down and her eyes on her plate and the nearby dishes as if she were trying to hide the smile. Once she glanced up and saw Jake looking at her. Her smile became wider, warmer. He grinned and looked back at his own plate.

"Have some of that slaw," Mrs. Griffeth instructed. "We got more of everthing out in the kitchen."

"These peas is good," Scotty said. "My mother makes them like this, in the same kind of white gravy."

"You oughta like them candied carrots, too. That's my mother's recipe. So is the cake Maxine made for dessert."

"I hope I can get around all this," Scotty said. "I'd hate to have to leave something unet."

"Well, we've got lots of time. You can always come back for seconds after you've rested up from the firsts."

Griffeth said, "Some women ain't happy unless you eat yourself to death."

"I wouldn't have no other kind," Scotty said.

"We grow a lot of our own food," Mrs. Griffeth said. "Everthing on the table we growed, except the sweet potatoes and the cranberry sauce. And the salt and sugar and stuff like that."

"We bought the flour," Max said.

"Yes, but we growed the wheat, or anyway some just like it."

"You have a real nice place here," Scotty said.

"When we die, Maxine gets it," Mrs. Griffeth said.

"Ya, you mentioned that."

"She's gonna be real well set up, ain't she, Jake?" the woman asked.

Jake had a mouthful of chicken and couldn't answer. He chewed, and no one else spoke. The parents were both watching him.

Maxine said, "Mother, Jake doesn't want to talk about that."

"How do you know? I'm interested in his opinion. What do you think of that, Jake?"

He managed to swallow the chicken. "It's okay, I guess." He picked up a forkful of potatoes and gravy.

"You guess? You sound like maybe it ain't a good idea."

He started to put the food into his mouth, but she was looking at him as if waiting for an answer. He lowered the fork, held it just above his plate, waiting.

"If it was my land and my daughter, I guess I wouldn't do it that way."

"Well, for goodness sakes! Why not?"

He said nothing for a moment, then put the fork and its load on his plate. "I guess I'd be afraid I'd be doing the wrong thing for the girl."

Max Griffeth asked, as if he were genuinely interested, "How can it be the wrong thing?"

"She wouldn't have nothing to look forward to. Except me dying. That ain't so good."

The woman said, "She can look forward to having this farm."

"Well, she has that now. She lives here and eats here and she can do about as much or as little on the farm as she wants, I reckon. After a while she'll still be here on the farm only she won't have no folks."

"She'll have a husband."

"Oh, yeah, but then he'll have the farm and she still won't have nothing to look forward to."

"Well, I ain't never heard of such a thing."

Jake reddened, but now that he had begun he plowed right on. "She couldn't never go nowhere. I mean, to live or work. She couldn't make no plans like that because she'd always have to think about how things was going on the farm. If she should go to Salt Lake or New York or some place and get a good job, first thing you know her folks would die and she'd have to quit and come back."

"But she wouldn't want to go off anyway, and leave her husband."

"She ain't married. If she was to get married, she'd have to find a farmer. If she was off in Salt Lake or somewhere and was to meet a doctor or a lawyer or something, he wouldn't want to come back here and farm. So the place wouldn't do her no good."

"She could sell it."

"Ya, if she didn't get took."

"She don't have to marry no doctor or lawyer. There's plenty of farm boys right close around here."

"Ya, but maybe she don't want to marry none of these clodhoppers around here. I wouldn't if I was a girl."

Maxine's grim look changed into a smile, almost a smirk, at that, but she kept her eyes lowered and went on eating. Mrs. Griffeth uttered a sound that was cousin to a sigh and nephew to a grunt and subsided into disgusted silence. Max Griffeth said, "How would you do it if it was up to you?"

"I'd keep on farming until I didn't want to farm no more. Then I'd sell the place for all I could get and give her half, and I'd take the other half and go someplace where it was warm all year, and be on vacation the rest of my life."

"That don't sound too bad," Griffeth said.

"Well, I think we've got it planned just fine," Mrs. Griffeth said.

Scotty said, "Jake's got a lotta theories about how to raise kids. That's the way it is with people that don't have no kids."

Jake shrugged. "I ain't got no land, either."

They took seconds, and from some of the serving dishes they took thirds. Lois Griffeth helped her daughter clear away the plates and serving dishes, and Mrs. Griffeth replenished the pitcher of milk, and Maxine brought out an array of desserts—pumpkin pie, mincemeat pie, cherry pie, apple pie, and a large one-layer white-frosted cake.

"We got whipped cream to go on that pie," Mrs. Griffeth said. "Max, go git the ice cream." He got up to do that. She said, "Max was at work all morning making that ice cream, and I come near forgetting we had it." He returned presently with the canister of ice cream and used a big spoon to scoop generous helpings onto each plate.

"I'll put this back in the pantry to keep cold," he said. "If you want more, just holler."

Jake finished chewing and swallowing a bit of cake. "That's raisin cake, ain't it. That's my favorite."

"There's lots more," Maxine said. "Have all you like."

They made a deep dent in the cluster of desserts before, one by one, they sank back in their chairs, overcome by the food. Max Griffeth said, "That was plumb good."

"You done a real good job, Maxine," Lois Griffeth said.

"I didn't do it all by myself," Maxine said.

Scotty said, "You're about as good a cook as Jake is."

Maxine shot him a quick grin. "And my rabbit's even better, isn't it?"

"Yes," he said through the laughter around the table, "I got to admit that it is."

Max scooted his chair back from the table. "Why don't we git away from the table and set down and let our food settle."

"We can go back in the parlor," Mrs. Griffeth said.

"Oh, no, let's just set in here for a while. Set there in that there rocker, Jake. That's a comfortable rocker."

"Maxine was rocked to sleep in that rocker more than once," Mrs. Griffeth said.

"Scotty, try that chair over there. I do believe I'll build up all the fires before I settle down, or we'll be settin' here in the cold."

Maxine said, "I'll clear the table."

"Oh, you can leave that a while," her mother said.

"I'd just as soon get it done."

Jake said, "I'll give you a hand."

"You don't need to do that."

"I know."

Mrs. Griffeth said, "Well, leave the whipped cream and one or two pies out here in case anybody wants more. Leave your plates and forks if you want."

They put most of the food in the pantry, which was on the far side of the kitchen. The kitchen was just off the dining room. It was a big room with white cabinets along one wall, a black coal range along the other wall, a worktable in the middle, and a set of wash-tubs under the windows at the far end. The pantry was to the right of the washtubs. To the left were a row of hooks on which hung a variety of coats and hats, and a door leading to the back yard.

"Put those pies right here," she said. "I'll cover them up with a dishtowel."

Jake said, "That was the best dinner I ever eat in my whole life."

She looked pleased and smiled warmly. "Thank you. I really did cook most of it. Mother wants you to think I did it all, but she did most of the vegetables and some of the pies."

"I liked the cake and the chicken best."

"I did those. Should we go back to the front room?"

"Okay."

Lois Griffeth greeted her daughter with a suggestion. "Maxine, why don't you set down at that piano and play us some music?"

Jake looked around the room. The piano, an upright of polished brown wood, was in the corner of the room farthest from the kitchen. It was open, and several pieces of sheet music were on the rack. There were a number of knickknacks on top of the piano. The round-topped stool was pushed underneath the keyboard.

Maxine said, "Nobody wants to hear me play."

"I'd like to hear you," Jake said.

She looked at him. "Oh? All right. What would you like to hear?"

"I don't care."

She went to the piano, pulled out the stool, sat, and began sorting through the sheet music. Jake stood watching her for a minute, then sat down in Scotty's chair at the table. He leaned forward on the table, his arms folded and resting on the white cloth, and did not take his eyes off her.

She turned on the stool and said to them, "I'll play if you'll sing with me."

"Sure," said Scotty. "Play away."

She pivoted back and played an introductory theme to a familiar tune, and they all chimed in:

"Over the river and through the woods
To Grandmother's house we go!
The horse knows the way to carry the sleigh
O'er the white and drifting sno-ow!"

CHAPTER EIGHT

They sang half a dozen songs. Then Maxine, as if oblivious to the rest of them, began playing music that had no words or to which they did not know the words. They listened quietly.

Max Griffeth, without saying anything, got up and went to a cupboard. He opened it and took out a deck of cards. He closed the cupboard and sat down at the table. With an index finger he motioned his wife and Scotty to the two unoccupied sides of the table. Scotty sat across from Jake, Mrs. Griffeth across from her husband. Max began to shuffle the cards. Maxine finished her tune and swiveled on the stool.

"I thought we might play some pinochle," Max said. "Go on playing."

"All right." She turned back to the piano and launched into some fast music. As the cards piled up in front of him, Jake watched her back bent slightly toward the keyboard, her fingers dancing swiftly from one set of notes to another. For almost an hour they played cards and she played music.

When she tired of her concert she turned and sat between Scotty and her father, silently watching them play a couple of hands. As the cards were being raked up from the second of those hands, her mother said, "Would you like to take my place, Maxine?"

"Oh, no. I don't feel like playing cards."

"There's other games. You want to play something else?"

"Does anyone want to play Chinese checkers?"

Scotty said, "Jake?"

Jake said, "You bet."

She stood up. "You guys play another hand while I go upstairs and get the board and set it up."

They played two games of Chinese checkers, pausing between them to dish up more pie and ice cream and whipped cream and milk, which they snacked on during the second game. When they finished the second game, Maxine began setting up the marbles for another. Her father left the table and went around the front room and kitchen and parlor lighting the kerosene lamps. When he returned to the table and said, "Ready to play," Maxine stood up.

"I don't think I'll play this time," she said. "I want to get those dishes done."

Jake stood up. "I might as well help," he said.

"You don't have to."

"I just as soon."

"Well, okay."

Mrs. Griffeth said, "Maybe you could get Scotty to help, too. With three of you, those dishes should take no time at all."

Scotty stood up. "I'm going to leave it to them. I get my fill of it. I'm the chief cook and bottle washer up at our camp. But I reckon it won't hurt me none to fill your coal buckets and split a little kindling." He went through the parlor to the hallway to get his coat.

Jake poured the hot water from the reservoir in the stove into the dishpan, then refilled the reservoir from the bucket so more water could heat. He poured the rest of the cold water from that bucket into a half-full bucket and handed the empty bucket to Scotty. "Might as well fill this, too," he said.

Maxine said, "The well's just out that back door to your right. You'll see a bunch of little sheds out past the garden. The coalshed and the woodshed are there."

"Okay." Carrying three coal buckets by their bails in one hand and the water bucket in the other, Scotty let himself out the back door.

"Where's your soap?" Jake asked.

"I can wash those."

"I might as well. I don't know where they go when they're clean, so you better dry them so you can put them away."

He rolled up his sleeves and they set to work. For a time they said no more than the work required them to say. Scotty came in with the water and a bucketful of coal and went back out again.

"Do you like teaching?" he asked.

"It's okay. Some of the children I like a lot. Especially the little ones. It's fun to watch them learn. They discover so much."

"How far is it to your school?"

"Six miles."

"Long ways."

"In good weather Dad lets me take the car. In bad weather I drive the horse and sleigh over on Monday morning and stay the week with a family that lives near the school. I come home Friday night. If it's rainy and muddy, Dad drives me."

"I like your folks."

"They like you. There aren't many people they let talk back to them like you did." She laughed happily. "I don't think Mother cared for it very much."

"I wasn't talking back. They asked me what I thought."

"I'm glad you told them. Wouldn't you like to inherit your father's farm?"

"There's other kids needs it more than I do."

"Most of the others are small, aren't they? If you had the farm, you could take care of them."

"I don't think Papa's going to die for a day or two yet, and I help take care of them what I can anyway." When Jake said "Papa" or "Mama" he pronounced the words "puh-puh" and "muh-muh."

"If you don't want to farm, what do you want to do?"

"I don't mind farming, but if I was to do that, I'd want to buy my own place."

Scotty came in with the other two buckets of coal and went through the kitchen to take them to the front room and the parlor.

"Have you known Scotty for a long time?"

"Long as I can remember."

"Does he tease you a lot?"

"We tease each other. He's a good guy."

"Does he like girls?"

"Oh, ya."

"Does he have a girl friend?"

"Quite a few. No one in particular."

"Do you?"

"I go dancing sometimes. No one particular girl."

Scotty came back into the room. "Where's your egg bucket? I seen your chicken coop and thought I might gather up your eggs."

Maxine put down her dishtowel. "Oh, Mother will appreciate that. She has to do that." She went into the pantry and returned with a small bucket. "She gathers them in this."

"Okay. I guess none of your hens is settin'?"

"No."

He took the egg bucket and went outside.

"Scotty seems very nice after you get to know him."

"Ya, he is."

She dried dishes in silence for several minutes before she said, "Are you the one in your family who doesn't want to get married?"

"Ya."

"Why not?"

"It don't seem like too good a idea."

She did not say anything for a time. She lifted a pile of dried plates into their place in a cupboard and closed the cupboard door. Jake bent over a food-encrusted pan, scrubbing at it to get it clean.

"I guess I don't understand," she finally said, "and I wish I did."

"It's just the way I feel."

"You don't want to have a woman in your home?"

"It ain't that. I don't think I should have kids. If you get married, you're likely to have kids."

"Don't you like children?"

"Kids is okay, but they're hard to raise."

"Your folks seem to have raised you well enough."

"It was hard for them, and it gets harder for ever kid. My folks work awful hard, and they never get nothing ahead."

"Well, they had a lot of children. If they only had three or four, it might be different."

"Maybe."

"You wouldn't have to have ten children."

"I know."

"But you don't want any?"

"Somebody's got to help the ones that's already born."

"And that's what you're going to do?"

"If I can."

"That won't leave anything for yourself."

"I'll probably have more that way than if I was to have kids."

"That seems sad to me."

"It don't to me."

"Well, I guess that's what counts."

Jake said nothing. He used his forearm to push back his hair and wipe perspiration from his forehead, and he filled the dishpan with another stack of dirty dishes. After a while he said, "Do you want to get married?"

"Someday. If I meet the right man."

"You never met him yet, though, huh?"

"I'm not sure."

Scotty brought in the eggs and the other two finished the dishes. They went back into the front room together. Both of the parents were sitting—Max in an easy chair, reading his magazine; Lois in the rocker, doing embroidery. She looked up at them.

"What do you young people want to do? Play some more cards? Maxine, you could play more for them."

Maxine said, "I'd like to bring down the phonograph."

"I can get it," Scotty said. "I seen it upstairs while we was washing up. Come on, Jake."

"There's a big pile of records up there," Maxine said. "Bring down all you can carry."

Max looked up quickly. "Yeah, but don't bring down no more'n you can carry. And watch your step on them stairs."

Lois said, "You'll need some light. Take that there lamp."

They set up the phonograph on the table. Scotty cranked it up while Maxine selected records. She stacked half a dozen on the table beside the machine while Scotty fitted a new needle into the arm. She put the record in place and set the needle in the groove. The music began. She turned to Jake.

"Will you dance with me?"

"Okay."

They were both good dancers. Lois Griffeth tapped her foot to the music and looked up now and then from her work to smile at the couple. Max got up from his chair and pushed it closer to the kitchen wall so there was more room to dance in the corner near the parlor door.

The record ended. She went to the phonograph to put on another one. She said to Jake, "You dance very well."

Scotty said, "Oh, he'll swing your shimmy tail."

She looked at Scotty with a challenging smile. "How about you?"

He shrugged. "I'll give it a try."

She alternated, dancing with one man and then the other until she said, "That's all. I'm worn out!" She pulled a chair from the table and sank into it, lounging back, laughing lightly, looking limply relaxed but graceful. With more restraint, Jake sat in another chair. Scotty lounged in the parlor doorway. Maxine leaned forward in her chair, took the record off the phonograph, and looked for another. "Let's just listen to some music," she said. Jake rose and went to the table to change the needle and crank up the phonograph again.

"Doggone," Max Griffeth said, getting out of his chair with some effort. "When I get this old hinder of mine sat down after a dinner like that, it's about all I can do to get it up again."

"Where are you going, dear?" his wife asked.

"I gotta do the milking before it gets any later than it already is. Them cows will think I've died."

Scotty stopped leaning against the doorframe and came alertly to life. "Oh, stay set down. We can milk your cows for you." Jake finished cranking the record player and stood erect.

"You don't need to do that," Max said, standing. "We brung you here for a holiday, not to do all our work for us."

Scotty waved a hand to motion him down. "A change is as good as a rest. When you need some rest, come on up and cut a few cedar posts with us. Let's go, Jake."

Jake started toward the parlor door. Max said, not very emphatically, "I can do it."

"You only have a couple of cows to milk, don't you?" Scotty asked.

"Ya. Two."

"We can divide them up."

They got their coats from the hall closet and put them on. Jake felt in a pocket for his gloves and came out with some envelopes. He went back into the front room ahead of Scotty.

"Does the mail come by here?" he asked.

"Ya," Max said, "ever day."

"I wrote these letters to my folks. I was wondering if I could mail them from here."

"Sure. Set them there on that cupboard. We'll see they get mailed."

Scotty, coming up beside Jake, said, "Where's your milk buckets?"

"In the pantry. When you get back in, Maxine will show you

where to put the milk. They's a blue pan in by the milk buckets. Fill it with warm water and take that rag that's hanging by it and wash their bags before you milk them. We try to keep the milk as clean as we can."

"Okay."

"There's a bin with some sacks of barley in it and a coffee can on one of the sacks. Give them each a half a can of barley. When you finish, let them out and throw some hay in that outside manger for them and the other stock. Maxine, show them where the lantern is. There's a nail by the second window that I hang the lantern on. The cows you're supposed to milk will more'n likely be by the door waiting for you. They usually go in by theirselves. They're both Holsteins. You won't have no trouble finding them."

It was warm and quiet, even snug, inside the small barn. The lantern hanging on the wall cast lights and shadows haphazardly. Each man had fitted himself against the side of a cow, burrowing his head in where the belly curved in to meet the hind quarter. They squatted on T-shaped stools made of two-by-fours and squinted down at buckets held between their knees. Twin streams of milk, alternating, sang against the metal bottom of each pail. As the buckets filled, the metallic singing changed to a deep-toned mellow plashy rhythm. Aromas blended in the barn—manure, fresh hay, cowhide, warm milk, and the clean sharp smell of a cold November night.

They worked without speaking for several minutes before Scotty's voice, muffled against the cow, came to Jake.

"You kind of like that girl, huh?"

A pause. Squirts of milk pushing into the foam that bubbled in the buckets. "Ya."

"I think she likes you."

No answer.

"Does that yellow dress make you change your mind?"

"About what?"

"Having kids."

"No."

"Maybe just getting married."

"Can't get married without having kids."

"Sure you can."

A long pause. "I doubt it."

"It's a big house. You sleep downstairs, and she can sleep upstairs."

"Ha ha ha."

Silence for a time. The milk streamed into the pails at a steady beat.

"I seen a watering trough out by the corral gate."

"What about it?"

"If you have any kids, you can put 'em in a gunny sack and drowned 'em, like they was puppies."

"That ain't funny neither."

Silence. Scotty, then Jake, finished milking. They stood, tossed their stools out of the way against the wall. Jake handed his bucket to Scotty and walked up to release the cows from their stanchions. The animals turned and walked quickly to the door. Jake followed them to open it, but it was not latched and the lead cow pushed it open with her muzzle. Both animals went out of the corral.

"If she paid as much attention to me as she does to you," Scotty said, "I'd be tempted to revise my thinking about getting married."

"She's a pretty girl."

"Well, maybe not pretty, but she's so homely she's cute."

"No, she's pretty."

A considered pause. "Ya, she is."

"If you want to get the hay throwed out, I'll find a shovel and clean out the gutter."

"Let me find a place to set this milk down out of the way."

When Scotty returned from placing the hay for the stock, the cow barn was dark. He saw the lantern glowing behind the manger and picked his way through corridors until he tracked it down. Jake was holding the lantern high with one hand, turning this way and that in a small room, looking here and there as if searching for something. Scotty remained quiet until Jake noticed him standing in the doorway.

"What's the trouble?" Scotty asked. "You lose your mind?"

"I was looking at these boxes and boards and stuff. Them's good orange crates."

"Kinda dirty."

"They'll wash off. Let's take some up to the house."

"We've got the milk and that pan."

"Can you take the milk and the pan?"

"Ya."

"Okay." Jake put an orange crate inside a deep apple box and placed another orange crate beside them. He selected several smooth boards, one-by-eights five to eight feet long, and arranged them under his right arm. He carried the lantern in his right hand. With his left hand, he picked up the apple box and the extra orange crate together. He awkwardly sidled out of the little room and made his way out of the barn. Scotty picked up the milk and the pans and walked with him, opening and closing the barn door and the corral gate.

There was a light snow falling. The sky was overcast, yet there was plenty of light. They could see the shapes of buildings and earthscape for some distance around them. The flakes that touched their faces were feather-soft. The snow drifted leisurely to the ground.

"It's a nice night," Jake said.

"Oh, yeah, but I think it's going to be a long hard winter."

They left the boxes and boards outside. Maxine had heard them coming; she opened the door and let them in. "Put the pan on the table," she said. "I'll wash it out later. Bring the milk in here."

They took the milk into the pantry and strained it into another bucket through a clean flour sack. From that bucket she poured it into an earthenware crock and covered it. By morning the cream would have risen and could be skimmed off for their cereal.

They put the buckets on the kitchen worktable. Maxine began pouring hot water to wash them out. Jake went into the front room, where the parents still sat, reading and stitching.

"I wonder if one of you could come look," he said.

They both got up and followed him to the back door. He stepped outside and picked up the boxes. They stood on the stoop watching as he held the lantern to each of the items so they could see them.

"These boxes and boards was in your barn," he said. "How much would you take for them?"

Max said, "You can have the boards. We got plenty of old boards around here. Lois will have to say about the boxes."

She pondered for a moment. "Oh, I guess a nickel apiece for the orange crates and a dime for the other."

"Heck, they're worth more than that."

"Oh, ya, but that don't matter. That's plenty. You've helped out quite a bit."

Jake put the boxes down and came inside, stopping to brush the snow off his coat. Maxine was washing the pails. Scotty was not in the kitchen. Jake hung his coat by the back door.

"Need any help?"

"I'm almost done."

He waited for her and they went into the front room together. Scotty and the old folks were playing rummy. On the next hand, Jake and Maxine entered the game. They played until Lois won.

"I wouldn't mind having some bread and milk," Max said. "I worked up a appetite doing nothing. Anybody else want some?"

"They's lots of pie left over," Lois said.

"I'll take some pumpkin pie if that's okay," Scotty said.

"I'd just as soon have the bread and milk," said Jake.

They all had bread and milk except Scotty. It was a silent supper. Tiredness and a night mood seemed to have come over them. Maxine finished first and went into the kitchen. They heard her go outside and come in, pour water, work with dishes, open and close doors and drawers. Max Griffeth broke another slice of bread into his bowl bit by bit and added milk and sugar and went on eating. Lois sat down in her chair and picked up her work but let it rest in her lap. Scotty picked up the deck of cards and dealt and played a hand of solitaire. Jake leaned on the table, his bowl and spoon pushed out of the way, and looked into the dark opaque glass of the window.

When Scotty had lost his game of solitaire and was gathering up the cards, Jake stood up. "I guess we better be getting back," he said.

Mrs. Griffeth said, "Ain't no need for you to go back tonight. They's a spare bed upstairs. Stay the night and have breakfast before you go."

"No, we got plenty to do tomorrow. We'd best go back tonight."

"It's a long walk in the snow."

"There ain't much snow."

Max Griffeth pushed his chair from the table and stood. "I'll get the truck and haul you as far as that ditch. I ain't gonna cross the ditch in the dark, though. You'll have to walk from there." He went into the kitchen to get his coat and hat and gloves, and went to start the truck.

Jake took a coin purse from his pocket and opened it. He counted out four nickels and closed the purse and put it back into his pocket. He held the coins in his fist and walked over to Mrs. Griffeth. "Here," he said. She held out her palm and he dropped the nickels into it. She got up and went to the cupboard. She opened the cupboard door and reached up to a bowl on a shelf even with her eyes. She dropped the coins into the bowl. They made the sound coins make when dropped onto a heap of coins.

Scotty got up. "I sure want to thank you for that dinner, Mrs. Griffeth. I ain't et so good since I don't know when."

"I never have, either," Jake said. "Thanks a lot."

"Don't thank me. Thank Maxine. She done all the work."

Jake went into the kitchen. Maxine was at the counter, her back to him, busy at an orange crate that stood on the counter before her.

"We're going now," Jake said. "Want to thank you for the dinner."

She turned, tossing her hair out of her eyes and smiling at him. "You've thanked me three or four times already. You gave me so much leftover thanks that I fixed up some leftover dinner for you." She turned back to the counter. Jake walked up to look into the orange crate. Maxine said, "Most of it's leftovers, anyway. I washed out one of your boxes. The heavy stuff is at the bottom. There's some fruit and a little bottle of jam and the leftover slaw and some gravy and the rest of the peas in white gravy. And I put in a little jar of pickles Mother made. I cooked one chicken we didn't even touch, so that's wrapped up in that waxed paper. You can give Scotty the gizzard. There are two pie pans that I wrapped up. One of them is a cherry pie that hasn't been cut, and the other one is full of different pieces of pie that were left over—mince and apple and pumpkin. Right on top here I put some fresh eggs. Right in this corner, on the bottom, there's some ice cream in a quart jar. Keep that someplace cold. This big package on the other side is another raisin cake that I baked." She put a hand lightly on his arm. "You seemed to like the cake, so I wanted to give you this one."

"Thanks. We'll be having Thanksgiving until Christmas." He looked down at her. Her eyes were gray, or seemed so in this light. She patted his hand and stepped away from him. Jake put on his coat and picked up the box.

Scotty came into the kitchen. "Whatcha got?"

"She fixed us our breakfast."

"That's plumb nice of her."

They heard the truck's engine outside, then the gravelly command of its horn. Scotty turned back to the front room. "Good night, Mrs. Griffeth. Good night, Maxine."

"Good night, Scotty. I'm glad you could come."

"So are we."

Jake said, "Good night, Mrs. Griffeth."

"Good night. You two know where we live now. Come back again."

"We will."

Maxine said, "You'll have to. You have a bunch of our bottles and baking pans."

"I'll bring them back."

"You can go out the front door. Dad will be out there."

Scotty said, "I'll go out back and get them other boxes and stuff. I'll meet you around in front."

Maxine walked ahead of Jake to open the front door, and Mrs. Griffeth followed behind. They stood on the porch, Mrs. Griffeth with her hands clasped at her waist, Maxine hugging herself at the shoulders against the chill air. The truck idled in the driveway. Its headlights cut a tunnel through gently falling snow. Jake made footprints in the fresh snow as he carried the box to the truck and placed it carefully in the center of the bed, leaning belly-boost across the edge of the truck bed to push the box into place. Scotty came around the side of the house and put the other boxes and the boards on the truck. They walked around to get into the truck on the passenger side. They could both hear, just barely, Mrs. Griffeth when she said, "Maxine, did you give Scotty that cake you baked for him?"

CHAPTER NINE

Two days later, Scotty got his deer. He had again left camp early, and when Jake arrived at the working place Scotty was dressing out the buck. They quit work early and carried it back to camp and slung it from a tree limb near the pig. They had pork for breakfast, venison for dinner, and a variety of side dishes that made their lives luxurious even after the orange crate and the last of its jars and pans and waxed-paper packages were empty. They dined for several days after that on pleasant memories of good food.

"I'm getting hungry," Scotty remarked one evening. "Why don't you go back and fall in love with that girl again?"

"This is Tuesday. I don't fall in love on Tuesdays."

"You don't care much for your friends."

"Anyhow, she's had her turn. Next time, it's a red-haired girl's turn to have me fall in love with her."

"You got anybody in mind?"

"I don't know no red-haired girls except Priscilla Smith, and she ain't too good-looking."

"That don't mean nothing. That girl Maxine ain't too good-looking."

"She's pretty."

"Well, maybe for a black-haired girl you might say she's pretty." Scotty chewed on a matchstick for a time. "Ya, you always get me there. She's pretty. I got to admit. In that yellow dress, anyway. She kinda reminds me of Colleen Moore."

"Who's Colleen Moore?"

"She's a movie actress. Don't you never go to movies?"

"Not much."

"Well, Colleen Moore ain't the worst of the litter." Scotty

lounged back on his blankets and played some introductory notes on his harmonica and sang:

> *"Can she bake a raisin cake, Billy Boy, Billy Boy?*
> *Can she bake a raisin cake, Charming Billy?*
> *Oh, she baked a raisin cake*
> *And she give it all to Jake.*
> *She's a young thing and cannot leave her mother."*

There was plenty of work in the juniper grove where the deer had been to last them another week and more. They did not have to spend any part of Sunday exploring for a new work area, so they spent it all working on the dugout.

They cut logs and laid them across the earthen banks to form a roof. Where the ground sloped down so much that the banks were too low to serve as walls, they had piled stones—the big, flat rocks that littered the ground in the vicinity—one on top of another to form rock walls. They laid the logs across the stone and earthen walls. Jake cut a piece of rope and tied it around one of the logs. That log formed the center part of the ceiling. When the dugout was finished they could hang their kerosene lantern from that rope so it would light the entire dugout. They used the lantern sparingly because they were afraid they might run out of kerosene and they might need the lantern some night to search for things or to go someplace in the dark in an emergency, but they used it for a while almost every evening.

Before midday they took down their tent. They spread the canvas over the logs and covered it with dirt. They took turns shoveling, each working for an hour or so while the other did something else.

They installed the camp stove at the far end of the dugout. Before they passed the stovepipe up through a hole they had made for it, Jake scrubbed off the boards they had brought from Griffeth's farm. He placed one of the longest boards across the back wall of the dugout, fitting it into niches he dug out of the earthen walls and tamping the earth back to help hold it flat against the wall. He used the back of an ax to drive nails into the board. From it he hung their pots and pans and dishtowels and tin cups.

He laid the longest board across the dugout, head high, to serve as a shelf. There, on that shelf above the stove, he put their condiments and dishes and some odds and ends.

Scotty arranged their beds along one side of the dugout. Jake had not dug that side down as far as the rest of the dugout, so their beds were raised a foot or so above the floor. They slept foot-to-foot. Scotty, who relished warmth, had his head near the stove. Jake, who could easily get too warm for comfort, slept with his head near the dugout door.

Scotty made that door with most of the remaining boards. The boards actually formed a wall that covered the end of the dugout except where a blanket hung to form the actual door. On nice days they could toss the blanket up onto the roof and let the place air out.

Jake washed out the other orange crate and the apple box. He stood the orange crates on their ends across the dugout from their beds and laid the last board across them, forming a desk. Each used one of the orange crates as his cupboard and dresser, laying their extra clothes and other belongings on the two shelves. They used the apple box to hold their flour and some other items of food and personal belongings. They leaned Jake's rifles and shotgun against the far end of the orange-crate desk and kept their axes just inside the door—Jake could reach out in the night and touch the cold steel of the ax heads.

The dirt for the roof came from a hole they dug near the dugout. They put their potatoes into the hole and kept it covered with logs and limbs.

They finished the dugout before the sun went down, and they lit the kerosene lamp and admired their new home. They had chicken and peas in gravy and cole slaw for supper—they had snacked on bread rather than pause for lunch—and they finished with a dessert of raisin cake and some of the bottled peaches Maxine had given them. They played cribbage until late, and Jake now and then reeled off some humorous poem he knew, and Scotty now and then played a tune on his harmonica or sang.

> *"Can she sweep and scrub the floor, Billy Boy, Billy Boy?*
> *Can she sweep and scrub the floor, Charming Billy?*
> *I must sweep and scrub the floor,*
> *For it would make her fingers sore.*
> *She's a young thing and cannot leave her mother."*

A period of sharp cold set in, and their digging was over for the winter. Jake had meant to plant a couple of posts and string a clothesline, but they never got around to it. But he ran a rope between two trees, and over this rope, on Sundays except one Sunday when snow fell heavily all day, they dried clothes and hung their blankets to air.

They stopped cooking outdoors except very occasionally. They kept all the firewood they could inside the dugout so it would dry and burn well. The days grew shorter and shortened their work days, but the piles of cedar posts grew. During the second week after Thanksgiving they shifted their work to a grove of juniper about a mile northeast of the dugout.

The snow fell now and then and built up to a depth of eight or ten inches. Then there was a long period of time without fresh snow. What had fallen formed a crust that became firm enough, in most places, to walk on. The snow did not hamper their work.

On the third Sunday after Thanksgiving they had come back from scouting a new grove north of the camp. At the crest of the ridge overlooking their gully Scotty stopped and looked around him.

"This would be a good hill for sledding right here," he said.

"We ain't got a sled."

"Maybe we could make one."

They tried several times. They cut tree trunks and heavy limbs and shaped them like runners. They used axes and their pocket knives—once they even tried the whetstone—to smooth the bottoms of the runners as well as they could. They saved bacon grease to smear on them. They nailed other sticks crossways on the runners. But they could not get a sled to work. A couple of times, when the snow was fresh, they had impromptu snowball fights. One day they tromped out a big fox and geese trail near where they were cutting posts. But sledding defeated them.

The effort, however, inspired them to try other means of working with wood. Scotty managed to make a bedstead, notching small logs together, lashing them with rope, fitting legs into holes that he laboriously dug out of the cross pieces with a pocketknife. He wove a rope back and forth from side to side, tied it tightly, spread his blankets on this framework, and lay down. The bed collapsed. They laughed for fifteen minutes. The bedstead joined all their sleds as firewood.

They tried to carve, but neither had much skill in that endeavor. They could whittle rough likenesses of, say, a four-legged animal, but they ended in long debates over whether they had carved a squirrel or a horse. Their one success was Scotty's. He whittled out twelve small round chunks of wood and twelve small square chunks of wood and drew a gridiron on the board across their orange crates, and they used the bits of wood and the gridiron to play checkers.

"Can she whittle on a stick, Billy Boy, Billy Boy?
Can she whittle on a stick, Charming Billy?
Oh, she whittled on a stick
Until she made me one toothpick.
She's a young thing and cannot leave her mother."

"Scotty, you going home for Christmas?"

"No. I don't think so."

"How come?"

Scotty turned from his side to his back and stared through the darkness toward the log roof. "I ain't got nothing to give 'em. I don't like to go home without nothing to give 'em."

There was silence in the dugout for long minutes. Scotty said, softly, "You asleep?"

"No."

Scotty moved again, turning onto his stomach. Jake said something. Scotty said, "What?" and turned back to his side.

"I said I could probably give you some money. You got it coming anyway, when we sell the posts."

"We ain't sold 'em yet."

"We will."

"You paid for all the food and stuff we brung up here."

"You'll pay your half when we sell the posts."

"I'm gonna wind up owing all the money we get for them posts."

"Two or three dollars ain't much. I could let you have two or three dollars. You could get something for that."

"I'd just as soon not owe you no more money than I do. Anyway, you're saving up for your truck."

"Two or three dollars won't make no difference toward the truck."

"Naw, keep your money. If I got them something, they wouldn't have no money to get me nothing, and they'd just feel bad."

After a while Scotty said, "You going to get something for that girl?"

"Hadn't thought about it. Anyway, I won't be going back there."

"One of us has to go back there and take back their bottles and dishes."

"They ain't all empty yet. Anyway, we won't be going back before Christmas. We won't use up all that stuff they sent before Christmas."

"I just thought you might plan on getting her a present."

"No, I don't think so."

In the darkness, Scotty found his harmonica. He experimented a little, then played "Little Town of Bethlehem" and "Silent Night." Then there was a silence until Jake said, "You might wash out them bottles and things and take them down to their house while I'm gone. Put the jam and the pickles in something else. They'd be glad to see you. Probably give you a big dinner."

"Oh, no. They had one shot at me. I don't plan on giving them no more. Even in a yellow dress she ain't going to get me to the church."

"I ain't so sure she wants to get married."

"I don't think her folks is gonna consult her wishes. They've got plans of their own."

"Ya."

"Seems a guy ain't happy till he has kids. Then he ain't happy till he has grandkids. He sees them little anklebiters running around pulling the cat's tail, and he figures as long as there's little kids with the same shape ears and the same big feet as he's got there's always gonna be part of him left in this world."

They heard the wind come up outside. They listened to it awhile.

"You know any poems about that?" Scotty asked.

"About what?"

"About having kids."

"Oh. Yeah.

'Over the hill to the poorhouse
We're wending our weary way.'

"I don't remember no more than that. Didn't figure I needed to know no more than that."

"You know what's gonna happen when you die?"

"What's that?"

"Everbody's gonna say, 'I sure miss Jake. He didn't have no kids. There ain't nobody ugly to look at no more.' "

"There's you."

"Oh, I'm gonna die before you do. I'm older."

"It's the good that die young. You'll live to be a old man."

"As long as the grub holds out, that's okay."

The wind was rising in heavy, whistling gusts, then dying down somewhat before picking up strength for another gust. It blew snow like scatter shot against the blanket that covered their doorway. Jake scrunched deeper into his blankets.

Scotty said, "I hope you give her a hug and a kiss before we left there that night."

"I plumb forgot."

"Didn't you even steal a little kiss across the dishpan when you was doing dishes?"

"She was standing too far away."

"You could of thought of some way to get her closer."

"She didn't seem interested."

The wind pushed the blanket aside and blew a fistful of snow across Jake's forehead. He found an ax and laid it on a corner of the blanket to hold it against the wind.

> "*Did she ask you to come in, Billy Boy, Billy Boy?*
> *Did she ask you to come in, Charming Billy?*
> *Oh, she asked me to come in,*
> *But a kiss would be a sin.*
> *She's a young thing and cannot leave her mother.*"

In the crisp, cold, cloudless air above the gullies and ridges the bite of the ax made a solid cracking sound like a shot. Jake, even as he worked, sometimes listened to the sounds they made, thirty yards apart, swinging their axes in rhythm until one or the other, for some reason, had the rhythm broken. The splitting sound of a falling tree put its own sharp report into the winter air. And when there was silence for a time, the silence was complete.

But once it was not complete. There was silence, but there was a humming sound. Jake had raised his ax to start work on another tree, but he lowered it, set the head gently into the snow, leaned on the handle, and listened.

He called to Scotty. "Do you hear something?"

"Ya." Both listened.

The humming was getting louder, slowly louder. Scotty said, "There it is."

Jake looked at him, saw him pointing upward and to the east. Jake looked up, searching the bright blue sky with his eyes. Then he saw it, too, very high, only a speck, flying a bit south of a westerly course. Jake shaded his eyes with his arm and watched for half a minute.

"Where do you think he's going?" he shouted to Scotty.

"I think he's going to crash in the desert if he don't change direction."

"Where's he from?"

"He's coming from the direction of Malad."

Jake watched and watched before he said, "It wouldn't be old Quin, would it?"

"I don't know. Could be."

The airplane, nearing them, turned left and began flying southeast.

Scotty shouted, "He's following the road. Must be going to Snowville."

"He's taking the long way around."

"Maybe just practicing."

The plane grew smaller. The sound grew fainter. Presently the crack of Scotty's ax began resounding across the snowy hills again. Jake looked after the plane for some time longer.

As they sat on a pile of posts eating dinner Jake said, "It more than likely ain't Quin. He probably ain't had time to learn enough that they'd let him go without a instructor."

"Ya. And this is a long way from Salt Lake."

"I wonder if he'll be home for Christmas. I wrote him a letter before Thanksgiving. Mailed it down at the Griffeths' place."

"Too bad you don't have a airplane and know how to fly it. You could hop right over and see that girl anytime you felt like it."

"I can do that now. I ain't never felt like it."

"She better not hear you say that. You'll break her heart."

"Her heart looks plenty tough to me."

"That ain't her heart. That's her pie crust. I'm gonna go over there on Christmas Day and ask her to write you a letter telling how much you broke her heart."

"You better not get smart with her. She'll give you the gizzard again."

"Well, I think you're just being stubborn. Go down and marry the girl."

"You're the groom they got picked out, not me. Anyway, I wouldn't have a chance."

"Why not?"

"She's older than me."

"Lotsa guys marry girls that's older than them."

"I don't know none."

"I do."

"Send one of them down to marry her."

> "*How old is she, Billy Boy, Billy Boy?*
> *How old is she, Charming Billy?*
> *Three times six and four times seven,*
> *Two times nineteen and eleven.*
> *She's a young thing and cannot leave her mother.*"

Another day. Another dinner. The day was Christmas Eve. They sat side by side on a pile of posts, warming their feet at a small fire, each holding a thermos cup of coffee between his palms, both looking northward toward nothing.

"You gonna go home by the road?" Scotty asked.

"No. The snow ain't deep and you can just about walk on the crust most places. I'll go up there where you killed the deer and follow that canyon that runs north off that ridge. It swings east a few miles down and picks up the road three miles from home."

"Will you happen to go by my place?"

"I will in a couple of days. I'm going to Malad."

"You might stop in and tell the folks hello."

"I will." Jake took a drink of his coffee, tossed out the drops that remained in the cup. "You can still come with."

"Noo." He pronounced it to rhyme with who. "I'll just stay up here and get some work done. Might sleep a little later, though."

"If you get lonesome, go see that girl."

"If I do, I'll give her a kiss and say it's a present from you."

"You do that." Jake stood, gathered up his ax and the dinner bucket and his thermos. He poured the rest of the coffee from his thermos into Scotty's. He put the cork in his thermos and screwed the lid on. He pulled on his gloves, picked up the thermos and ax and dinner bucket, and took a few steps away from the pile of posts. He looked around him at the landscape and the sky.

"Be careful," he said. "Don't cut your foot off or nothing. There's nobody to help you until I get back."

"I'll be okay."

"I figure I'll get back late Saturday."

"Take your time."

"Merry Christmas."

"Merry Christmas."

Jake walked back to camp. He put the ax inside the dugout, cleaned out the dinner bucket, rinsed out his thermos and stood it upside down on the shelf above the stove. He rolled up his bedroll. He put into his pockets a few things he wanted to take with him.

When he got to the patch of trees where they had seen the deer he paused for a moment to glance at the piles of posts they had left here, all of them waiting to be hauled out in the spring. Then he started along the ridge above the canyon that led to home. Not far along the way he began to sing.

"Oh, where have you been, Billy Boy, Billy Boy?
Oh, where have you been, Charming Billy?
I have been to seek a ———"

He walked along, silent, head down, for several paces.

"I have been to see my girl———"

He looked up, looked all around him, walked on without singing for some distance.

"I have been to see Maxine.
She's the prettiest girl I've seen.
She's a young thing and cannot leave her mother."

CHAPTER TEN

Under the circumstances, it was a swift and easy walk down the ridge. The snow was heavily crusted, and his heavy shoes crunched into it only an inch or so at each stride. Once in a while an unexpected patch of soft snow sent him sinking to his calf or his knee, once to his hip. He reached the road before it was completely dark. He figured it was eighteen miles home on this direct line, and he figured that he walked it in not much more than five hours. On bare ground he could have cut an hour off that time.

The road he took would have led him into Holbrook. A couple of miles along it he left it, turning east on a side road. The snow was not as firm and the going was slower. The road sloped gently downward for nearly half a mile. After he'd gone a quarter mile of that he could see, off to his right, barely visible in the darkness, the shape of a building. It was a one-room cabin that had once been someone's house but was now abandoned.

Almost half a mile from the main road, this side road dropped steeply to a creek. The creek was frozen, but the ice where the road crossed the creek was thin. It was broken twice a day by Jake's father's cows, which were driven here morning and evening to be watered. Jake broke through the ice but the creek was shallow. He waded across without getting his pants wet, although the water spilled into his shoes.

Then the road made a steep ascent for a hundred yards before leveling out to a gentle climb. Half a mile from the creek he crossed another road and came to his house. The shape of the house and the shapes of the barn and sheds were plain, but there was no light showing in the house or any other building.

He walked to the door, scraped his feet on the cement step, and went inside. When he shut the door he was surrounded by warmth. They could not have been gone long; there was a red glow flickering from the cracks in the potbellied heater across the room.

"Anybody home?" he shouted. No answer came.

Jake took off his coat and felt his way toward the table in the middle of the room. He dropped the coat over the first chair he encountered. There was a kerosene lamp on the table. He lifted the chimney, lit the lamp, and replaced the chimney. When he had adjusted the wick slightly, he looked around the room.

Not much had changed in his weeks away from home except for the Christmas tree that stood in the corner at the foot of the couch. There was a generous pile of packages under the tree. It was decorated with red and green paper chains, popcorn strings, glass ornaments, tinsel, and some homemade paper decorations.

The room contained a set of cupboards, five chairs around the table, a rocking chair near the heater, woodbox, bureau, door to the kitchen, door to the bedrooms.

Jake carried the lamp into the kitchen. Cabinets ranged along the outside wall. He had helped his father build them. A long wooden table covered with oilcloth stood in the middle of the room. There were chairs at each end and one chair and one long bench on each side. He had made the benches himself. A highchair stood against a wall. Beside the chair stood a washstand—a table with a basin and a bucket of water standing on it, a second bucket of water on the floor beneath it, and some towels and washcloths hanging on hooks screwed into the wall. The washstand stood beside the back door.

The stove and a woodbox were also near the door.

The floor was covered with old linoleum, so worn in spots that the pattern had vanished entirely and only the reddish-brown core of the material remained.

Jake put his lamp on the table and cleared off the top of a heavy cupboard. He put a bench near the cupboard and stepped onto the bench and from there climbed onto the cupboard. Rising from a crouch, he used both hands to push upward on the trap door that led to the crawl space above the ceiling.

His head was in the attic. He placed the trap door out of the way, gripped the rafters with both hands, and hoisted himself into the attic.

He knelt beside the trap door and struck a match. In the light from its flame he could see the shapes of several boxes and bundles in the gloomy crawl space. It was cold up here—it felt even colder than it had outdoors.

He pulled one box closer to him. The match was burning close to his fingers. He blew it out, spat into the palm of one hand, and dampened the head of the match so it would be cool before he tossed it away.

He opened the box in the darkness and put the lid aside. He struck another match, and before it burned out he had removed a number of packages from the box and placed them near the edge of the trap-door opening. Each package was wrapped in white tissue paper and tied with colored string—red, green, blue, yellow.

In darkness again he put the lid back on the box and pushed it as far back as he could reach. He lowered himself back down to the heavy cupboard. Two at a time, he took the tissue-wrapped packages from the attic, knelt, and placed them on the cupboard near his feet. When they were all down he replaced the trap door and climbed back down to the bench and the floor. With a bandanna from his pocket he wiped clean the bench and the top of the cupboard, where his feet had been. He put the bench and the bandanna back where they belonged.

It took three trips to the Christmas tree, carrying packages by the armful, to put all the presents under the tree. There was enough light to enable him to make out his own name scrawled or printed on some of the tags on the other packages.

He left the lamp burning in the kitchen and went out the back door. There was a lean-to built against the back of the house. The door to it was near the back door. In the lean-to he lit another match, found another kerosene lamp on a chest of drawers, and lit that lamp.

In this room there were two double beds and a cot, a chest of drawers, and three wooden boxes. There was no stove. It was very cold here.

He went to one of the boxes, opened it, and took out some clothing—socks, long underwear, a pair of slacks, a dress shirt. Closing the box, he blew out the lamp and took the clothing out of the lean-to and back into the kitchen.

There was warm water in a boiler on the stove and Jake gave himself a sponge bath. He dried off and put on clean clothing, laced up his shoes, put his coat back on. The dirty water he tossed out the back door into the snow. He put the pan back where it belonged, picked up his dirty clothing, took it to the lean-to, and tossed it into the darkness.

Jake put the lamp back on the front-room table, blew it out, and pulled on his gloves. He groped in the woodbox for a big piece of wood. The embers sprang to flame as soon as the wood hit them. He watched the fire take, then closed the heater door and went outside, carefully closing the front door behind him.

The family's cows and pigs were penned in the corral on his right. The road he followed led past small sheds and between fields. A mile north it curved to the left and joined the road he had walked along earlier that evening. It was four miles more to the church at Holbrook.

A number of people turned to look at him as he slipped quietly into the last pew. Some smiled, some nodded a greeting. He gave them all a general, unsmiling nod in return. Concentrating, his tongue between his teeth, he took off his gloves and quietly wiggled out of his coat. His eyes focused on the stage.

The pulpit and the benches that were usually on the stage had been put aside for tonight. Now there was a manger scene. Jake saw his sister, wearing a white sheet, representing one of the angels. There was his brother, a towel draped over his head, a stick in his hand, portraying a shepherd. Someone was reciting words from the Bible. A woman seated at a piano in the front corner of the church began to play. Another woman stood, faced the crowd, and when the piano introduction had concluded she led them in singing.

"We three kings of Orient are.
Bearing gifts . . ."

The wise men shuffled onto the stage. Another of Jake's brothers was among them. They knelt at the manger and presented their gifts, then rose and stood back to form a tableau. The song ended. More words from the Bible were recited. Again the piano and the song leader.

"Joy to the world! The Lord is come.
Let earth receive her king!"

The music ended. With a jerky, mechanical sound the curtains were closed. Someone turned on the lights above the audience.

There was a brief silence, then people began to whisper to one another.

A man in front of Jake turned around and extended his hand. Jake shook hands with him.

"Hi, Jake. It's good you got here. Merry Christmas."

"Thanks. Merry Christmas. How you doing?"

"Can't complain. I seen your folks come in before the program. Your sister sang a song. She done a real good job."

"Good for her."

Other people nearby turned to whisper their greetings to him, and he returned them. Thumps and scraping sounds and giggles sometimes reached his ears from behind the curtains, and the curtains themselves bumped and rustled often and were sometimes pulled aside far enough to allow an eye to peek out. One little boy came onto the apron of the stage from one side, pushing the curtain away to make a passage. He stood, fists on hips, scowl on face, surveying the audience angrily, until a woman followed him and led him firmly back behind the curtain.

A young woman got up from a pew toward the front of the church and came back to Jake. She sat beside him, a big smile on her face, and hugged him. "Hi, Jake."

"Hi, Joanne."

"It sure is good to see you again. How long you gonna be home?"

"Rest of the week. Only I'm going to Malad for a couple of days."

"Want to come up and sit with us?"

"Ya."

He followed his sister toward the pew where the rest of the family was sitting. One man from another pew got up, walked back, and intercepted Jake.

"Hi, Jake."

"Hi, Willard."

Willard put his mouth close to Jake's ear and whispered. Jake thought a moment, then nodded. "Ya, that would be okay," he said.

The man walked back toward the front of the church. Jake sat down with his family. His mother reached across his father and his sister to squeeze his arm with her hand. "I'm glad you got here," she said. "We didn't know when you'd come, so we come on ahead."

"I got a late start from camp."

His father said, "Have you et?"

"Not supper."

A boy sitting beyond his mother leaned forward so Jake could see him. "I got a apple in my pocket," he whispered loudly. "Want it?"

"I'll wait till later."

Another boy leaned forward and said, "Hi."

"Howdy."

Someone turned off the lights. The curtains on the stage began to open. Jake whispered to Joanne, "Where's the baby?"

"Oh, she was the baby in the manger. Wasn't she good? We was all afraid she'd cry."

There was a play now, in which Santa Claus was preparing to make his trip around the world and faced some difficult problems. The audience strained to hear some of the young performers, relaxed and laughed at the jokes when some of the stronger-voiced children appeared, and joined in the singing of jolly Christmas songs as the pianist and the song leader gave the cues. Santa solved his problem and was off on his trip, and the curtains closed.

The lights were switched on again. The song leader led everyone in two more Christmas songs. Then the man named Willard walked up to her. He talked with her in low tones. The pianist turned sideways on her bench, her hands in her lap, and watched. The song leader sat down, and the pianist left the bench and sat beside her. Willard walked to the front and center of the audience.

"Ever since I can remember," he said, "Jake Mortensen has give us 'The Night Before Christmas.' We didn't know whether he would be here this year so we didn't ask him, but he's here and he says he'll give it again."

There was a murmur of approval through the audience as Willard sat down. Jake looked at his parents, who looked pleased about it, and got up from his seat. He went to the front of the church and looked around at the audience. The people looked friendly, ready to listen to him.

" 'Twas the night before Christmas
And all through the house
Not a creature was stirring,
Not even a mouse . . ."

He put his hands in his pockets and went on reciting, looking here and there at people in the audience. They had been straining for-

ward in anticipation before he began. Before the poem was many lines along they were relaxing back in the benches, listening, many of them smiling. He saw his brother Jerry listening, moving his lips, reciting silently the words Jake was saying aloud.

". . . but I heard him exclaim
Ere he drove out of sight,
'Happy Christmas to all
And to all a good night!' "

There was a sound of warm applause, which Jake acknowledged with a nod as he went back to his seat. Before he got there the piano started again, and, as Jake sat, the audience began to sing "Silent Night."

Joanne leaned toward him. "You done real good. You always do it good."

"Thanks."

The song ended, and Santa Claus came in from outside, ho-ho-hoing and striding down the center aisle, a gunny sack slung over one shoulder. He waved at the crowd and sat on the apron of the stage. The children who had been in the program came out from backstage. Someone opened the curtains. Santa Claus held several children on his knee, asked them what they wanted for Christmas, repeated their answers to the crowd. Jake's sister, the angel in the program, sat on his knee and stared at his beard with an amazed smile, but he could not get her to talk. When he put her down, the brother who had been a shepherd took her hand and led her to the family.

The little girl saw Jake and leaped upon him. He picked her up. "Hi, Jake! Merry Christmas!"

"Merry Christmas, Julia!"

"I was a angel!"

"I seen you up there."

"Jimmy Junior was a shepherd and I was a angel."

"Well, you should be a angel, because you are one. Hi, Jim."

The little boy smiled a big, shy smile. "Hi!" He crawled past Jake's knees and past Joanne and huddled up against his father, who put a hand on his shoulder and patted him a couple of times. The little boy looked up at his father and whispered, "Jake called me 'Jim.' "

"I heard him."

The boy put a finger into his mouth and rested his head on his father's leg.

Another boy came down the side aisle carrying a baby. "Hi, Jake," he said, sidling past Jake and Joanne and reaching across his little brother and his father to hand the baby to his mother. "She was real good, Mama."

Mama said, "She didn't cry none at all, did she."

"Nope."

Jake said, "Hi, Joe. You was a good wise man."

"I got to be because Harold got sick."

"That wasn't too wise of Harold."

Joe grinned. He squeezed past Joanne and Jake and sat on the end of the pew beside Jake. Jake scooted in against Joanne, but still there was almost no room for his brother. "Good thing you got a skinny little hind end," Jake said.

Joe scowled up at him. "I ain't so skinny."

"I guess you growed since I left."

Joe jerked his head in a nod of emphatic affirmation and said nothing.

Santa Claus was moving around the church, reaching into his gunny sack and taking from it small brown-paper bags tied shut with string. He handed them out to children, who eagerly tore them open and began eating the peanuts and hard candy they found inside. Santa came to the Mortensens' pew, and Jimmy Junior reached for and got the first sack.

"Don't eat it all up tonight," Mama warned her children. "Save some for tomorrow. Don't make yourselves sick."

Joe and Julia got their sacks. Santa Claus shouted, "Janet! Catch!" A young girl with braided blond hair leaned forward just past the brothers in the middle of the pew and caught the sack that was tossed to her.

Santa Claus said, "Jake, you been a good boy?"

"If you ain't caught me, I guess I have."

"Here. Have a sack for that good pome you told about me."

"Thanks, Santa Claus." Jake took the sack and Santa went on to the next pew. Jake turned and looked down the pew. "Howdy, Janet. How come you're hiding out down there and not saying nothing to me?"

Janet leaned forward again. "You're too far away."

"No, I'm right here. You're the one that's far away."

Papa said, "How's your work been going?"

"Just fine. I figure we've got better than two thousand posts cut. We ain't counted the ones yet where we are now."

"You're doing good."

"Ya."

Janet said, "Don't it get lonesome out there all alone?"

"Oh, we ain't alone. We got a pet rabbit and a tame rattlesnake and there's a coyote and a bear living in the next cave over. They come to supper on Sundays."

Jimmy Junior looked up in wonder, his finger out of his mouth. "What's their names?"

Joanne and the nearest brothers laughed aloud, and Papa tousled his youngest son's hair. "Are they teasing you, son?" he asked. "Tell 'em they better not tease the shepherd or you'll let the sheep out."

"I'll let the sheep out," Jimmy said, and put his head back down.

Jake opened his little sack and began to shell and eat the peanuts inside, stuffing the shells into a pants pocket. It was his first food since dinner with Scotty on the pile of posts. He ate casually, but he ate steadily.

Santa Claus finished his rounds. With a last wave and a "Ho ho ho!" he went out the door to complete his circuit of the world.

Willard stood up again and climbed onto the stage. He stood looking down at the crowd. The church fell silent.

Willard said, "Let us pray." Heads bowed. "Our Father, Who art in heaven. Be with us now as we go to our separate homes. Let no harm befall us along the road, and guide us safely to our own firesides. Help us remember Him Whose coming we celebrate tonight. Help make us ready for when He comes again. Bless these children who have done so good in the program here tonight. We ask in the name of Jesus. Amen."

There was a sudden bustle of people standing, putting on their coats, visiting their friends. Jake pulled his jacket on and buttoned it up. He tucked his gloves under one arm and went on eating his peanuts.

Papa said, "Did you walk in?"

"Ya."

"Then you can ride home with us. Let's go, kids."

Jimmy Junior was suddenly alert, no longer sleepy. "Hurry up, everbody! We gotta go home and open our presents!"

CHAPTER ELEVEN

The front room was still warm, but the fire was no more than a few dull embers. While Papa lighted two lamps, Jake stuffed sagebrush into the heater and put a log on top. He tossed in a match and the sagebrush caught. He closed the heater door against the sudden roar of flame.

"Are we gonna open our packages, Papa?" Jimmy Junior was asking. He had partly unbuttoned his coat and was jumping up and down. He grabbed for his father's coattails to get his attention.

"Don't grab my coat," Papa said. "I'll spill this coal oil and start a fire."

"Are we gonna open our presents?"

"Oh, why don't we open 'em in the morning?"

Jimmy's wail of "No!" was joined by Janet and Joe. Janet added, "We *always* open them the night before!"

Julia had been peering under the tree. "There's more presents here," she said.

Joe hurried to the tree. "Let me see," he said. He squatted and began to examine the packages wrapped in white tissue paper. "These is from Jake! Jake brought home some presents!"

"They ain't nothing," Jake said. "They's just pieces of firewood and stuff I cut from them juniper trees over there."

"Oh, I'll bet," Janet said. "I'll bet you got something real nice."

Mama said, "Where was there over there to get presents?"

"I got 'em a long time ago," Jake said. "They was in the attic. I got 'em down tonight."

"Next year, I'm gonna look in the attic," Joe said.

Jake said, "What I got for you was a bottle of milk. It's been up there since September. I hope it ain't clabbered."

They heard the back door slam. In a moment Jeff came in from the kitchen, pulling off his coat. He had stayed outside to drain the radiator of the family pickup. Julia said, "Jeff, Jake brought more presents."

"That was good of him," Jeff said. "I needed some presents, and he said I could have all he brought."

"No he didn't," Joe said. "One's got my name on it."

"That there's a mistake," Jeff said. "They're all mine. Jake told me so in his letter."

Mama said, "Oh, that reminds me. You got some letters from Quin." She went to a cupboard and took down two letters from a shelf and handed them to Jake. He looked at the envelopes, then stuck both letters into his shirt pocket.

"I'll read them later," he said.

Joanne had been sitting in the rocking chair, holding the baby. Jimmy had squeezed himself onto a corner of the chair and had snuggled up against his big sister. Papa said, "You kids better get ready for bed. Jimmy Junior looks plump tuckered out."

The little boy raised his drooping head and frowned. "I ain't tired," he insisted.

"Well, you will be before long. We better not take a chance."

"Papa!" Janet begged. "Don't tease like that! Let's open our presents!"

Papa looked doubtful. "You better ask Mama," he said.

"Mama, can we?"

"Sit down around the tree. Not too close. Give Papa some room to hand them out."

There was a scramble as Julia, Jimmy, Joe, and Janet hurried for choice places. Jeff and Jerry moved more slowly, but they had already positioned themselves—they were old hands at this game. Jake stood a moment near the heater, then walked to the door and slowly sat down with his shoulder against the doorframe. Joanne remained in the rocker. Mama said to her, "I can take the baby if you want to get by the tree."

"I don't mind."

"I better hold her. She ought to have some milk, anyway."

Mama took the baby and settled herself to nurse it. Joanne pulled her coat a little closer around her and sat down in the space between Jake and Janet. Papa said, "Joe, you hand out the presents this year."

Joe grinned like an imp and made a move forward. "Okay," he said.

Janet grabbed him by the shoulder and held him back. "No! Papa, you do it. You always do it."

Joe said, "You're hurting my shoulder."

"Get back where you was."

"Okay." Joe settled back. Janet released her grip. Joe lunged for the tree. Janet grabbed him, knocked him over. He landed on Jimmy, and Jimmy fell against Julia. Jimmy wailed, and Julia shouted in protest.

"Let go of me!" Joe said angrily.

"Well, you stay where you was."

Papa said, "Here now!" The command in his voice silenced everyone. "If you kids is gonna fight, you can all go to bed."

The silence held for a moment, the only sounds being those of children righting themselves and settling poutily into position. Then Papa stepped over Julia and Jimmy and sat down on the linoleum. He peered under the tree, then reached for a package, and another. He looked carefully at the tags on each one, then handed them over. "Julia," he said. "Jimmy Junior."

Little sounds of happiness began to escape from the youngest children as they began unwrapping their presents. Joanne looked at Jake, then leaned close to whisper, "Are you okay?"

"Ya."

"You look sad."

"I'm fine."

Jake carried Jimmy Junior to bed. The little boy had barely opened the last of his presents before he fell asleep. Joanne had wakened him to a dazed and semiconscious state and helped him hang one of his clean socks over an arm of the rocker. One of Julia's long brown stockings hung over the other arm.

Jeff went ahead, and by the time Jake carried his little brother out the back door and into the lean-to Jeff had lighted the lamp and was starting to get undressed. Jake sat on the edge of one of the double beds and began taking off Jimmy's clothes.

Jeff said, "I started sleeping in your bed when you went up to cut posts. Do you want it back?"

"No. I'll sleep in this bed with Jimmy. Joe, you sleep over there with Jerry."

"Good. I don't like sleeping with Jimmy. He kicks."

Jerry said, "You stay on your side of the bed, or I'll kick you clean out to the corral."

Jake was the last one into bed. He moved the lamp to an orange crate that stood on end between the double beds. He opened Quin's letters and read them.

"Dear Jake. Well, school is going okay for me. I am taking history, English composition, trigonometry, physics, R.O.T.C., and physical education. That keeps me pretty busy. It is hard to study because I am in a dormitory with five roommates and it seems like they are all noisy and never want to study, just have a good time, so it is pretty noisy in here. But I am doing okay. So is our football team. We have beat all our games but one so far, and lost that one by just a couple of points. I have gone to all our home games. You should hear those bleachers rock and rattle with the cheers when things get exciting! I have not found a girl friend yet but I am looking at all candidates. Ha ha. How about you? I'm glad you did so good in the wheat harvest and was able to save so much money. You will have that truck before you know it. Then you can drive down here and see me. Ha ha. I sure miss you and the old gang, but I am glad to be here in college, too. The best part is on Tuesday mornings. I fixed it so I do not have any classes before ten on Tuesdays and I go out first crack out of the box to the airfield and take my flying lesson. My instructor is mean as he can be, but I suppose he's got to be that way. If you do not learn to keep your head when he is yelling at you there is no telling what you might do in a real emergency. The first time I tried to land the plane I thought he was going to bite my head off. I am doing better at landings now. One morning we did nothing but, just landing and then hitting the throttle and taking off again and circling around and landing again. One of these times, after I solo, I will fly up there and look for you and land and give you a ride somewhere. You would really like it if you had a chance to fly in an airplane. Well, I had better try to study in spite of these noisy roommates of mine. Thanks for your letter. Write soon. Your friend,

Quin."

"Dear Jake. It was good to get your letter but you made me homesick. I wish I was up there making camp with you and Scotty and helping you cut posts. We would make quite a crew all three working together. Do you remember the time we cut all that wood for old lady Mansfield and she gave us that pie. How was your Thanksgiving dinner at those people's house? Did that girl catch old Scotty and get him married up? More power to her if she did. Scotty is pretty hard to catch. I think you and me have the best idea—be bachelors all our lives and teach our kids to do the same. Ha ha. I have been going out some with a little girl I met down here, though. She is in my English comp. class and is a real cutie. You will have to meet her someday if you come down here. My flying instructor says I am doing pretty good for a dumb kid. He has not said anything yet, but I think he might let me solo about Christmas or soon after. I have bad news about Christmas. I am not going to come home. I am going to take a flying lesson that week, and also my folks want to see where I live and go to college and all so they are coming down here and we are all going to stay with my cousins for a few days. So I will not be seeing you. I hope to see you in the spring, or maybe sooner if I solo and get a chance to fly up there. I am saving up a little money so maybe I can rent the airplane that I take my lessons in and someday I can fly up there and see you and the folks and all the guys. Well, have a good Christmas and think of me. Write soon. Your friend,

Quin."

Jake put the letters back into their envelopes and put the envelopes on the orange crate. He got out of bed and put the lamp back on the dresser. The other boys were already asleep. He could hear faint sounds coming from somewhere else in the house. Perhaps Santa Claus was at his work. Jake blew out the lamp and went to bed.

"Jake! Jake! You gotta wake up!"

"Huh?"

"Come on, Jake! Everbody's awake but you!"

"That's okay. I wanna sleep."

"You can't sleep, Jake! We gotta see what Santa Claus brought!"

"I don't think he come this year."

"Yes he did! Come on! Get outta bed!"

"Hey! Gimme back them covers!"

"No! Get up! Come on!"

"In five minutes."

"No! Now! Please, Jake!"

"Okay, Joe." Jake sat up. "Where's the others?"

"Jeff and Jerry's milking. Papa got Jimmy up and took him to the toilet."

"Well, I better go there myself."

"Oh, do you hafta? We'll never get to see what Santa Claus brought."

"Just hold your horses." Jake began pulling on his clothes.

Outside, he saw Jeff and Jerry driving the cows back to the corral from the stream a half mile down the trail. The animals plodded past him, steam rising from their nostrils into the cold air. The sun was not yet up, but the dawn had advanced far enough to give light to see by.

Jake said, "Joe thinks you oughta come in now so we can see what Santa Claus brung."

Jerry laughed loudly. "Tell Joe we're gonna feed the pigs and chickens and gather the eggs and paint the barn, and then we'll be right in."

"You're still watering the cows at the crick, huh?"

"Ya. I guess we will be all winter. We ain't been able to find another twin pinion and fix the windmill yet."

"I'm going into Malad this week. Maybe I can find one."

"I hope so. We gotta haul either snow or crick water for the house, and I'm getting tired of it."

The kitchen was still cold, but the fire in the cookstove was burning well, and Mama had the coffee on. Jimmy Junior was sitting on one of the benches drinking a glass of milk.

"Where's the girls?" Jake asked.

Mama said, "We ain't let them come out of their room yet."

Jeff and Jerry came in carrying fresh milk. They put the buckets on the kitchen counter and went to the washstand to clean up.

Papa come in from the front room. "Is everbody ready?" he asked.

Jake said, "I'll get Joe."

He went out the back door and looked into the lean-to. He saw no one. "Joe?" No answer.

He shut the lean-to door and looked around the back yard, then yelled loudly, "Joe!"

The answer came faintly to his ears. "I'm in the toilet! Hold your horses!"

"Mama! Look! I got a teddy bear!" Julia came skipping out of the crowd around the Christmas tree, clinging to one arm of the bear and waving it at her mother. She got halfway to Mama, then reversed direction and plunged back into the mob.

"I got a *train!*" roared Joe. He pulled its wooden cars from their box and arranged them on the floor and huddled over them, working on hooking them together.

"Oh—oh—I got a farm!" shouted Jimmy. "I got a farm! Come look at my farm!"

"I've already seen it," muttered Jerry to his older brothers, grinning.

Julia came out of the crowd again, carrying a homemade Raggedy Ann doll. "He even brung something for Baby Jill!" she shouted. "Here's a dollie, Jill!" She stood at her mother's feet, waving the doll upward as if expecting the baby to reach down and take it. Mama took it and tucked it between herself and the baby.

Jake had received a pair of wool socks as his gift from Jeff and had hung one of them over the back of a chair last night. He sat down in the chair now and looked at the stocking. There was a popcorn ball wrapped in waxed paper at the top of it. He set that aside and found an apple. He took a bite out of the apple and put it down on the table beside the popcorn ball. He looked around him. Jimmy was setting up his farm. It consisted of a barn and some animals cut from pieces of lumber and painted.

Jake took another bite from his apple and poked deeper into his sock. He pulled out another waxed-paper package and opened it; there was licorice and homemade candy in it. Then his fingers encountered peanuts. He held the sock and poured the peanuts out onto the table.

His hand had located something hard and round inside the stocking. He gripped it so it would not fall out with the peanuts, and when the peanuts were gone it was the only thing left. He put a hand down into the toe of the sock and took it out.

It was a pocket watch, silver-colored with a yellow face, dark black numerals, and dark black hands. It shone with newness. Jake sat holding it in his cupped hands, turning it over, examining it carefully and fully. He took out his pocketknife, opened it, and pried the back cover off the watch. He wound the watch and looked at the workings move. Carefully, he replaced the back cover and studied the face of the watch.

Jerry said, "What did you get, Jake?"

"A watch." He held it up so everyone could see it.

Joe said, "Boy! That's pretty! Look at my train!" He had hooked most of the cars together and was working on a caboose and a flatcar.

Joanne came over to Jake and bent down to look at the watch. "Isn't that nice!"

Papa walked up to him and took his own watch from his pocket. He held the watch where Jake could see the time. Papa said, "Pull the stem out easy and you can set it." Jake began setting his watch. Papa said, "Wind it once a day. Try to wind it at the same time ever day. Just snug. Don't force it."

Jake said, "It sure is nice. Thanks, Papa."

"Don't thank me. Thank Santa Claus."

Jake finished his oatmeal and pushed his bowl away so he could lean on the table. Mama said, "You want more mush?"

"No, that's plenty."

Joanne said, "This must seem like a real vacation to you, Jake."

"It feels pretty good."

"When you going back?"

"About the end of the week. I thought I might go into Malad in a day or two."

Papa said, "How you going?"

"Walk over, I guess."

Mama said, "Maybe you can get some things for me."

"Give me a list."

Jeff looked out the window. "Milkman's here," he said. Some of the others looked out the window. A truck had stopped between the house and the barn. Presently a man came out of the barn carrying a ten-gallon can of milk. He lifted it onto the bed of the truck.

Mama said, "This is egg day," and got up from the table. She opened a cupboard door, bent down, and lifted out a crate of eggs. She put it on the counter.

Joanne said, "Are you going to see Jean in Malad?"

"Ya. I thought I might stay over a night with her."

"She'll be glad to see you."

"Charlie's out of work," Jeff said.

Joanne said, "He was the last we heard. He might have a job now."

There was a knock at the back door and Mama called, "Come in." The milkman came in.

"Hello, Henry," Papa said.

"Hello, Jim. Got any eggs, Jennie?"

Mama said, "Them on the counter. Four dozen."

"They're not laying too good, huh?" Henry reached into his pocket and took out a coin purse.

"We've et quite a few, but they always drop off in winter."

"Ya." Henry counted some coins into Mama's hand. She put them into her apron pocket. Henry closed the purse and put it back into his pocket. "How you doing, Jake? I ain't seen you in a long time."

"Not bad."

Henry walked to the counter, picked up the box of eggs. "They tell me you're cutting posts out by Juniper Row."

"Ya. Scotty Tubbs and me."

"Quit for the winter?"

"Nope. I'm going back after Christmas."

"You'll get snowed in over there. It's gonna be a bad winter."

"We don't go noplace anyhow."

"Lotta guys is already hauling hay in case they can't get through this winter."

"Well, we ain't coming out till spring, anyhow."

Henry was at the back door now, and Mama opened it for him. "I'll bring back your crate in the morning, Jennie."

"Okay. 'Bye. Merry Christmas."

"Ya. Same to you."

Papa said, "Have you got enough food up there to last you till spring?"

"I'm gonna have to buy another half a pig off you. Scotty got us a deer, though. That's been good."

"That's too bad," Jerry said.

"Why?"

"Christmas dinner won't be special for you."

"Why?"

"Jeff killed a deer this fall. We're gonna have venison steaks for dinner."

Mama said, "Janet, don't you feel good?"

"Oh, ya. I feel okay."

"You ain't hardly touched your mush."

"I'm not hungry for mush."

"Well, you should eat your breakfast."

"I'm tired of oatmeal all the time."

Jeff said, "She's just trying to save room for more deer meat at dinner."

Joe said, "That ain't fair. She'll eat more than me. Mama, make her eat her mush."

Jerry laughed. "Joe, there ain't any two people here that's going to eat more than you do."

Joe said, "They better not."

Janet said, "Can I be excused?"

"Okay. Drink your milk."

Janet finished her milk and left the kitchen. The talk went on. A couple of minutes later, Jake got up from the table and went into the front room. There was no one there. The door to the bedrooms was closed. He opened it a crack and said quietly, "Can I come in?"

Janet said, "Come in."

She was lying on her stomach on one of the two double beds in the back bedroom. Jake closed both the front-room door and the door connecting the front and back bedrooms. He walked over to Janet.

"Are you sick?"

"No."

"What's wrong?"

"Nothing."

"Something is." He sat down and patted her lightly on the back.

"I'm okay."

"Have you tried on your new dress yet? It sure looks pretty."

She buried her face in her arms and began to cry with body-shaking sobs. "Oh, Jake, I wanted a doll so bad!"

"Instead of the dress?"

"It's a beautiful dress, but I wanted a doll so bad." She lost her voice in her sobs, and for a while she just cried. Jake sat with his hand on her shoulder, now and then patting her gently. She sniffed and wiped her eyes on her forearm and raised her head a little. Choking back more tears she said, "All my life I wanted just one big china doll, and this year everthing went so good and Papa done so well with the farm I was sure I would get it, and I didn't, and now I'm gonna be too old! I'm never gonna get one!" She broke into renewed crying.

Jake sat silent for a long time, patting her shoulder absent-mindedly. At last he said, "They give us a awful lot."

"I know. I'm sorry. I just can't help it."

"There's a lot of us. They done the best they could."

CHAPTER TWELVE

Jake said, "Them was sure good steaks."

"I thought you had 'em all the time up at your camp."

"Not like Mama cooks 'em."

Jerry looked at the wrench in his hand and the pieces of machinery lying on the platform before him. "I can't make it work," he said.

Jake shook his head. "No. It ain't gonna work till we get a new twin pinion for it. I'll look for one in Malad."

Jerry said, "You know what I liked best about them steaks?"

"What?"

"Watching Papa eat his. I like to watch Papa eat. He takes a big mouthful and he don't say nothing, he just chews and chews on it, like it was just so good!"

"He ain't always had much good to eat."

Jerry said, "Well, I'm gonna go get warm before I have to drive the cows down." He stepped onto the ladder that led from the windmill platform down to the ground, and began to descend. When his hands were out of the way Jake stepped onto the ladder and followed him.

Jake said, "I'll drive 'em down."

Jake stopped in the kitchen to get two water buckets and carried them with him as he let the cows out of the corral and followed them down the half-mile slope to the creek. As they picked their way into the stream and broke the thin ice and drank, he went upstream a few yards and scooped both buckets full of water. He set them down on some flat ground away from the cows until the animals had finished drinking and he had started them back to the corral. Then he retrieved the buckets and walked behind the cattle. He put the buckets on the back step before he chased in the adventurous calves and closed the corral gate.

He helped Jeff and Jerry and Papa do the milking.

Jerry said, "Joe's gonna wonder how come we get the milking done so much quicker now than we used to."

"Joe won't think nothing about it," Jeff said.

"Why is it quicker?" Jake asked.

"Oh, we been spending extra time out here mornings and evenings making that stuff for Joe and Jimmy Junior. The train and the farm. We worked up in the hayloft so he wouldn't catch us by surprise and find out what we was doing."

Jeff said, "Joanne took it all down to her school last week and painted it."

"You done a good job."

"We gotta fix that boxcar. The wheel's on crooked."

Papa said, "We gotta teach Jimmy Junior to keep his farm off in one corner someplace. He leaves it all out in the middle of the floor. Somebody's gonna step on it."

"If somebody steps on it after all that work," Jeff said, "I'll kick their butt."

After dinner, Papa sat alone in the kitchen and practiced on his old fiddle. The rest of the family sat in the front room, cracking nuts from a paper sack full of them that had been Santa Claus's present to Mama and Papa.

Joanne went to the door. "Papa, come in here and play us a tune."

"I'm just gonna practice a little."

"Oh, come in and play."

He came in, carrying the fiddle and bow in one hand and his music stand in the other and arranged a chair so he could sit. He held the fiddle in his lap and looked through his music. "I guess I'll play 'The Old Spinning Wheel,'" he said. He played it through, slow in tempo, keeping time by tapping his foot.

When he finished Joanne said, "Play us another one."

"What should I play?"

Jeff said, "Play 'The Old Loom.'"

"I guess I'll play 'She'll Be Coming 'Round the Mountain.'"

Mama said, "Jerry, you should get the accordion. You play that real good on the accordion."

Papa said, "Go get it. We'll play a duet."

Joe said, "I'll get it." He dashed through the doorway leading to the bedrooms and returned in a moment lugging the black case that contained the accordion. Jerry opened the case, took out the instrument, and made some tuning-up sounds before he murmured, "Okay."

Papa tapped his foot a few times, held the bow poised, then nodded to Jerry and they began to play. Almost at once, Jeff began to sing, and the others joined in.

"She'll be coming 'round the mountain when she comes.
She'll be coming 'round the mountain when she comes.
She'll be coming 'round the mountain
She'll be coming 'round the mountain
She'll be coming 'round the mountain when she comes.

Joanne got up and grabbed Jeff by the hand. "Dance with me," she commanded, and they began an impromptu dance full of do-si-dos and clap-your-hands and bows and swing-your-partners.

"Oh, we'll all have chicken and dumplings when she comes.
Oh, we'll all have chicken and dumplings when she comes."

Jake said, "Janet, want to dance?"

"There's not room."

"Joe, help me move this table out of the way."

They finished the song, and Jerry, solo, began another. This time Joanne led the singing.

"Go tell Aunt Rhody. Go tell Aunt Rhody.
Go tell Aunt Rhody the old gray goose is dead."

Then Jerry lit into "Turkey in the Straw," and even Mama got up and danced a few steps in the crowded front room. When that was over, everyone sat down again, on chairs and on the couch and on the floor. Jerry began putting the accordion away. Papa played another song, and Jeff sang along.

"From this valley they say you are leaving.
We will miss your bright eyes and sweet smile.
You are taking away all the sunshine
That has brightened our lives for a while."

Jerry had begun to softly whistle the tune. Jake and Joanne joined the singing.

"Come and sit by my side if you love me.
Do not hasten to bid me adieu.
But remember the Red River Valley
And the cowboy who loved you so true."

Papa got up and went back into the kitchen. Presently they could hear him playing scales and exercises and working haltingly on a new tune. Jake and Jeff put the table back where it belonged. Jerry put the accordion back into its cubbyhole in the back bedroom.

Jake went into the kitchen, got his coat, and went outside. Jeff followed him. They walked toward the barn. Jake leaned against the corral fence. Jeff came up and leaned beside him.

Jake said, "You want to go to Malad with me?"

"I got to help Baker fix his barn tomorrow."

"You been working for him pretty regular?"

"Some."

"That sure was a nice farm you made for Jimmy Junior."

"Jerry done most of it."

Jake let his gaze wander over the darkened buildings and landscape until Jeff said, "You must be doing good cutting posts."

"I figure we've got better than two thousand. We'll have maybe eight or nine thousand by spring."

"Can you sell that many?"

"If we can haul them to Weston, Tremonton, Downey, places like that, I think we can sell them all. Maybe Rockland or American Falls. Thirty cents apiece."

"That's a lot of money."

"Well, we gotta pay expenses out of that, groceries and hauling and all that, and I've gotta split it with Scotty. But I might come out with five, six hundred dollars or better for a winter's work."

"Boy." Jeff shook his head in disbelief. "That's doing okay."

"Maybe we can put away a little money. Get Joe through high school or let Janet go to teachers college when she gets old enough or something." Jake looked around at the dark shapes of the buildings. "Fix this place up some."

His watch told him it was nine in the morning when he left home and half-past four in the afternoon when he walked into Malad Thirty miles in seven and a half hours.

On the way he had stopped three times. Once at Quin's place on the chance Quin might be home, but no one was. Once at Scotty's place to say hello to his folks, but they were also not home.

The third stop had been when Colin Baker greeted him from the front porch of the Baker house.

"Hi, Jake. Come on over."

"Can't stay. I'm going to Malad."

"It's a long walk."

Jake walked through the snow to the front porch.

"Good to see you," Colin said. "How was your Christmas?"

"Just fine."

"I hear you been working up in the hills."

"Ya. Cutting posts."

"Quit for the winter now?"

"No. Just come home for Christmas. I'm going back."

"Lotta snow up there to be working in."

"We ain't got too much now."

"You'll get more. You're gonna get snowbound up there."

"We don't figure to come back out until spring thaw."

"Seems like it would get lonesome."

"It don't seem bad."

"You got any snowshoes?"

"No. We tried to make some skis once, but we don't know how."

"I'll sell you my old skis. I got some new ones for Christmas."

"How much?"

"Two dollars."

"I'll buy them. Will you be home tomorrow night?"

"Ya."

"I'll stop by and get them and pay you for them then."

"Okay."

There were lights in some of the house windows by the time he entered Malad. Jake paused to look long at one old house. He saw light coming through its windows, and once the shadow of a person passed between a lamp and a window.

He turned and looked across the street to the small candy shop that stood there. Two people went into the store, and Jake heard the bell ring as it did whenever the door was opened. The light from the candy shop was bright; it came from electric lights. Jake breathed deeply of the fragrance that spilled out with the light—peppermint and chocolate and other candy smells.

He turned and walked on and soon entered the business block. He paused there once, in front of an automobile and truck dealership, and looked through the window at a Model T Ford parked just inside the window. It glistened under the electric lights of that room.

Farther down the block he stopped again and read the posters on the front of the motion picture theater.

Two blocks beyond the business block he turned left and followed the street up the hill, block after block, until he came to the house he wanted. He walked up the two front steps to the porch and knocked at the door. He waited, listening to the footsteps inside, until the door was opened.

"Jake! Come in!"

"Howdy, Jean."

"It's good to see you!" The young woman gave her brother a warm hug. "Take off your coat. I was just starting supper. I'll peel some more spuds."

"I can peel them." Jake pulled off his coat and gloves. Jean reached for them. "Just a minute," he said. He took two packages out of the coat pockets, then gave her the coat and gloves.

"What are those?" she asked, walking across the room to a closet.

"Your Christmas presents."

"You didn't have to give us nothing."

"I done pretty good in the wheat last fall. How's Charlie?"

"He's working again."

"That's good."

"He's the janitor at the hotel. He don't really like it, but he figures it'll get us by this winter and he might have better luck in the spring." She hung up the coat, stuffed the gloves into a pocket of it, and closed the closet door.

"Are you doing anything?" Jake put the presents down on a small table that stood in the center of an almost bare room. There was a small davenport under the side window and another small table near the front window. A lamp was burning on a chest of drawers against the back wall. There were two old mismatched chairs in different parts of the room, standing on linoleum not yet so worn that it had lost its red and yellow pattern. Jake looked up at the ceiling. An electric wire hung down, but there was no bulb in the socket.

"No," she answered. "Come on in the kitchen. We got a stove in there. It's kind of chilly in here."

"It don't feel too bad."

It was much warmer in the kitchen. She sat on a stool beside the sink, took several potatoes out of a gunny sack, and began peeling them.

"You ain't got a cellar, huh?" he said.

"It's gotta be cleaned up. It's real bad down there."

"Seems like it'd be too warm under the sink to keep them spuds."

"Is it? I guess we could put them out in the shed."

"They might freeze. I'd think in the front room or the bedroom where it ain't so warm."

"I better mention that to Charlie."

Jake lounged against the drainboard beside the sink and looked around the room. A small drop-leaf table stood against one wall. The back door and the stove were opposite the sink. There were two chairs tucked under the table. A new calendar, already showing January, hung near the door to the front room.

"The folks give me a watch for Christmas," he said, and took it from his pocket. It was tied to his waist overalls with a bootlace. Jean took the watch in her hand. "Oh, Jake, how nice! You've always wanted a watch."

"I sure didn't expect it."

She handed back the watch. "The folks sent over them potatoes for us. It sure does help."

"Do you remember them potatoes Papa sent us for Christmas that year he couldn't come home?"

"Oh, yes, I sure do! They was really good."

"Mama boiled them with the skins on."

"I remember. That was a nice Christmas."

She finished peeling the extra potatoes, rinsed them under the faucet, and carried them to the stove to add them to the contents of a pot that was already cooking. Jake looked at the faucet. "It sure must be nice to have running water," he said.

"It is. It's real handy."

She put grease into a skillet and, as it heated, she got flour and water so she could make gravy. "What brings you to Malad?" she asked.

"I come to see you guys, and I want to buy a truck."

She stared at him. "A truck? Have you got enough money to buy a truck?"

"I can make a down payment if they'll let me make payments."

"Will they do that?"

"I don't know. I'm going to find out."

"You mean a big truck?"

"Yup."

"Not a pickup."

"I need it to haul them posts we're cutting, and I figure I can do custom hauling and pay for the truck easy."

"That would be real nice."

Jake stood up and walked around the kitchen. "There's a movie on downtown tonight. I thought I might take you and Charlie. Kind of a extra Christmas present."

"What movie is it?"

"It's one called *Lilac Time*. It has Colleen Moore and Gary Cooper in it."

"We'd like to go. Anyway I would, and I'm sure Charlie would."

He walked to the stove and looked down at the full woodbox. "What do you do, buy your wood?"

"Charlie's folks give us this."

"Maybe in the spring I can haul you over a load. We got quite a bit of waste with the post cutting, and a lot of it would make good firewood. I thought of hauling some home to the folks."

Jean was stirring the gravy in the skillet, waiting for it to reach a slow, bubbling boil. She said, "I've got a surprise for you, too. Almost as big a surprise as your truck."

"Oh?"

"I'm gonna have a baby."

"Oh." Jake sat down on the stool and looked at her. "Have you told Mama yet?"

"No. I'm kinda scared to. And I'm afraid she'll worry." She laughed. "But you're the worrier in the family. Don't you worry none about me having a baby, Jake. I'll do fine."

He looked at the floor and said nothing.

She said, "I know how you feel about more kids, but I wanted to tell you."

He said, "Are you glad about it?"

"Yes, I kind of am. I'm kinda glad about it."

"Then I'm glad, too." He looked up at her. "If you need any help, let me know."

"I hope I don't, but if I have to, I will."

She went on with her work and he moved away from the stool and the sink to be out of her way. "You got a real nice place," he said.

"We was lucky. The rent ain't too bad. How's all the folks?"

"They all seem fine."

"Did everbody have a nice Christmas?"

"I think so. Except maybe Janet. She was disappointed she didn't get a doll."

"I bet she never told nobody she wanted one."

"Probably not."

"Janet's that way."

"It sure made her cry for a while. Don't tell nobody, though."

"I won't."

"I thought of getting her a doll, but I'm afraid they're too dear."

"They're real dear. Anyway, it might not look good if you give her so much and the others nothing."

"Ya. That's right."

They heard the front door open and the screen door slam and the front door close. Jean moved toward the front-room door. "Charlie? Is that you? Come on in and wash up for supper. Jake's here. He wants to take us to the pitcher show!"

CHAPTER THIRTEEN

Jake walked slowly around three vehicles, squatting to examine tires and opening doors to look at seats and dashboards, before a man approached him.

"Good morning. Can I sell you a new car today?"

Jake closed the car door and turned to face the man. "I'm Jake Mortensen. I'm Jim Mortensen's boy from out to Holbrook."

"How do you do, Jake. I'm Glen Evans." The man extended a hand and Jake accepted the handshake.

"I come to buy a truck."

"Okay. Let's walk out back. We have quite a few used trucks for sale. The prices aren't too bad, either."

The man started to walk away, but Jake remained where he was and said, "I want to buy a new truck."

Evans turned back to him. "We don't have any new trucks in stock. We have to order them."

"Oh." Jake tucked his upper lip between his teeth and frowned over the news for a moment. Then he said, "Well, okay. I guess I better put in my order. I want a new Ford ton-and-a-half truck. How much are they?"

"Let's go into my office and look at some things."

Evans led the way into the manager's office and offered Jake a seat. He shuffled through papers on his desk and came up with the one he wanted. He studied it carefully and said, "New Ford truck . . . let me figure . . ." He made some pencil calculations on the paper he was studying. "That would be eight hundred and fifty-two dollars."

"That's about what I figured."

"That's without a spare tire."

"Oh." Jake heaved a sigh. "Well, I gotta have a spare."

"That's another fifty dollars."

"Okay."

"Nine hundred and two dollars altogether."

"Okay. I figured I'd pay you three hundred dollars down if I could pay the rest on time."

Evans did some more calculating. "Three hundred dollars. That's not too bad. What do you want—a year to pay?"

"A year would be good."

"Year to pay." His pencil moved quickly. "Well, that'd be sixty-eight dollars carrying charges. Make the total nine hundred seventy dollars. Three hundred down, that leaves six seventy. Fifty—fifty-five—well, figure fifty-five dollars and—uh—eighty-five cents a month, and a few cents less the last month. Fifty-five sixty-five the last month." He smiled. "Give you a little bargain there at the end."

Jake did not smile. "Okay." He put a hand into his coat pocket and came out with a wallet. "I brought the three hundred."

Evans raised a restraining hand, dropped his pencil on the desk, and leaned back in his wooden swivel chair. "Just a minute, Jake—that's the right name, ain't it?"

"Ya. Jake Mortensen."

"Okay. First of all, tell me how old you are."

"Eighteen."

"Well, that isn't legal age, you see."

"Ya."

"I mean, you can't sign a contract. It wouldn't be any good if you did sign it. If you didn't pay on time, there'd be a problem."

"I'd pay."

"I'm sure you would, if nothing went wrong. It's when things go wrong that a contract is important. Anyway, you need a good contract for your own protection."

Jake chewed his upper lip again. "I don't want to wait three years."

Evans leaned forward, folded his arms across his desk. "Oh, you don't need to do that. We do have to get you a co-signer, though."

"What's that?"

"Someone else to sign the contract with you. Someone who's over twenty-one and has good credit. A friend in town, maybe, or your father, or someone you work for."

"I work for myself. That's why I need the truck."

"I see."

"I been out on my own pretty much since I was fourteen. I kinda figured I could buy the truck on my own."

Evans made a little gesture with his head. "Well, I'm sure anxious to help you, but I gotta look out for my business, do things in a businesslike way."

"Ya, I understand."

"Do you think you could get somebody to co-sign?"

Jake looked at the floor. "Well, my dad, maybe."

"If you want me to, I'll make out the papers and you can take them along."

Jake thought about it. "Okay."

Evans pulled a pad from a desk drawer, found some carbon paper, and fixed two sheets of it between pages in the pad. He picked up an indelible pencil, licked its tip, and began to fill in the blanks on the contract form on the pad. He broke a pencil lead pressing to get through the carbon paper and paused to sharpen the pencil with his pocketknife before he turned to the pad.

Jake said, "There's one thing. I'm working up in the hills and I'm likely to be snowbound till April. So I guess I couldn't get the truck until April. I couldn't start making payments till May."

"That's fine. I'll fix it up that way." Evans continued to fill in the blanks.

Jake said, "I guess I better not pay you the three hundred dollars until we get the contract signed."

"That's right."

Jake put his wallet back into his pocket.

Evans finished writing and carefully removed the carbon paper and tore three sheets from the pad. He handed them to Jake.

"You take these with you," Evans said. "If you get a co-signer, have him sign all three copies and bring them back to me. Have somebody—two people—watch him sign so they can sign right there as witnesses. Or else bring him with you and we'll all sign together in here."

"Okay." Jake started to get up.

"Sit down a minute." Evans sprawled back in his chair and Jake sat down. "What does your dad do?"

"He farms out to Holbrook."

"What's his name?"

"Jim Mortensen."

"Does he own his own place?"

"He's buying it."

"Who's handling the mortgage?"

"The bank here in Malad."

"You have any money in the bank?"

"No. I keep it put away at home."

"Might not hurt to put it in the bank."

Jake considered. "Yeah. Might not."

"What do you plan to do with the truck?"

"Custom hauling."

"Anything particular?"

"Me and a friend is cutting posts this winter. We'll wanta haul them out and sell them first. Then whatever work I can get—hay, wheat, potatoes, whatever there is."

"Do you know how to drive a truck?"

"Ya. I drove for Bob Baker and Blaze Tyler. We got a pickup at home. I drive that sometimes."

"Who else have you worked for?"

"Oh, just about ever farmer in Holbrook."

"Lynn Sweet?"

"Ya. Him."

"You a pretty good worker?"

"Ya."

Evans let his chair swing upright and he stood up. Jake stood. Evans said, "I guess we can sell you the truck if you get that note co-signed by your dad or someone else reliable. Let me know."

"I will."

Evans walked Jake to the front door and shook hands with him before Jake went back to Jean's house.

"Well, where's your truck?" she asked when she met him on the front porch.

"They've got to order one."

"When will it come?" She led the way into the house and closed the door behind them.

"I gotta get Papa to co-sign my note."

"Oh. Do you think he will?"

"I don't know. All I can do is ask him."

"I hope he does."

"So do I."

Jean led him into the kitchen. She pointed to a paper bag on the counter. "I made you some dinner you can eat on the way. I put it there in the sack of stuff you got for Mama."

"I guess I better take it and get going."

"Did you find that part you need for the windmill?"

"No. There ain't one in town, I guess."

"Your whole trip was a kind of a failure, wasn't it?"

"I got to visit you and see a pitcher show."

"Oh, I really liked that movie. I'm glad you took us."

"Well, I better go."

"I put some candy in with your dinner. We got some for Christmas."

"Thanks. They still got that candy store across from our old place."

"Oh, I know! I go by there sometimes."

"It sures smells good down there. I remember when we lived there, I used to stand in the yard and just smell the candy smells from across the road. I come by there last night. It smells just as good."

"Joanne went in there one time."

"Did she?"

"Mama gave her some money to go to the store and get bread, and she sneaked over there and bought some candy. I guess she just couldn't stand it no more." Jean broke into giggles. "She sure got a licking."

"I don't remember that."

"You was just little."

Jake put an arm around Jean and gave her a hug. "Tell Charlie good-bye for me, and take it easy. Do you want me to tell Mama you're going to have a baby?"

"No. I'll write her a letter."

"Okay. 'Bye now."

He walked again past the house where he had once lived and stopped again to breathe in the fragrance of the candy. Then he walked across the street, hesitated a moment, and entered the candy store. The bell attached to the door tinkled, and a tall, gray-haired woman came immediately through a door and stood behind the counter.

"Good morning," she said. "May I help you?"

"Thought I might look around."

"That's just fine."

She did not move but stood erect behind the counter and watched him. Jake moved slowly around the small store, looking at everything —glass cases and large glass jars of candy, boxes of candy, even three small wooden kegs of candy. Peppermints, taffy, chocolates, gumdrops, hard candy, fudge, divinity, all sorts of candy. He looked at it all and walked back to the door.

"Don't see anything you like?" she asked.

"Oh, there's plenty I like." He paused with his hand on the doorknob and looked around the room again. Then he removed his hand from the knob and walked to the counter.

"Give me a quarter's worth of peppermints," he said.

"All right." She picked up a small white paper bag and opened it.

"Give me two quarters' worth," he said. "Put each one in a different bag."

"Each peppermint?"

"Each quarter's worth. Two bags."

"All right."

She weighed the candy on a scale and put it into the two sacks. As she twisted the tops of the sacks shut Jake said, "Give me five of them penny candies right there, too."

"Certainly."

She put the stick candy he pointed out into another bag. He paid the fifty-five cents and carefully put the sacks into his pocket.

At Colin Baker's house that evening Jake paid Colin the two dollars and took his old skis.

He found Scotty's parents at home. The old man answered the door.

"Who? Oh. Hi, Jake."

"Howdy."

"Come on in."

Jake went inside.

"Hello, Jake."

"Hello, Mrs. Tubbs."

"Did you come home alone?"

"Ya. Scotty figured he better stay up there and work. I had to come get some stuff before we get snowed in."

Mrs. Tubbs said, "Sit down."

Jake sat on a kitchen chair. The house was one room, with a door leading into a lean-to. Mrs. Tubbs was working at the stove. She said, "Want to have supper with us?"

"My folks is expecting me home. I been to Malad."

"How's everything in Malad?"

"Just the same."

Mr. Tubbs said, "How's Scotty?"

"He's fine. We're doing pretty good. We'll make quite a bit off them posts."

"That'll be good."

Jake took a sack from his pocket. "Scotty give me some money and had me buy this for you. Christmas present. Sorry it's late."

"Where'd Scotty get money?"

"Hung onto it, I guess. I don't know. It was just a dime."

Mrs. Tubbs opened the sack and looked into it. "Peppermint candy! Look, Michael! Peppermint candy!"

Michael Tubbs looked into the sack. "That's a lot of candy for a dime."

Jake shrugged. "I never bought none before. That's what they give me. Scotty said you'd like it for Christmas."

Mrs. Tubbs said, "We didn't even get him nothing."

Jake stood up. "I don't think he even thought none about that. Well, I gotta be going."

"Thanks for coming by, Jake."

"That's okay." Jake reached the door, then stopped and turned back. "Come to think of it, you could get Scotty something if you wanted."

"What's that, Jake?"

"I got to thinking. Colin Baker was trying to sell me his old skis. He got some new ones. I didn't have no money, but Scotty was trying to make hisself some skis up at our camp. He'd probably like them if you wanted to buy them."

Michael Tubbs grunted. "Ya. Reckon he would."

Jake said, "I could go by Colin's place and get them and take them up to Scotty if you wanted to buy them for him."

Michael said, "Well, I'll think about it."

Jake said, "Okay," and turned to go.

Mrs. Tubbs said, "How much does he want for them, Jake?"

"Fifty cents."

Mrs. Tubbs said, "What do you think, Michael?"

Michael said, "I dono. Have to think about it."

Jake said, "I wouldn't mind going halves. I'd like to get him something myself."

Mrs. Tubbs said, "You don't need to do that. I got fifty cents put away."

Michael said, "Where'd you get fifty cents?"

"Never you mind. I got it." She went across the room to a chest of drawers that stood beside their bed. She opened a drawer, rummaged through it, and came back with a quarter, a dime, and three nickels. She handed the money to Jake. "You get the skis for him, okay?"

"You bet." Jake put the money into his pocket.

"And give him our love. Is there anything he needs?"

"We're doing pretty good. He shot a deer, so we been eating good."

"I'm glad to hear that. You tell him we're doing just fine."

"I will."

Jake let himself out the front door and walked down the snow-covered front path and out the broken gate. He looked back at the house. The door was closed and the blinds were drawn. He picked up the skis from the borrow pit, where he had left them, and walked on through the early night.

It was after supper the next night before he poured a glass of milk for himself and sat down at the kitchen table beside Papa, who was drinking a glass of milk and writing in a school tablet.

"Whatcha writing, Papa?"

"Some stuff for Sunday school. I got to give the lesson."

Jake took his truck contract from his pocket and unfolded it, leaning on his forearms on the table. "I got something I wish you'd take a look at."

"What is it?"

Jake handed him the papers. "I want to buy a truck. I got the money for the down payment. They need you to co-sign with me."

Papa studied the papers carefully, looking at each carbon after he had carefully read the original.

"You'd be paying on this for a year," he said.

"A year starting in April."

"What if something was to go haywire?"

"I don't think nothing would."

Papa read some more on the contract. "If you can't pay this, I'd have to."

"Ya, but I could pay it. When I sell them posts I'll have enough to pay quite a few months. I can haul hay for guys, and I can get a lot of work in the wheat. I won't have no trouble."

"What if you was to wreck the truck?"

"I won't."

"Yeah, but what if you did?"

"Well, I guess I'd have to go talk to them."

"There's lots that can go wrong. I've had some bad luck on contracts I signed."

"If something goes wrong, Papa, I'll get a job here, or go to Malad and get a job, and pay them off."

"Jobs ain't always easy to find."

Jake sat in silence. Papa read the contract a third time.

"I'm kinda scared to sign it," Papa said. "If something was to go haywire, they could come and get the farm. Then there wouldn't none of us have no place to go."

Jake said nothing for a moment, then, quietly, "I think it would be okay."

"I know you'd do your best, son, but I don't think I better. I'm just scared about it. I don't think I better."

CHAPTER FOURTEEN

Jake skied into camp with the last of the daylight, balancing a sack of potatoes on his shoulder and with a flour sack full of stuff tied with a piece of rope around his waist. He kicked his feet out of the skis and slogged the last few steps through the snow to the door of the dugout as Scotty came out to meet him.

"I wondered why the birds stopped singing and all the critters run off," Scotty said.

"Howdy," Jake said. He let the potatoes drop to the ground. He stood erect, flexed his shoulders, and began to untie the rope around his waist. "How'd it go?" he asked.

"No trouble. I got quite a bit done."

Jake took off the sack and handed it to Scotty. "Set this on my bed."

"I unrolled your bed and let it air out in case you come back tonight."

"I said I would."

"Well, I thought you might, anyhow."

Scotty took the sack and carried it into the dugout. Jake walked back and picked up the skis and carried them to the dugout.

"Where'd you get the skis?"

"I borrowed them from you."

"Me?"

"Your folks bought them for you for Christmas."

"No they didn't."

"Yes they did. Here." Jake leaned the upright skis toward Scotty and let them fall. Scotty caught them.

"My folks didn't buy me no skis."

"They bought these."

"They couldn't afford 'em."

"These was secondhand."

"Who from?"

"Colin Baker."

"My folks wouldn't even talk to a Baker."

"I knowed about them. I told your folks and they give me the money to buy them."

"Where'd they get the money? My old man stick up the store?"

"They was only four bits."

"How much?"

"Four bits."

"How much?"

"Four bits. Colin got a new pair and he didn't want these no more."

Scotty stared hard at Jake for a long moment, then said, "If you say so." He looked at the skis. "How do they work?"

"You put them on the snow and put your feet in the straps and go forward. It don't do no good to go backward."

"You have any trouble coming over here on them?"

"I only come from the road. It's awkward going uphill, but it sure is nice going down."

"Who brung you over?"

"My dad hauled me in the sleigh. We brought some more supplies. They're hid under a tree down close to the road. We'll have to go after them in the morning."

Scotty looked at the skis again. "Four bits, huh?"

"Ya. And you owe me a dime."

"What for?"

"I figured you'd want to give your folks something for the skis, so I bought a dime's worth of peppermints and give to them."

"How much peppermints do you get for a dime now? Six pounds and all the broken pieces?"

"Just a little sackful."

"I ain't got a dime."

"I'll take it out of your share of the posts."

Scotty studied the skis, then put them down and fitted his feet into the straps. He skied slowly down a little hill, then took them off and walked back up.

"You can walk them uphill if you know how," Jake said.

"I know how, but I'm lazy."

"We get a little more snow and it'll be too deep to walk far. Them skis will be nice to have then."

On Sunday, after they had brought up the supplies and hung the fresh pork in the tree beside the venison and what was left of the first pig, they took the skis on their weekly reconnaissance. It was an easy matter to pick a place to do their work the coming week. They spent the rest of the day skiing, taking turns, sometimes trying with little success to ride tandem or to ski on one ski alone.

Jake made supper for them that night and divided the large piece of cake his mother had sent with him. They sat on their beds, eating the cake and sipping coffee.

"How was your Christmas?" Scotty asked.

"It was real nice. Look." Jake took the watch from his pocket, untied it, and handed it to Scotty. He examined it carefully, front and back.

"That's a nice watch," he said.

"First one I ever had."

"Now we'll know when it's quitting time around here."

He handed back the watch. Jake reached over and placed it on the middle shelf of an orange crate. Jake said, "I ain't going to take it to work."

"Why not?"

"I'm afraid of losing it in the snow. I'll leave it here."

"And we'll just work until it gets dark, huh?"

"Same as always."

"You're a hard taskmaster."

"Did you do anything Christmas?"

"I tried to catch you a rabbit and decorate it in red and green ribbon for when you got back, but he outrun me."

"I thought you might go down to them people's place."

"Nope."

Jake drank the last of his coffee and got up to put his cup into the dishpan and brush off his hands. He lay down on the bed, wiggled and adjusted a few times until he was comfortable, put his hands behind his head, and lay looking at the candelight flickering on the ceiling.

"I reckon we'll have to hire Bud to haul our posts for us," he said.

"I thought you was gonna buy a truck."

"So did I, but I ain't old enough. I got to have a co-signer. Can't buy on time until I'm twenty-one."

"Won't your dad co-sign?"

"No. He's afraid something might go wrong."

"What can go wrong?"

"Oh, wreck the truck. Not be able to make no money. Lotsa things could go wrong."

"Yeah, but they won't."

"Well, I can see his point."

"I can't," Scotty said. "He knows you're careful. Anyhow, you was gonna give almost all the money back to your family, wasn't you? You wasn't gonna keep hardly nothing for yourself."

"Well, he's had some hard luck. He don't want to sign up for none of mine."

"I'd sign with you if they'd let me. I'm over twenty-one. But they want somebody that has some money or a farm or something."

"Yeah—that's what he's afraid of—losing his farm."

"Well, I guess that's worth worrying about." Scotty bent over his hands, cleaning his fingernails with his pocketknife. "You oughta get that girl to sign with you. They wouldn't even ask if she has no money. They'd just take a look at her knees and that yellow dress and give you whatever you asked for. You smile at her just right, and she'd do it for you."

"Sure she would."

They cut each post eight feet long, and their eyes had become so accustomed to that length that a pile of posts, each cut without having been measured, varied in length scarcely three inches between the longest and the shortest. If they had applied a tape measure to any given post it would probably have shown an error of less than two inches.

From almost any high point around them now they could see piles of their posts, some of the old piles nothing more than white or speckled bumps (speckled if some of the wood showed through the snow) on a snow-covered landscape. The newer piles were black spots on the white background. But they had not begun to exhaust the available patches of juniper. Juniper Row, the long wide belt of the stunted trees, had hardly been touched. There was enough work for the winter.

They took New Year's Day off from cutting posts and spent it cutting firewood and hauling it to make a big pile beside their dugout. Jake said, "That'll give some of it a chance to cure some."

"It don't seem to need much curing."

"We've found a lot of old stuff that burns good. If it snows much more we won't be able to find none of that."

"Oh, juniper burns good anyhow. That and posts is all it's good for."

"If we was to do this again next winter," Jake said, "it might not hurt to pick out a place in the spring and cut a bunch of firewood then, so it'd have the summer to cure in. Some of the wood we got gets a little smoky."

"A little smoke don't hurt nobody. Makes the meat taste better."

Scotty asked, "You wanta play cribbage?"

"Soon as I finish this."

"Whatcha writing?"

"A letter."

"You can't mail no letters up here."

"I thought after I wrote a bunch I might walk over to them people's place and have them mail them."

"I was wondering when you was gonna go see that girl again."

"They live closest. If somebody else lived closer, I'd go there."

"I wouldn't. I'd go right back to that yellow dress."

They got another inch or two of snow late in the week, the first snowfall since before Christmas. On Sunday's reconnaissance, Jake moved them a long walk northwest of their camp. "Save the closer stuff for later," he said. "When that snow gets much deeper we're not going to want to walk very far in it."

"I can always ski."

"Okay. You ski out and do the work, and I'll stay close and keep the fire going."

Jack set up his snares for rabbits again, but many of the amimals looked too thin to make good eating. "Rabbits is best in the fall," he said.

"Rabbits is best left alone," Scotty said.

Twice in the week that followed, new snow fell. There was not a large amount either time, but Jake wore a frown when he looked at the sky.

They slept late on Sunday and breakfasted leisurely. They cleaned up around the dugout, and Jake built a fire outside and used both that fire and the camp stove to boil water.

"Why all the water?"

"I want to take a bath."

"In January? You'll freeze."

But Jake rolled up their beds so he would not splash water on them and took a bath in the dugout. He dried himself thoroughly, then sat close to the camp stove for almost two hours, writing.

"More letters?"

"Ya."

"You must be writing to everybody you know."

"Ya."

In early afternoon Jake sealed the last of his letters and put a stamp on it. He had a small pile of letters lying on the orange-crate dresser. From one of his shelves in that dresser he took a package. He had brought it back with him from his Christmas vacation, and it had rested unopened on the shelf since then. He untied the string, and the brown-paper wrapping lay loosely over the contents of the package. Jake took off the clean work clothes he had put on after his bath.

Scotty had been washing more clothes in the big pan in the center of the dugout floor and hanging them to dry. He looked up as Jake finished opening the package.

"What's that? Your suit?"

"My good clothes. I brung 'em up this time."

"You trying to impress the rabbits?"

"You can come with me if you want."

"Where you going?"

"I thought I'd go look for a place to work this week, and then go on down to them people's house and mail my letters. I better do it now before the snow gets much deeper."

"It's pretty deep now."

"Ya, but it ain't bad to walk in, and there'll be a road to their place still. Pretty soon we're going to get a real snowstorm, and that road might get closed."

"I'll come with you to look for a place to work, but I don't think I'll go see that girl with you."

"I ain't going to see that girl. I'm going to mail my letters."

"I know what you're going for."

They put on their coats, and Jake took one more thing from his package before he put the wrappings back on the shelf. It was a small white sack, which he put carefully into a coat pocket.

CHAPTER FIFTEEN

He had long since placed in a flour sack the jars and pans in which Maxine had sent the food back with them at Thanksgiving. He picked up that sack now, and they left the dugout and set out to the northwest. They crossed two ridges following their own footsteps, footsteps they had made going back and forth to work during the past week. After the second ridge they veered off the old path.

"Some of the snow is getting pretty deep," Scotty said. They had struck a deep drift and were floundering through it, walking with effort against soft snow that came past their knees.

"It drifts in a little and then don't make a crust," Jake said.

They came out of the drift and found easier walking, angling up another ridge until they came to a clump of juniper.

"This looks good," Scotty said.

"Ain't much of it," Jake said. They walked slowly past the clump, inspecting the size of the trees, and came out beyond it with a good view of the land to the north.

"There's quite a bit down there," Scotty said.

"Ya. Okay. How about if we start with that bunch of trees right there"—Jake pointed—"then swing over there, then work back this way this week?"

"Don't sound bad."

"Okay."

They stood silently, looking over the sweep of the land as if contemplating their decision. They had about reached the western limit of the system of ridges and ravines in which they had been working. To their right the land was folded and broken. To their left the ridges played out into the edge of the long north-south valley that contained the road from Utah. Scotty looked south, looked northwest, and pointed and said, "Look."

Jake followed his direction. About a mile away, a vehicle was moving slowly northward.

"Hauling hay with a sled," Jake said. "Four horses."

"I bet they're hauling hay to Holbrook the same way."

"Yup. Not today, though. I don't know nobody in Holbrook that'd haul hay on Sunday."

"I would if you'd pay me."

"You're like that guy out there, though. You're a heathen. Ain't got no religion."

"Well, being a heathen don't pay good, but it don't cut into my Sundays so much."

"I seen you at church once."

"Don't tell nobody."

"They wouldn't believe it anyhow."

They watched the sled until it disappeared behind the next fold in the ground. Jake carefully slung the sack of bottles and dishes over his shoulder. He could hear a slight clatter from inside the sack.

"Guess I better get over there before it gets too late," he said.

"Kiss her once for me."

"If I was to kiss her, it wouldn't be with you in mind."

The road westward from the main road had been packed down recently, but no one had driven over it since the latest snowfall. Jake found good footing on the road and walked rapidly. If he looked to the side he could see the barbed wire and fence posts move by him at a steady flow. His feet at every stride kicked up a cloud of snow and settled to the instep into the snow. A couple of times he turned and walked backward for a few steps, looking back at the long line of footprints he had made.

A dog, silent, trotting, wagging its tail, came out to the road to greet him at the Griffeth place.

"Hi, boy. Good dog." The dog trotted beside him as he started for the front porch. Then Jake veered around the house to the back door. He kicked his feet against the steps to get the snow off them and scraped the soles on the boot scraper that was fastened to the back stoop before he knocked sharply on the door. He waited, his head down as he listened. He heard someone moving in the kitchen, then Maxine opened the door.

"Well, Jake Mortensen! How do you do? Come in!"

She stepped back, holding the door open. She was wearing a dark green dress, something she might have worn to teach school, or to go to church. She looked pleased to see him. He gave his shoes one last kick and one last shuffle on the cement stoop and went inside. She closed the door. He walked to the table in the middle of the kitchen and put down his flour sack.

"I brung back your dishes and stuff," he said.

"Well, thank you. I wasn't worried about them, but it's nice to see you again. You must have had a long walk. Take off your coat. Can you stay awhile?"

"Oh, a little while, maybe." He took his letters from his coat pocket. "I wonder if you'd mail these letters for me."

"Certainly." She took his letters and went into the front room with them. He hung his coat on one of the hooks near the back door.

She came back into the kitchen and said, "Do you like bread pudding?"

"Yes."

"Mother made some. Let me fix us each a bowl." She went into the pantry to get the pudding and the milk.

"That was sure good cake you give us."

"I'm glad. We have half an apple pie on the shelf in here. Would you like to take that back with you?"

"No. I better not take back no pans nor nothing. We're gonna get snowbound pretty quick would be my guess, and I wouldn't be able to bring them back."

"I don't mind. We've got pans. Take it."

He shook his head and dragged out the word "No."

She came into the kitchen with her hands full and pushed the pantry door shut with her foot. At the table she dished up two bowls of bread pudding and poured two glasses of milk. She returned the rest of the food to the pantry and put two spoons on the table.

"Did you have a nice Christmas?"

"Sure did. We all did. Well, Janet was a little unhappy part of the time, but we all had a good Christmas."

"Janet? She's one of your sisters."

"Ya. She's the middle girl."

"What made her unhappy? Sit down, Jake. Mother makes delicious pudding."

Jake sat and picked up his spoon. "Oh, she was hoping to get a china doll. She ain't never had one. And she didn't. Now she figures the folks will think she's getting too old, and she won't never get one."

"That's too bad." Maxine tasted the pudding. "It's even better than usual."

"It's real good."

"You certainly look nice. Did you get those clothes for Christmas?"

Jake looked down at himself. "Oh, no. These ain't new. They just ain't been wore much. It's my good clothes."

"You look very handsome."

"Oh." He took a big spoonful of pudding and looked around the kitchen, taking in cupboards and calendar and the beginnings of a supper being prepared.

"What did you get for Christmas?" she asked.

"A watch. Ain't never had one before."

"A watch! How nice! May I see it?"

He took it from his pocket, untied the string from his belt, and handed it across the table to her.

"That's very nice."

"I guess it ain't one of the real dear ones, but it keeps good time."

Maxine looked up at a kitchen clock that was ticking on top of the warming oven. "It certainly does. Or else we're both wrong." She handed the watch back to him. He fastened the string back to his belt and put the watch back into his pocket.

"I bet you got a lot of nice stuff," he said.

"I got clothes, mostly, and some books."

"I got a little book of funny poems from my sisters. Somebody almost always gives me a book of poems. The folks give me one for my birthday."

"Do you enjoy poetry?"

"Ya. I like to learn the poems and say them by heart."

"I write poetry sometimes."

"I'd like to read some."

She smiled. "Oh, no. No one reads it. It's just for myself."

"I bet it's good."

"The world will never know."

"My sister writes poems."

"Which sister?"

"Janet. She don't show them around much, neither. She's showed some to me."

"You should feel honored."

Jake looked toward the front room. "Where's your folks?"

"They went off in the car to see some people."

"They must of gone west. There ain't no car tracks to the east."

"Nobody goes out of the valley much in the winter. The road's closed a lot."

"We ain't really had much snow yet."

"Dad says we'll get a lot more."

"I think he's right."

Jake finished his bread pudding and a glass of milk.

"Would you like some more?"

"Oh, I better not."

"There's plenty. I'd like you to have some if you'd like it."

"Okay. Not too much."

She dished up more for him. "How's your work coming?" she asked.

"We're doing good. We're getting close to having four thousand posts. We'll have nine thousand or better by spring."

"Dad was saying after you left here on Thanksgiving that he might buy some from you."

"That'd be good. Wouldn't be too far to haul."

"You two made quite an impression on him. He says it isn't everybody who'd spend a winter working like that, all alone."

"It isn't everbody that has to."

She sat across the table from him again, her elbow on the table and her cheek resting on her hand, looking across at him as he ate. "I've been thinking a lot about what you told Dad at Thanksgiving dinner."

"What did I tell him?"

"That I should be free to leave this place if I wanted to. Go off somewhere and seek my fortune."

"Oh. Ya. I'd forgot about that."

"I haven't forgotten it for a minute." She folded her arms on the table. She was wearing short sleeves, and her arms were still somewhat brown even so late in the winter. They were slender, strong-looking arms, with smooth skin. She looked down at the table top between them. "I think I'm going to do it."

"Go off?"

"Yes. All my life I've dreamed about going places. I've been to Salt Lake. I might like to go back there. But someplace farther, I think. San Francisco. St. Louis. New York. I might go to Canada. I've read about Canada. I think I might like it."

"If you like snow."

"I was thinking of the big towns in the east. Montreal or someplace."

"What would you do?"

She looked up, smiling, and leaned a little toward him. "Do you know what I'd do first? I'd just look. I'd walk all over, looking at things. I'd take tours and go to museums and libraries and places, and see as much as I could see."

"Wouldn't you have to get a job?"

"Oh, yes, after a while. I don't care what job. Teach or wait tables or anything I could get. I'm not worried about that." She looked down at the table again and was silent for a time, lost in her own thoughts. Then she looked back at him, her face serious now. "I've thought about that so much, and until you said what you did on Thanksgiving it had never occurred to me that I could really do any of it. It was as if you opened the world to me."

He looked into his bowl, slowly chewing. He took another bite.

She said, "I think that just the minute school lets out in the spring, I'm going to go."

"You told your folks?"

"No. There'll be enough of an argument when I leave. I'm not going to fight with them about it all winter."

"Well, good luck."

She reached across the table and gripped his arm. "Oh, you're the one who brought me good luck, just by coming here. You're my lucky charm. I should fasten you to a silver chain and carry you in my pocket."

He looked at the hand that clutched his forearm. "I wouldn't fit," he said.

Laughing, she withdrew her hand. "I could put your picture in my pocket, if I could talk you out of one."

"Maybe I could get one from the folks. I don't have one with me."

She pushed back her chair and sprang to her feet. "I'm going to get my camera and take a picture of you. Don't go away."

She hurried from the room, and faintly he could hear her footsteps on the stairs. He finished his pudding and his milk and got up. He was looking out the kitchen window when she came back downstairs.

"Let's go outside," she said.

She had him pose beside the back steps. He squinted into the sun and looked into the camera.

"Don't squint."

"The sun's too bright."

"Well, then, I'm going to move." She found an angle that let him look more natural and snapped the shutter. "Stay there." She wound the film and moved closer and took another picture.

"Okay," she said, starting toward the house, "now I have your picture. Let's go inside where it's warm."

"Let me take one of you."

She posed, hugging herself against the cold, and they went inside.

"When you get them developed," he said, "send me one of them."

"All right. I'll send you one of your own, too. And when I get where I'm going, I'll send you a picture postcard."

"I've got a friend in Salt Lake I write to a lot."

"Oh? Fellow or girl?"

"He's a guy I went to school with. He went on to high school. He's at the University of Utah now. He's learning to fly."

"Oh, that must be fun!"

"Ever time I see a airplane I think about him. One of these days I'm figuring on getting a airplane ride from him."

"I'd really look forward to something like that!"

She gathered up the dishes and stacked them ready for washing, then led him into the front room. "We could play cards or checkers or something," she said.

"I better be getting back before long."

"Don't run off so soon! You just got here! Sit down."

They sat, and he looked around the room again. Except that it was clean of the Thanksgiving things it seemed no different than when he had left it.

"This sure is a nice house."

"Dad's talking about piping in running water this year."

"My sister's got running water."

"Where does she live?"

"In Malad. Jean, the married sister. She's going to have a baby."

"I'll bet she's excited."

"Yeah, I guess."

Maxine was in the rocking chair, and she rocked a few times, looking at him closely, before she spoke again. "Does it bother you that she's going to have a baby?"

"No. She's kinda glad, so it's okay with me."

"Have you thought any more about whether you'd ever want to get married and have children?"

"Some."

"Do you still feel the same way you did?"

Jake looked away from her for a moment, looked at the ceiling, looked back at her. "Ya."

She smiled. "Well, I feel sorry for the girl you didn't marry."

"She didn't miss nothing."

"How's Scotty?"

"He's about the same."

"Has he eaten any more gizzards?"

Jake grinned. "I put out my snares again after Christmas, but most of the rabbits is too skinny to be good eating. Scotty kids me a lot about them."

"He must be a very good friend."

"Ya. I don't know nobody else I'd want to be up here with all winter but him and Quin."

She rocked quietly for a moment, looking across the room at him. Suddenly he stood up. "I better go."

She stood and walked around the table to him. "You could stay for supper. The folks would like to see you."

"No. I better get back to camp."

"Will you come see us again?"

"Maybe not. If we get more snow, it ain't gonna be too easy to get places."

"Well, come in the spring."

"Maybe. I appreciate all you done. I hope you have good luck wherever you go."

"I hope you do, Jake Mortensen."

He walked into the kitchen and got his coat. She followed him.

"I hope you'll get in touch with Dad about the posts. Maybe I'll see you then."

"Ya. I hadn't thought of that." He pulled on his coat. They were facing each other, although Jake looked over her head as he buttoned his coat. He put his hand into a pocket of the coat and took out a small package. He handed it to her. "I got these for you for Christmas. It's kinda late, but here you go."

"What are they?" She unrolled the package and it became a sack. She opened the sack and looked inside. "Oh! Peppermints! I love peppermints!" She held out the open sack to him. "Would you like one?"

"No. I wanted for you to have them all."

"Oh, Jake, I certainly thank you. It's been an age since I had peppermints."

"I hope you like them."

"I will."

He looked carefully at her face, a long, appraising look. "I don't think I ever knowed a nicer girl. Or a prettier one, too."

She placed the palm of her hand against his cheek. "Just because you're never going to get married, Jake Mortensen, doesn't mean you're never going to get kissed."

CHAPTER SIXTEEN

The snow was falling heavily enough to limit visibility. Scotty walked almost up to Jake before Jake noticed him. Jake had been swinging his ax in rapid blows, swinging it horizontally from the end as a power hitter would swing a baseball bat at a low pitch. He had felled three trees without cutting them into posts and was working on a fourth. He happened to glance up and see Scotty approaching. He stopped his work. In spite of the cold, sweat streaked his face. Jake said nothing.

Scotty said, "You swing like you was mad at the tree."

Jake put his axhead into the snow and leaned on the handle. His breathing was a little heavy. "Just trying to get more done."

"This snow keeps falling like this, you'll lose sight of them others before you get them cut up."

"I'll get them cut up. Don't worry."

"I ain't worried. Just seemed funny to me."

"I know what I'm doing."

Scotty said, "I thought it must be about dinnertime."

Jake squinted upward into the falling snow, looking for a sun that could not be seen. He looked back down. "Maybe so. I don't know."

"I thought you had a watch built into your head."

"Well, I don't."

"You wanna eat, or should I go work some more?"

Jake swung his ax so it bit into a tree stump and held. "Let's eat."

They waded through snow to a pile of posts. Jake brushed fresh snow away with his hand and revealed their dinner bucket and thermos bottles standing on the logs. He took the bucket and his bottle and walked to the other end of the pile. He cleared a place to sit and sat down on the pile.

Scotty picked up his bottle and looked around. "Mind if I set by you?" he asked.

"Go ahead."

Scotty made himself a seat a couple of feet from Jake and sat down. Jake had pried the lid off the bucket and taken a piece of rabbit from it. Scotty reached for a sandwich.

Scotty said, "I guess there ain't no use trying to build a fire."

"Everthing's too wet to burn."

"Ya." He took a bite and chewed. "That rabbit good?"

"Ya, for cold rabbit."

"I'm surprised you found a fat one. There's been so many poor ones."

"This one knowed where the hay was hid."

"It don't look like the snow slowed you down none this morning."

"I been doing pretty good."

"I can't seem to get up no speed. It's like the snow was hard to cut through."

"You're probably just tired," Jake said. "You ain't had no time off since we come up here. I had that week at Christmas."

"I don't feel tired. Just logy, I guess, from the cold."

"It'll get worse, I reckon. It don't get too cold when it's snowing."

"The way it's coming down, it ain't gonna stop snowing till summer."

Jake went on eating for a while before he said, "I guess it was about noon. I'm hungry."

"The way you was working, I'd be hungry too."

"How much do you reckon Bud will charge for hauling out these posts?"

Scotty shook his head. "I got no idea."

"Well, I got a idea, but I wonder just how much. Trouble is, we gotta pay him for his time. The further we haul them, the more we gotta pay."

"Well, charge more money over in Weston and places."

"They won't pay no more. Holbrook posts ain't no better than Cub River posts."

"Is that where they get them now?"

"Wherever they get them now. I don't know where they get them now."

"Weston Canyon, maybe."

"It don't matter none where they get them. We just gotta haul them over and pay Bud and make what we can off them."

"Or else not sell them."

"Ya, and that's a winter gone to waste."

Scotty took a bite of a sandwich and chewed thoughtfully. "Maybe you could buy a secondhand truck."

"I don't want a secondhand truck."

"Well, I don't blame you for that, but you could get a secondhand truck for the three hundred dollars you got, and then earn enough to buy a new one later."

"Ya, maybe. And maybe the thing would fly apart on me the first trip and I wouldn't have three hundred dollars nor a truck either one."

"There's always that."

"I'm not going to monkey around with no secondhand truck. If it was that good, they wouldn't of sold it back to the dealer anyhow. You don't know how long a old truck is going to last, if it's going to last at all. I'd be money ahead to get a new one, and then take care of it. It won't be breaking down on me right when I need it most. Even if it don't cost a lot to fix, a breakdown can cost me a job. I want a truck I can depend on."

"I guess you're right."

"I ain't gonna buy no secondhand truck."

"Well, I'm just trying to help. I don't know how you're gonna buy a new one."

"Neither do I."

Scotty took another bite of his sandwich and looked off through the curtain of snow.

Jake had set a candle on the corner of the orange-crate dresser. He sat next to the corner on a chunk of log and bent over his work. He was sewing together a large tear in a pair of waist overalls. He worked slowly, putting the two sides of the seam together a little at a time and making his stitches carefully. His thread was long, and he extended his arm three or four feet from the cloth each time he pulled the thread through.

Scotty pushed aside the blanket at the dugout door and stood in the doorway a moment, his back to Jake, brushing snow off himself before coming inside. Then he turned, stamped his feet a couple of times to remove more snow, and came inside. He picked his way around Jake, careful not to step on either bed in the narrow quarters, and took off his gloves and coat.

"Fixing them pants again, huh?"

"Looks like it."

"Same pants?"

"Ya."

"You're about going to have to give up one of these days and chuck 'em in the fire."

"Maybe."

"You got plenty of pants. You got two more pair, ain't you?"

"Might as well wear these out first."

"I think you've wore them out."

Jake went on sewing. Scotty hung his coat on a nail near the stove. "It's plenty warm in here," he said.

"It's okay."

Scotty opened the stove, looked inside, and closed it again. He sat down on the blanket. "I knocked a bunch of snow off the roof."

"I could hear you."

"I figured I better not let it get too heavy up there. Wouldn't want the roof to cave in on us."

"Yeah."

"It's probably okay, but maybe if it was to get too heavy over them rock walls she'd all come tumbling down. Right on top of you."

"Yeah. Maybe."

Scotty got his harmonica and began to play.

> *"From this valley they say you are leaving.*
> *We will miss—"*

Jake said, "Don't play that."

Scotty stopped playing and took a long look at his partner.

It was common now to sink calf-deep into snow at every step. They walked toward the camp in the last dim light of day and looked like dark shapes swaggering, their arms and shoulders moving in exaggerated rhythm as each leg in turn was lifted high to clear the snow and find a new foothold. Their axes were carried over their shoulders, and the heads swung back and forth with the rocking motions of their bodies. The bucket Jake carried moved in a rising arc across his body and a descending arc back as he labored through the snow. Sometimes one led the way, sometimes the other. The one trailing had a little easier time of it, walking in his partner's tracks.

Jake, leading the way this evening, stopped and set his ax and bucket in the snow. He walked a few feet off the trail and peered into some brush.

"I got one," he said. He removed the rabbit from the snare and rearranged the wires. He added the rabbit to his load and they walked on.

Closer to the dugout, Scotty stopped. "You gonna check this other snare?"

"Might as well." Again Jake put down his load and left the trail. He returned with another rabbit.

"Ain't too many times I catch two," he said. "Both in good shape, too."

"If that's what you call good shape," Scotty said.

"What's wrong with the shape it's in?"

"It's rabbit-shaped."

"You want me to cook you the gizzard?"

Scotty moved ahead to break trail the rest of the way into camp. "You can have the whole rabbit. The only part I want is the hop."

"I don't know how to cook the hop."

"You don't cook hops. You put them in beer."

Jake finished trimming the limbs and twigs off a post and picked it up to carry it to the pile. Immediately, he had to put it down again and turn his back to the wind. He rubbed his glove across his eyes to remove the snow that had been blown into them by the sudden flurry of the wind. The wind had been rising, but he had paid it no attention until now. He turned back to face it. The snow that had been falling all morning was still coming down heavily, and now the wind was sharp, never gentle, and gusting more and more often into angry blasts. Eyes squinted and head lowered against the storm, Jake carried his post to the pile. He went back and picked up his ax, feeling the blast of the wind on his back pushing him at every step, staggering him once. He went back to the pile, teeth gritted against the irritation of the storm, and dug under the snow until he found the dinner bucket and thermos.

He stood for a moment at the end of the pile of posts, getting his bearings. Then he began lumbering through the snow, quartering the wind and trying to peer through the driving snow for Scotty. The wind died for a second and he heard the chunk of an ax to his right. He turned in that direction and had the wind slightly at his back and kept on walking and peering. He saw Scotty dimly, working on a tree, and slogged through the snow until he was a few feet from him. Jake shouted above the wind, "We better go in."

Scotty jumped, startled, and turned around. "What say?"

"We better go in. If this blizzard gets any worse we won't be able to find our way."

"I thought you could find your way anywhere." But Scotty pushed through the snow to another tree, Jake following, and dug his own thermos out of the snow.

"Not in a blizzard," Jake said. "I don't wanta get caught in one."

Their way lay eastward and southward, so they had the wind coming in behind their right shoulders, helping them more than it hurt them. It was still hard, though, to see through the driven snow, and the force of the wind added to the snow depth to make them stumble as they picked their way. Every hundred yards or so they changed leaders. Only in their own canyon were they partly sheltered from the storm, and even there the wind blew and the snow flew. They hurried the last twenty yards and burst into their dugout with sighs of relief.

"We better just sit her out until that wind dies down," Jake said. He began pulling off his coat. Scotty went to the stove to get the fire going.

The blizzard remained heavy all that night and had not much abated by morning. The young men came out of the dugout and considered, then Jake said, "Let's knock off until noon."

Before he went back into the dugout, Jake made his way through the storm to the tree in which the meat was hanging. There were three rabbits there now. He took down one of them and carried it back to the dugout. He put it on the shelf above the stove, where it would thaw and be ready to be cooked later in the day. From the same shelf he took down a sack of beans. He cleared a space on the orange-crate dresser, poured beans out onto it, and began pushing clean beans off the edge of the dresser into a pot, flicking away the bits of rock and stems and other foreign matter that had been sacked up with the beans. The beans landed with a rattle in the empty pot, but when the bottom had been covered they dropped in with less noise. When he had enough to make a meal and was ready to wash them, add water, and put them on the stove to simmer through the day, he turned from the dresser and saw that Scotty had fallen asleep on top of his bed.

The storm died down a little in the afternoon, and they went to work.

"We better not go far," Scotty said. "It's hard to walk, and that storm can blow up again. I figure we ought to stay in this canyon."

Jake thought about it, the tip of his tongue held between his teeth —something he often did when he was concentrating. "Ya," he said, "that's good. If the wind don't blow so much tomorrow, though, I think we oughta go two canyons north. That ain't too far, and there's lots of juniper there. I kinda figured we might work there when the snow got deep."

They went up the canyon to the first large grove beyond the dugout and cut there for the rest of the day. Because of the storm it got dark earlier than usual, and they returned to camp. Jake stopped at the tree to cut down another rabbit.

"You got one on the shelf already," Scotty said.

"I figured I'd cook this one tomorrow in the stew pot. Just let him simmer all day."

"If the fire don't go out."

"I can usually bank it up so it'll keep some heat."

He put the rabbit on the shelf and they got out of their heavy clothes. Jake walked back out and cut some venison for Scotty and returned to fix supper.

Scotty said, "Your pants tore again."

"I know."

"You're gonna run outa thread before the snow melts. Maybe you oughta wear a different pair."

"Maybe."

Jake fried the rabbit and the venison and opened a can of peas and heated them. Scotty made coffee. They sat on their beds and ate without conversation. Scotty poured hot water into a pan and began the job of washing the dishes. Jake sat on a log stool and got out paper and pencil. The pencil broke on the first stroke. Jake took out his pocketknife and began to whittle a new point.

Scotty said, "Gonna write another letter?"

"Kinda looks that way."

"I wouldn't mind a little help with these dishes."

"I'll dry them. Keep your shirt on."

"The wind ain't blowing so bad no more."

"I noticed."

Jake finished sharpening his pencil and put it aside. He got up, took the dishtowel from its hook above the stove, and began drying the dishes as Scotty washed and rinsed them. They worked in silence until the task was almost done.

"Why don't you say that poem about the guy that got froze to death. Sam McGee."

"I don't feel like it."

"You sick?"

"No, I ain't sick."

Scotty finished washing the last dish, the skillet, and sloshed hot water in it to rinse it. He said, "Who you gonna write to? That girl?"

"I wish you'd lay off me about that girl. No, I ain't gonna write to that girl. It ain't none of your business anyhow."

Scotty lowered his hands to his sides and looked at Jake. "Maybe it ain't none of my business, but you been on the prod ever since you come back from seeing her that last time. What's eating on you, anyway? You catch her with one of them farm boys from down the valley?"

A trained prize fighter could hardly have thrown a left jab faster, straighter, or harder than the one with which Jake hit Scotty in the nose and mouth. It made Scotty reel and step back onto his bed. He brought his hand to his mouth and stared over it at Jake in astonishment. Jake, looking just as surprised, lowered his fist and stared back. Scotty took his hand away from his face and looked at it. It was covered with blood.

Scotty put the hand back to his face and, with his other hand, began groping in his pockets. Jake pulled a red bandanna from his own back pocket and held it out to Scotty. "Here," he said. "Here's my hanky."

Scotty rejected it with an angry gesture. "Get away from me," he said. He shouldered past Jake to the orange-crate dresser and began fumbling through it for a handkerchief. "Just get away from me."

Jake looked down at the kneeling figure, then walked around him, trampling on both their beds, and grabbed his coat and hat and gloves. He pulled the cap onto his head and was putting his coat on as he left the dugout. He was eight or ten steps away when something hit him in the back, making him lurch even more than usual in the deep snow. He stopped and looked over his shoulder. Scotty, in the dugout opening, snapped, "And take your darn rabbit with you."

CHAPTER SEVENTEEN

Jake plowed his way to the ridge above the dugout and walked down it toward the west. It was easier walking on the ridge; the wind had swept away much of the snow, and he did not sink in as far at every step. Still, it was difficult, and the wind itself was blowing against him, although it no longer was blowing a blizzard.

Half a mile or so from the dugout he stopped, went a few feet off the ridge, and leaned against a tree. He stared off toward the west, although there was nothing he could see in that direction except a very dim landscape of snow broken by dark shapes here and there.

The night was cold and growing colder. After a while he began walking in little circles between the tree and the ridge, stamping his feet and swinging his arms. He packed down a circular path in the snow. Then he leaned against the tree again, his arms folded with his hands in his armpits. After a while he was again walking, stamping, swinging his arms.

Finally he gave that up and walked back up the ridge. Near the dugout he struck a match and searched through the snow for the rabbit Scotty had thrown at him. The match was blown out by the wind and he lit a second and a third, cupping them in his hand and looking. He gave up, threw away the third spent match, and walked up to the dugout.

A candle was burning on the orange-crate dresser. Scotty was in bed, silent. Jake let himself in. He took off his cap and gloves and unbuttoned his coat. He sat on the log stool and began to unlace his boots.

Scotty, his voice muffled a little by a blanket over his mouth, said, "I cleaned off your rabbit and put it back up there."

Jake looked up at the shelf over the stove and saw the rabbit. He said, "Thanks." He pulled off one boot and put it down beside the dresser. "I'm sorry I hit you," he said.

"I had it coming."

"I know, but I'm sorry I done it."

"It's okay."

"You get the bleeding stopped okay?"

"Ya."

"That's good." Jake took off the other boot and stood up to take off his coat.

"I won't tease you none about that girl no more."

Jake hung up his coat. "Ain't much to say about her. She's going away in the spring."

"Where?"

"I dono. She don't know. We ain't likely to run across her no more."

"Oh."

Jake took off his outer clothes, blew out the candle, and got into bed.

Scotty said, "I guess that would make me hard to get along with, too."

In the morning, the wind had died down. Jake got up first and made breakfast. As the bacon was frying he prepared his rabbit for the stew kettle. As Scotty sat on his bed with his plate in his lap and began eating, Jake put his own plate on the shelf and stoked the fire again. He closed the stove, took his plate, and sat cross-legged on his own bed to eat.

"You've got her pretty warm in here," Scotty said.

"Gotta build up some coals and start that water boiling. Then I can bank the fire and fix it so she'll smolder away all day and keep the rabbit cooking."

"I bet she goes out."

"Oh, maybe. But she'll last a long time, anyhow. I'll just have to warm her up a little tonight and she'll be ready to eat."

"That old rabbit's likely to just hop off the stove and hop on home while we're gone."

"Them's the best kind. More flavor."

Scotty drank coffee and put it aside. "I'm surprised you don't just hop across the snowbanks one of these days like a rabbit."

"It don't seem to add no special strength to my legs. Can't figure why."

Scotty bit off a piece of bacon. "Probably just as well. If it was to affect your legs it might affect your ears, too, and you can't stand no more'n you got."

"That's true."

"It's kinda too bad you ain't gonna get married and have kids. You and that girl might have some pretty good-looking kids if they didn't all go to ears and feet, like you did."

Jake looked at his plate and continued eating. Scotty said, "I don't learn things none too fast, do I," and reached for his coffee cup.

They finished breakfast in silence and put on their coats. Jake lifted his kettle off the stove and worked at the firebox again, arranging embers and fuel to get the kind of fire he wanted. Scotty had filled the thermoses. Jake picked up the dinner bucket he had packed earlier and started to leave. He saw the dishtowel still lying in the corner where he had dropped it last night when he hit Scotty. He picked it up and hung it on its nail above the stove.

They were sitting on a small pile of freshly cut posts, eating dinner, when they heard another airplane motor. It took them a minute of scanning the cloudy-bright sky before they could pick it out. It was flying due north, high up. Jake sat, Scotty lay back on the posts, and both shaded their eyes and watched the small speck plod northward.

"Sure don't seem to be going fast," Scotty said.

"I know, but they do. Well, you can tell. Look where he was when we started watching him and look where he is now. Figure out what was below him then and what's below him now. That's a lot of ground if you was to cover it on foot."

"Yeah, but he seems to be just chugging along peaceful as can be up there, like he's got all the time in the world and ain't making much progress."

They watched the plane until it was out of sight.

The day had been warm, and their work made them warmer. Jake took off his coat not long after lunch and worked in his shirt sleeves. Scotty, nearby, laughed aloud. "Jake, you sure do wear bright underwear. If we was to need help, all you'd have to do would be bend over, and they'd see the signal for miles around."

Jake twisted around and looked at his backside. His torn pants were in worse shape than ever. He said, "Back where I come from, clothes this nice is a Sunday-go-to-meeting suit. You oughta see what the poor folks wear."

Scotty said, "I'm glad I ain't back where you come from."

But the sun never did break through, although Jake and Scotty could always detect its location by the bright spot above the clouds, and late in the afternoon a light but chilly wind began to blow. Jake put his coat back on and worked the last hour and a half bundled up against the cold. When it was too dark to see, he called a halt.

Only two ridges now lay between their work and their camp. Carrying their gear, they waded through the deep snow up the first ridge, down through the intervening canyon. Scotty said, "I'll sure be glad when this gets a crust on it."

Jake said, "I've saw the snow with such a hard crust you could drive a car on it."

"Heck," said Scotty, "over where we live nobody drives a car except when there's a crust on the snow."

"You can go to hell for lying just as quick as you can for stealing."

"I ain't going to hell. Just before I die, I'm gonna repent, and the Lord will welcome me into his arms." Scotty waded a few more steps as he gathered his breath, then resumed. "The trouble with you good guys is you miss all the fun. You're good all your lives and heaven ain't exciting for you. You figured on going there all the time. But guys like me, we take risks. We sin. Now, you couldn't have churches nor ministers nor police forces nor nothing else if you didn't have sin. You couldn't even have good guys without sinners. There wouldn't be nothing to compare you to." He stopped talking again, blew out his breath in an exhalation, and slogged on through the snow. Again he picked up the thread of his conversation. "The Lord welcomes a sinner to heaven quicker'n one of you guys that never knowed how to be anything but good. You don't represent no challenge for Him. He's got you cornered all the while. When He gets somebody like me to repent, it's a triumph for Him. And in the meantime, I'm the one that has the fun." He stopped now to let Jake move past him and begin breaking trail up the last part of the slope of the second ridge. "But it all evens out in the end. There we'll both be, side by side, on the road to glory there at the end."

"The road to glory, huh?"

Stars had begun to appear in the sky. The wind grew a little stronger, a little colder, as they crossed the ridge and began the descent toward their camp.

Scotty sniffed the air and said, "I guess your fire kept going all day. Your rabbit oughta be about done."

"How do you know?"

"I can smell wood smoke."

Jake entered a trail they had broken earlier, and the going became easier. They picked up a little speed and came around the last bend and could see their dugout in the dim remaining light. The wood-smoke smell was strong now. They were within a few paces of the dugout when Jake said, "Look."

Scotty came abreast of him and looked. The blanket was gone from the entrance to the dugout. The entrance was a black hole against the white snow of the canyon wall. Smoke still poured from the hole.

CHAPTER EIGHTEEN

They walked up to the mouth of the dugout and peered in. They could see nothing except the smoke issuing from the hole. There were no flames, no sparks, and not enough light to see inside.

"I guess she's through burning," Jake said.

"Just a lotta smoke."

Jake crept a couple of steps into the dugout. Scotty said, "See anything?"

"No. I'm gonna strike a match."

The match flared in the darkness and Jake advanced further into the interior. Scotty stepped just inside the door.

"The ground feels hot to stand on," Jake said. The match moved back and forth across the dugout. It glowed off charred logs that had been the ceiling of their home. Jake shook the match out and lit another.

"The lantern's gone," he said. Then: "I'm coming out."

Scotty backed out the door and Jake came out after him. Jake took off a glove and wiped his eyes. "It makes your eyes smart," he said. "It's too hot to walk on in there. My feet was starting to feel like my shoes was on fire." He looked down at his feet, and stood quietly for a moment in the snow.

"Don't look like we can sleep in there tonight," Scotty said.

"Oh, ya. Not way inside—that won't cool off for a while. But we can sleep close to the door, I think."

"Maybe the ashes is too hot for our clothes."

"I don't think so. If they are, we can pile up some juniper limbs and sleep on them."

"What if they catch fire?"

"The ashes ain't that hot. Let's build a fire out here and cook some supper. Then we can figure what to do."

Scotty said, "I bet that rabbit of yours is done."

Jake said, "Yeah, I bet. That mighta been what done it. I guess I built that fire up too hot."

"She's been hot before and never caught fire."

"There's always a first time." Jake turned and looked into the black hole. "I dono. I don't know."

They brought wood from their firewood pile and laid the fire. Scotty knelt and whittled a pile of shavings and struck a match to them and got the fire going. Jake cut pieces of meat from the deer in the tree and found sticks to stick through them so they could hold the meat over the fire and cook it.

"We got any dishes left?" Scotty asked.

"I dono. Here. Hold my stick. I'm gonna have another look."

Jake stayed inside the dugout a little longer this time. Scotty glanced over his shoulder now and then and saw the glow of a match in the black interior. Presently Jake returned.

"You gotta crouch down in there," he said, rubbing his eyes, "or you get too much smoke. You get a lot anyway."

"Rub your eyes with snow," Scotty advised. "That's better than rubbing them with your dirty hands. You'll just smear the smoke around."

Jake held soothing snow to his eyes as he crouched beside the fire. He took his own stick back and held it with one hand, moving the snow from one eye to the other with his other hand.

"It looks like all the dishes melted," he said.

"Musta got pretty hot," Scotty said.

"Hot enough to mess up tin, anyway."

"It shouldn't of melted the skillet. That's iron."

"I didn't see it. There's a big mess back by the stove. I think what happened is the dishtowel above the stove caught fire. Maybe I left it touching the stove. It looks like the fire run up the dishtowel and caught on that shelf. Then the shelf fell down with all that stuff on it and hit the stove so hard it knocked it over and spilled the fire out. Then everything burned. There's a big pile of melted dishes and burned food and stuff back by the stove."

Scotty adjusted to a more comfortable position. "There ain't no blankets left, is there?"

"No. Ain't no clothes, neither. Them orange crates burned up.

The wood all burned. The lamp and the coal oil looks like they blowed up."

"I wonder why we didn't hear it?"

"It's right there in the mountainside and we had that and another hill between us. We was likely chopping."

"Your bullets and shotgun shells must of gone off, too."

"I guess. I didn't look for them. The guns is ruined. Stocks burned off. The barrels is still hot to touch."

Scotty brought his meat close to him and inspected it, then put it back over the fire. Jake tossed away the snow from his hand and concentrated on his own cooking.

Scotty said, "You didn't have no money in there, did you?"

"No. Just some coins—a couple of silver dollars and some change. I put most of my paper money in the bank at Malad. I left some at home."

"That's good."

"I can't find my watch, though. Your skis is burned up."

"I figured they would be."

Jake squatted in silence for a while. Then he handed his stick to Scotty. "Hold this. I'm gonna have another look."

He was gone even longer this time. When he came back to the fire he said, "I better not go in anymore. I'm using up all my matches."

"We had some matches in there."

"They must of burned up. Just about everthing did."

Scotty handed Jake his stick. "I think this is done." Scotty cautiously touched his venison with his fingertips, then stood and stretched and waited for the meat to cool before he tried to eat it. Jake held his away from the fire but continued to squat near the flames.

Jake said, "Some of the peas blowed up. There's three or four cans left. It looks like the beans got pretty well baked. The rabbit burned up. The flour sack burned and the flour looks all charred, but if we was to dig down into it we might find some good flour. The ammunition is gone."

"There musta been quite a racket around here for a while."

"Yeah."

Scotty tried touching the venison again and began to cautiously nibble at it, still leaving it impaled on the stick.

"I found the money," Jake said. "It's too hot to pick up, and it's black, but it'll be okay. I can't find my watch."

Scotty said, "Maybe it'll turn up." He started to take another bite, but interrupted himself by laughing. "Maybe it'll turnip," he said. "Will a turnip watch turn up?" He chuckled again and ate.

"It was keeping good time," Jake said.

"It was a good watch. I wish I had one like it."

"I wish I could find that one."

"You lost about everthing you had, didn't you."

"Ya. Everthing but a few clothes I left at home."

"And them raggedy pants you're wearing." Scotty took another bite, chewed, and swallowed. "When you come into this world you didn't have a rag on you. Now you're all rags." He laughed.

Jake joined in the laugh and began to eat.

They did make one more trip into the dugout, together this time, striking matches and examining the ashes and blackness and ruined mess inside. The skillet they found in good shape, but the other dishes were warped and twisted by the heat. Their staples had been destroyed by the fire. Flames had eaten the bark off the logs that formed their ceiling and had charred the logs but had not burned through them. Everything else of wood, and everything of cloth, had burned. There was little that could be salvaged. Jake put his money in the snow to cool, then put it into his pocket. They could not find the watch.

When they emerged Scotty said, "What do we do now?"

"Get some sleep, I guess. Maybe we can clean it up some in the morning."

"Where do we sleep?"

"In the dugout." Jake went back into it and, with his feet, began scraping ashes aside. He cleared away enough space so they could lie down with their feet just inside the doorway, their heads toward the middle of the dugout.

They had been there only a minute or two when Scotty sat up. "I don't think I can take the smell all night. I don't like the smell of burned stuff."

"Ya, you're right. Want to face the other way?"

"Yeah."

They turned around and lay with their heads near the opening. Jake tucked his hands into his coat pockets and lay on his back.

Scotty rolled over on his stomach and rested his chin on his gloved hands. Scotty said, "I wish we'd built that fire closer to the dugout."

"Wanta move it?"

"Too much trouble."

"I'm warm enough."

"My legs is warm. I ain't too sure about my face."

"We can scoot further in the dugout if you want."

"It's okay. Say a poem."

Jake pondered a while before he spoke.

> *"There are strange things done in the midnight sun*
> *By the men who moil for gold.*
> *The Arctic trails have their secret tales*
> *That would make your blood run cold . . ."*

Jake woke in the night. He was still on his back. The night was very quiet. There were few clouds. The sky was filled with stars.

Scotty was curled up on the ground beside him, huddling in a ball, shivering.

Jake whispered, "Are you awake?"

"Ye—ye—yes."

"I'm kinda cold."

"I'm freezing."

"Let's get further in the dugout."

Jake sat up, got to his feet, and walked farther inside. Scotty, more slowly, got to his feet. He stayed bent over, hugging himself, shivering.

Jake said, "There ain't no more smoke, I don't think."

"There ain't no more heat, neither."

"Ya, it's cold in here." Jake walked all the way to the back of the dugout, groping through darkness, stepping carefully, until his boots encountered the debris at the rear.

"Whatcha doing?" Scotty asked.

"Seeing if it's warm anywhere."

"I-I-Is it?"

"No." Jake turned and walked carefully out again, his groping hand touching Scotty and guiding himself around him.

The fire had not even embers left. Jake said, "We must of slept awhile."

"I been awake awhile."

"You shoulda said something."

"No use b-both of us being m-miserable."

Jake went to the woodpile and brought more wood to the mouth of the dugout. He laid a fire. "Whittle me some shavings," he said.

They build the fire near the mouth of the dugout and crouched beside it to warm themselves. Then they added more wood and got back into the dugout and lay down again. They huddled close together for warmth. Before long, they were again asleep.

Scotty woke. He wiggled closer to Jake, tightened his grip on his companion, hugging him for warmth. Jake said, "Huh?" in a sleepy voice, turned his head so he would have been looking upward if his eyes had been open. He, too, squirmed to get closer to his friend. He turned his face back toward Scotty and came awake. He leaned his head back away from his friend.

Scotty opened his eyes and said, "Whatsamatter?"

Jake grunted, untangled himself from Scotty, and sat up.

"Everthing okay?" Scotty said.

Jake rubbed his eyes. "You sure got a rough beard. I'd hate to be your wife."

"I'd shave for my wife, if I liked her."

Jake twisted and propped himself on one hand so he could look outside. "What time do you think it is?"

"Nighttime." Scotty sat up. "It don't get no warmer, does it."

Jake glanced at the fire. Red embers remained. "I can build that up," he said. He stood up, stretched, and walked stiffly out of the dugout. In a moment he was back, adding wood carefully to the embers, poking them into life. The fire blazed up fresh.

Scotty crept out of the dugout and squatted by the fire, which was three or four feet from the opening. He looked up at the sky. "I think it's coming on morning," he said.

Jake looked up. "Ya."

"Maybe an hour, hour and a half to sunup."

"Maybe."

Scotty turned and peered back into the darkness of the dugout. "That sure ain't much of a house no more," he said.

"We can build a front on it today out of some logs," Jake said. "Clean out all them cinders. See if the stove will still work."

Scotty looked at him. "We can't stay here," he said.

"How come?"

"We ain't got nothing. No blankets nor nothing."

"If the stove works, we can keep warm."

"Ya, if we don't burn the place down again."

"There ain't nothing much to burn."

"That's what I mean. We got no blankets, no dishcloths, no clothes. All you got is them raggedy pants, and they ain't gonna last."

"Maybe we could kill a deer and get a skin."

"I ain't gonna sleep under no stinky skin. And I ain't gonna chew on it for a month to make it soft to use. Anyhow, your guns is ruined."

"Well, we could fix up something."

"And we can't cook," Scotty said.

"We've got all that meat in the tree. We've got potatoes and apples and them few carrots down in the hole. There's some peas left. I think the flour's good once we get under the scorched part."

"Ya, but we got nothing to cook in. All the dishes is ruined."

"We got the skillet. When we empty some peas we can use the can to boil coffee and stuff."

"The coffee burned up."

"Oh, ya." Jake stared into the dugout, his fists on his hips. "Well, we won't go thirsty. There's plenty of snow."

"Yeah, and there's more coming, and we're like to freeze to death if we try to stay up here without no blankets or extra clothes."

Jake turned, his fists still on his hips, and looked at the shapes of the trees in the darkness. "I hate to leave and lose so much time. We gotta hire a truck, and we gotta buy new stuff to take the place of what burned. I hate to lose time. We need to cut posts."

"Ya, I know it," Scotty said, "but we can't do much if we can't sleep and stay well. We're gonna wind up cold and sick and miserable and maybe die up here if we don't get blankets and stuff. We gotta go home."

Jake sighed deeply, still staring down the dark canyon. He let his hands fall to his sides and took a step forward. He lowered his head, spat into the snow. "Ya," he said, "I guess we better."

CHAPTER NINETEEN

They built up the fire and cut several slices of meat and began to roast it on sticks. Jake got into the hole they had dug and brought out apples and carrots, with which they filled the pockets of their coats.

"Should we take a can of peas?" Jake asked. "They might taste good on the way."

"Naw. They're just heavy to carry. The apples is fine. We can take some of this meat once we get it cooked."

They ate their fill, and each put two or three pieces of extra meat into his pockets. Jake tucked his into a pocket with some apples and said, "It ain't gonna help the flavor of them apples none."

"The apples might help the meat," Scotty said. "Matter a fact, you oughta put in a couple apples whenever you cook a rabbit. That might improve the taste."

"You don't even know what rabbit tastes like."

"Some of us is just lucky, that's all."

"Well, I take that back. You've eat the gizzard and I never have."

"Your day is coming."

Jake picked up his ax and hefted it. "Think we oughta take a ax with us?"

"Why?"

"I dono. Just thought we might could use it on the way."

"It's just more to carry."

"I guess so." Jake put the axes inside the dugout, leaning them against the stone wall.

The sky was beginning to lighten. Jake looked at it, looked at the fire, which was beginning to die. He kicked snow on the fire, stamped on it, killed it.

"We might as well go," he said.

Scotty said, "You know, we might be just as smart to go over to them people's place and not try to get home."

"Why?"

"It's closer."

"Yeah, but I don't think there's a road. When I went over there last time there was snow on the road, and Maxine said not many people uses it in winter. We'd have to go ten miles through snow."

"It's further the other way. Twenty miles or better."

"Twenty-five by road. That's the thing. There's a road going home."

"Maybe it ain't open neither."

"It's gotta be. They haul hay over it all winter from Snowville and Stone. If we're about half lucky, we can catch a ride on a sleigh going after hay."

"That don't sound too bad."

Jake took one more look around him. "Okay. Let's go."

He led out. They had not tried to go south toward the road since the heavy snow fell, and there were no trails to follow in that direction. There was deep snow in the canyon bottom and up most of the next hillside. Jake moved through it in a rhythmic walk, lifting his legs out of the snow as far as he comfortably could and kicking through the top layers of snow to get a new foothold. His shoulders and arms swung in rhythm with his legs; it required one's entire body to push a path through this deep snow. Scotty followed behind, walking in the trail Jake made, having an easier time of it.

They crossed the first ridge and began the descent. Jake said, "Soon as we finish those gullies to the north of us we might as well come down in here. There's plenty of trees in here."

"Ya."

The snow deepened again, and Jake stopped and leaned aside. Scotty passed him and took over the trail-breaking job. They crossed the bottom of this wide canyon and started up the south side. Scotty said, "It's gonna be good to get on the road."

"It'll sure be easier walking."

Scotty stepped higher than Jake when he broke trail and had a way of lunging forward a little at each step. He lunged now, and sank down farther than usual into the snow, and stopped.

"That was a deep one," Jake said. "What'd you do? Find a hole?"

Scotty mumbled something. Jake walked up next to him and said, "What?"

"I said I'm stuck," muttered Scotty. He had not moved since he sank into the snow. Now he tried to bring the trailing leg up even with the other one. He grunted and swore and held still again.

Jake said, "What's the matter?"

"I got my foot stuck in a hole."

"Let me look." Jake pushed through the snow to get in front of Scotty.

Scotty said, "I think it's a badger hole."

Jake bent over close to Scotty's leg and brushed some snow aside. "I can't see nothing," he said.

"Let me lean on you a minute."

Jake stood upright. Scotty supported himself with a hand on Jake's shoulder and moved his free foot closer to the other one. He winced in pain.

"It hurting you?"

"Ever time I put weight on that foot it makes the ankle hurt."

"What happened? Your toe get wedged in, or what?"

Scotty looked down at the leg that disappeared into the snow. "It's kinda like a fishhook. The heel went in the hole first, and my toe's pointing up and wedged against the side of the hole."

"You can't pull it up?"

"It just pushes the toe in harder. The ground's all froze up. There ain't no give."

"Can you push your heel down and your toe up?"

"That's when it hurts, when I try to do that."

Jake drew a deep breath and let it out. "Well, just hold still," he said.

"I ain't got much choice."

Like a dog at a rabbit hole, Jake began digging out the snow in front of Scotty's leg. He used both hands to push it between his legs, so it rose in a little flurry behind him. As the hole through the snow deepened, snow from the sides of the hole slipped to the bottom and had to be scraped out. Jake widened the hole. He worked his way all around Scotty, digging out the snow behind him so he could keep the hole clean as he worked his way down.

"It's kinda crusty here toward the bottom," he said, punching into the snow with his fist to loosen some of the old crust.

Then, presently: "I've come to some dirt."

He widened the bare spot until Scotty stood in a funnel-shaped hole in the snow about three feet deep and wider in diameter, at the top, than a tall man's height. Jake crouched in the hole, scraping more snow away with his fingers, trying to get a good look at the trapped foot.

Jake said, "Well, I'll tell you what. I'm going to try to get my hands under your foot and help pull."

He changed position and tried to slide a hand around the foot. "Hole's too small," he said. He pulled at the frozen earth with his hand but could dislodge none of it. He took out his pocketknife, opened it, and began to jab at the ground, cutting out little chunks of it and tossing them aside.

"Maybe you could just cut away the dirt and get me out that way," Scotty said.

Jake did not reply at once. He kept working with his knife, throwing away more dirt. Then he stopped. "I can't cut you loose," he said.

"Why not?"

"That badger knowed what he was doing. Your toe's against one rock and your heel's against another. Can you turn your foot sideways?"

Scotty strained and grunted, then said, "She won't budge."

Jake bent down again, still working with his knife. After several minutes he closed the knife and put it back into his pocket. He said, "I can get my hands under your foot and pull up. Just hold still and let me see if I can pull your toe out."

Jake slipped his hands down through the holes he had cut beside Scotty's foot, got hold of the shoe, and tugged. He released the foot, adjusted himself into a better position, and pulled again. He relaxed and looked up at Scotty.

"I think you're lifting up on your heel when I pull on your toe. Try not to do that."

He took hold again and pulled again, longer than before, then, with an exhalation of breath through his lips he relaxed. He knelt on one knee, studying the foot, then stood up.

"What now?" Scotty asked.

"Just a minute."

Jake walked around behind Scotty and knelt again. He reached around Scotty's leg with his hands, fitted them into the hole, and again took Scotty's foot in his hands. Now he placed his shoulder against the calf of Scotty's leg and, pushing against the calf with his shoulder, he pulled upward on the toe.

Scotty winced and swore. "That hurts," he said. Jake did not relent. His shoulder pressed harder, his hands pulled harder. He wrenched a half scream from Scotty, a howling "Ouch!"—and he wrenched the foot free from the hole.

Scotty stood on his other foot, taking rapid, deep, jerky breaths and saying over and over in a kind of sob, "Oh! Oh! Oh!" His stomach tightened visibly and spasmodically as he uttered a short series of crying sounds. Then he took and released an especially deep breath and said emphatically, "That hurt."

Jake rose slowly to his feet. "It was about all I could do," he said "except wait for the badger to come up and eat your foot off."

Scotty put a little weight on the sore foot, took a short hobbling step, and put his weight back on the good foot. He let out a long "Whew!" and stood with his mouth open, taking deep breaths and staring off into the distance.

Jake said, "You gonna be able to walk?"

"Just give me a minute," Scotty breathed. He continued to breathe deeply and stare off at nothing. With one hand he rubbed the thigh of the injured leg, as though rubbing the thigh somehow relieved the pain in the foot.

Jake said, "Maybe we better go back to camp."

Scotty made an impatient gesture. "Just hang on a minute."

They stood for several minutes, Scotty getting control of himself and of the pain, Jake waiting.

Scotty said, "We can't go back to camp. We got all the problems we had before and this one, too."

"Yeah, but it's nearly twenty-five miles from here to my place. Can you walk that far on that leg?"

"I ain't got no other," Scotty said. He took another hobbling step or two. "I don't think nothing's broke. It sure do hurt."

"Maybe if you was to take off your shoe I could feel around and see if anything's broke."

"No. I think my ankle's sprained. If it's gonna swell up and I take my shoe off, I'll never get it back on."

"We could pack it in snow and take down the swelling."

"It's gonna be in snow awhile anyhow."

"Are you gonna be able to walk?"

Scotty, his tongue between his lips, leaned his head back and stared at the sky. The sun was up now, a ball perched on the eastern horizon, sending streaks of red-gold light and black shadow across the snow of the shallow canyon. Scotty took several deep breaths and lowered his head. "Can you cut me a stick to lean on?" he asked.

"I wish I had a ax," Jake said. He turned in a slow circle, looking toward the trees in all directions, then struck out westward through the deep snow. Thirty yards away he came to a few junipers and examined them. He found a branch that suited him, tromped out a working area in the snow, then grabbed the limb and pulled backward and down with all his might. The limb cracked off and left Jake sitting in the snow, holding the broken limb.

"You don't need no ax!" Scotty yelled across the snow. "Break a few fence posts across your knee while you're there. No use wasting the day."

Jake carried the limb back to Scotty, dragging it beside him and stripping off twigs and branches as he went. When he reached Scotty he took out his knife and cut away a few of the more stubborn branches, then handed it to Scotty. "How's this?"

Scotty held it in both hands, put the base down near his injured foot, and leaned on it. He returned his weight to his good foot.

"It wants to be about a foot shorter," he said.

Jake took the stick and went to the badger hole. He inserted the small end a foot into the hole, pulled it so it was braced against the two rocks that had held Scotty's foot, and gave another pull. He stumbled but caught himself as the end broke off. He jabbed the stick down against one of the rocks to break off a jagged end that had been left and gave the stick back to Scotty.

Again Scotty tried leaning on the stick. He stood back on his good foot and looked to the south, the direction they had to go.

"Well," he said, "I think I can hobble along okay. My ankle don't feel so bad. I ain't going to be able to break trail, though."

"It ain't much more than a mile to the road. I can do that okay," Jake said.

It was not much of a strain on Jake, it turned out. He plowed forward, leaving his feet farther in the snow than he normally would in order to make a better path. Every twenty yards or so he stopped to let Scotty catch up. That gave him a breathing space before he cut out the next section of trail for them.

They passed one of the piles of posts they had cut, and Scotty said, "Let's stop." He leaned against the pile and used one hand to brush away snow from the posts. He searched among the posts and pulled one loose. "I think this might be a better stick for me," he said.

He tried it, took a few steps.

"It seems awful long," Jake said.

"Yeah, it's no good." Scotty tossed it back onto the pile, hobbled back to the pile, and reclaimed his first walking stick.

They made their slow way through Juniper Row. The snow was a little deeper here, and at times Jake waded waist-deep in it, forcing a passage with his thighs, his arms raised like wings and rolling forward and back in time with the motion of his legs. He stopped midway and looked at the trees on both sides of him. "We didn't cut into this too bad," he said. "There's still lots of trees for another time."

"They make a kind of snow fence, too," Scotty said. "It shouldn't be so bad on the other side."

He was right. The snow was noticeably less deep south of the row, although they still plowed through a deep drift here and there.

"Watch out," Jake said. "Here's the fence."

The fence itself was covered by a snowdrift. Jake used hands and legs to feel his way through it, find a firm foothold, and cautiously step over the fence, holding the top wire down with his gloved hands. "Be careful," he said. "If the snow gives way you're like to set down on a barb."

Scotty used his walking stick to hold the wire down, but he didn't look at the wire as he stepped across. His gaze was wandering across the landscape just to the south of them. When he had cleared the fence he followed Jake a few more steps as they crossed a ditch and stood on a level, snow-covered patch of ground.

Jake stood with his hands on his hips, facing the rising sun and squinting into its glare. Scotty stood a few feet from him, his body facing south but his head looking toward the west, then toward the east, then back toward the west, and finally at Jake.

"I thought you said there'd be a road here," Scotty said.

"I thought there was gonna be."

CHAPTER TWENTY

It was the road they had ridden over in the truck to get here. From where they stood it rose to a crest in the west, rose to another in the east. But there was no road. The snow lay across it in folds and furrows and long flat stretches; only in spots could they see the fence lines that ran along both sides of the road. It was clean white unblemished snow, touched with long shadows here and there where the sun, now well off the horizon, still stood behind peaks and crags and junipers.

"Ain't nobody been hauling hay over this road," Scotty said.

"Not for a while."

They stood for a long time in silence, Jake facing eastward and contemplating the waves of snow that glistened in the sunlight; Scotty turning in a slow, limping walk to survey the landscape in all its bleak and empty directions.

Jake looked up, looking at the sky and speaking to the man behind him. "Wanta go back to camp?"

"No. If we go back there we ain't gonna get out."

Jake nodded his head slowly a few times and stared at the crest toward the east.

Scotty said, "I'll tell you what I think we ought to do. We oughta go to that girl's place."

"No."

"Why not?"

"Because that road's more likely to be snowed shut than this one is. They don't even try to use that road in winter. From right where we stand, it's a good ten miles to her place. I ain't gonna break trail through this kinda snow for ten miles. Anyhow, I don't think I could if I tried. I don't think I could last that long."

"But it might be open."

"No."

Scotty hobbled closer to his companion. "Look, Jake, it's ten miles there, but it's pretty near twenty-five miles to your place, and there ain't no other place closer in that direction."

"It's more like twenty-one miles."

"Okay, twenty-one. That's still better'n twice as far."

"Ya. But we're just six miles or so from the junction with the road to Stone. That road will be open."

"How do you know?"

"Because folks in Holbrook has to go to Stone and Snowville to get stuff."

"They can take the other road."

"The other road ain't as good."

"Then they can do without. Jake, sometimes the snow gets so bad people just don't go nowhere."

"Snow like this ain't gonna stop people. Did you ever know snow like this to stop people?"

"No, I guess not."

"They just hitch up their sleighs and go ahead. Snow like this ain't gonna stop nobody."

Scotty turned and faced the west. "I still think a sure ten miles is better than the risk of twenty-one."

Jake stared straight ahead toward the east. "It wouldn't do us no good to go there. We'd still be stuck. We got to get blankets and clothes and stuff. We got to go home for that."

"They have all that stuff."

"I ain't got no money."

"You're good for it. They like you. They'd let us borrow it and pay them later."

"They ain't got our size clothes."

"Oh, some of his clothes might come close enough to get us by. Anyhow, they got neighbors."

"I don't wanta buy nothing from them."

"Then they could give us a ride to Holbrook. They got horses and a sleigh and stuff."

"They wouldn't want to make the trip."

"How do you know they wouldn't? I bet they would."

Jake maintained his silence for a moment. Scotty had turned back to him now and was waiting for him to change his mind.

Jake said, "I ain't going to that girl's house in these pants."

"Oh." Scotty turned slowly and looked toward the west again, then turned back. "We don't even know if there's gonna be a road when we get to the junction," he said.

Exasperation showed in Jake's voice. "There will be a road. There always has been."

Scotty thought a moment, jabbed at the snow with his walking stick. "Okay," he said. "Let's go."

The snow was not quite as deep on the road as it had been in the rough country. It varied in depth. Sometimes calf-deep, sometimes knee-deep, sometimes in drifts that were deeper. Jake moved through it often in almost a casual walk, his lower legs kicking forward to clear a path. In the drifts he worked harder. His legs lifted higher and kicked harder, his arms swung in larger arcs. In the very deep drifts it was as if his thighs had to hit and push the snow to break through it. His arms sometimes flailed with exertion; more often, he put his palms on the snow as if bracing himself or pulling himself forward. When he broke through a large drift he might accelerate his pace for several steps as if the effort of forcing himself against the snow had, once the resistance was removed, made him unable to keep from lunging forward with uncontrollable speed.

And every twenty or thirty or forty yards, he stopped to wait for Scotty.

Scotty was moving faster now. He had developed a knack with his walking stick. In the shallower areas of snow he simply held it with his left hand, leaning on it a little as his right leg swung forward and found footing, then lifting it as he lifted his injured foot, swinging the stick ahead, planting it firmly into the snow, and resting on it again as he walked. In the deep snow he slowed down, and he held the stick with both hands, putting more weight on it to support his injured foot and taking shorter steps with his good foot.

They crossed the first ridge and descended into the long swale that led up to the second ridge. On that ridge, Jake waited for Scotty to finish the climb, and both stood on the crest, resting together.

Jake said, "Are you going to be able to keep going?"

"If you can make it, I can make it." Gripping the stick for support, Scotty leaned down and rubbed his foot. "It don't hurt so bad now. I think the walking does it good."

"Well, we're like to cure it completely before we get where we're going."

In spring or summer these rolling hills were gray-green with sagebrush, spotted with dark green juniper trees, and the fragrance of sage was thick in the air—especially after a rain. Late in the summer and through the early fall, when the grass had turned brown and there was no rain, a walk along this road would send up from each footstep a puff of the thick dust that lay on the road. A truck or a car driving the road would raise a cloud of dust that would obscure visibility for a quarter of a mile behind the vehicle before the dust would settle enough so that a following driver could see through it. Vehicles meeting each other blinded each other. And on such days there was always sound—a breeze rattling the dry weeds, the quick rustle of a rabbit starting from his station, and once in a while the buzz of a rattlesnake—or was it the whir of a grasshopper? Overhead, birds of prey soared and circled, sometimes diving and swooping. The sun would be warm, and even without exertion the person abroad in this fragrant living desert world would find a fine film of perspiration on his face.

Nothing of that remained except the sun, which was climbing higher and higher in a bright blue sky, and the dark splotches of juniper that jutted up through the snow. There was no fragrance. There was no warmth. There was no sound, except the soft sounds of their legs pushing through the drifts and the soft thump of Scotty's stick each time he brought it down to help him along his slow and painful way.

There was, however, the brightness, more glaring than the brightness of summer. Jake waited for Scotty on the uphill side of one large drift he had broken through and said to him, "That sun's getting brighter and brighter."

"It sure do glare off the snow."

Jake took off a glove and fumbled in a pocket. He came out with a match. "Put your stick over here," he said.

Scotty planted the stick between them, and Jake scratched the match to life on it. He held it, letting it burn until the flame was near his fingers, then gently blew it out. Smoke curled up from the twisted black stem of the match. Jake held it between them, letting it cool. Scotty took off a glove, letting the stick rest across his shoulder.

Jake said, "I wish them skis of yours hadn't burned up. They'd be a lot of help now."

"We could only one of us ski at a time."

"Even if you just used them to ski down each hill, that would help some."

Jake crumbled the blackened match in the palm of his hand and held the hand up and open between them. Scotty limped closer, and each man rummaged a bare index finger in the black ash and used that index finger to paint blackness beneath each of his eyes. They continued the painting until all four eyes were nearly encircled with dark black smudges. Each inspected the work of the other and touched up places the other had missed.

Jake brushed his palm back and forth on his pants leg to get rid of the remaining ash. "That oughta cut down some on the glare," he said. "I'd hate to go snow-blind."

"I knowed a guy once that went snow-blind," Scotty said. "He couldn't see for about a week. He was with some other guys or he'd of got lost and might never of got home."

Jake turned and began trudging up the road again, approaching still another crest on this up-and-down road through the low juniper-covered hills. He called back over his shoulder, "It's a good day. I wish that somebody would take a notion to take a sled to Snowville and bring back a load of hay."

"Well," called Scotty from a few yards behind him, "They better take a notion pretty quick or it'll be too late. Anybody going to Snowville oughta be through here in the forenoon."

Jake squinted up at the sun. "It ain't ten o'clock yet."

There was the brightness, and there was the perspiration. For each of them, walking was an effort. Scotty was moving more rapidly on his crutch now, but the set of his mouth indicated both determination and pain, and his face glistened. Jake did not often have to breathe hard through even the deepest drifts—although when he piled into snow that reached his stomach, as it did in a couple of places, he was puffing before he reached the other side—but his face, too, was shiny with sweat. When they stopped to rest they customarily wiped their foreheads with their coat sleeves. Sometimes one of them removed a glove so he could use his palm and fingertips to get the sweat out of his eyes or wipe it from his face.

But progress was steady, and extremely deep drifts only occasionally slowed them down. Jake had already glanced toward the sun and estimated aloud that it was a little better than an hour and a half to noon when they began descending the last of the hillsides. Here on the eastern side of the range of hills the road descended in a long final slope and emerged upon a wide plain that looked flat in any season and looked especially like a table now, covered as it was with snow, unbroken and white as far as they could see except for occasional dark spots that were tall sagebrush or small trees or possibly a few fence posts. To their left, the edge of the hills met the plain in a line that meandered northeast. To their right the slopes fell back slightly toward the west and extended southward, meeting the plain in almost a straight north-south line. Off in the east they could see the next range of mountains rising from the valley floor, a good twenty miles away.

Jake said, "It's all downhill and flatland from here."

"That's good. Them hills was getting me down."

"No, they was getting you up. Now we can let you down easy."

Scotty scanned the valley floor carefully, his head moving slowly from left to right and back to the left. "I don't see no sign of a road," he said.

"You can't see it from here. It's behind that little ridge."

"I don't see no ridge."

"It's hard to see, but it's there. That valley ain't as flat as she looks."

Jake walked more swiftly now. It was downhill, and there were fewer deep drifts to slow him, and he walked with more appearance of purpose, of determination. At one point he built up more than a sixty-yard lead over Scotty and stopped only when he heard Scotty's shout of "Hey! Wait up!" catch him from behind.

The road reached the foot of the last hill and leveled out, rising and falling only slightly, rarely causing the walkers to lose sight of the ground beyond the next slight rise. They came to a sharper, but very short, incline and dipped from it into a gully less than ten yards wide. The gully had served as a trap for the snow, and the drift that lay across it might have been six feet deep or more. Jake waded into it, sank deeper and deeper, and found himself floundering and falling and crawling through it, getting snow on his face and in his mouth, stopping to regain his balance, joining his hands in front of him like a snowplow and pushing out in a swimming motion to help force passage through the snow. Scotty struggled along behind him, moving slowly and carefully and with effort. Jake crawled up the ridge on the other side, then found a foothold and braced himself and reached back to take Scotty's hand and help him up the last couple of steps. They stood on the ridge beyond the gully, catching their breaths. Their view once again was unobstructed, and they surveyed the valley floor in front of them.

Scotty said, "There ain't nobody been using that road, neither."

CHAPTER TWENTY-ONE

They stood in the center of silent white immensity, looking. Knee-deep in snow they stood, in the center of the junction where what should have been the road from Stone to Holbrook joined what should have been its branch to Black Pine. The snow lay in giant ripples across both roads, making them of one substance with the sagebrush fields on either side. Now there was scarcely any relief to the white landscape. The sagebrush was too small to stick up above the snow except in a few spots. There were hardly any junipers on these flatlands. The snow had drifted over most of the fence posts. There was nothing in sight but endless snow and the hills they had just come over.

Jake said, "Well, what do you think?" He looked beaten.

Scotty shook his head. He looked defeated, too. "I don't know. I don't know what to think."

"I thought for sure they'd be using this road."

"There must not be nobody that wants to go nowhere."

"Except us."

"I'm having second thoughts about that myself."

Jake looked back up along the road they had followed, marked now by the track of their passage. "She's eight miles back to camp. I guess we could go back."

"Yeah, we could. And we'd get there just about dark and spend the night freezing to death."

They stood in silence for a long time. Jake stamped out a little circle in the snow, his hands on his hips and his head bowed. Then he swore aloud and raised his head. "Rotten, stinking, no-good luck." He tramped his circle once again. "Of all the two-bit, low-down, clabberlapping, lousy, stinking, no-good, rotten luck." He kicked at the snow. "This takes the knotheaded stinking cake."

Scotty said, "Is there something that don't just set quite right with you?"

Jake kicked the snow again and turned away. He put his head back, twisted it as if to ease aching muscles in his neck. He turned to face Scotty.

"We can go back to the dugout. We can go to them people's house—that's about sixteen miles up hill and down dale. We can head for home. From this spot right here to where we turn off to get to my place, it's fourteen miles. It's another mile down across the crick and up to the house. Fifteen miles on the flat to go home, sixteen miles through the hills to go the other way. The dugout's closest."

"It's the coldest, too," Scotty said. "How you feeling, besides being mad? Can you break trail the rest of the way home?"

"I don't know." Jake lowered his head and turned again to face northeasterly, toward home. "I don't know. I don't feel bad. I ain't as tired as I thought I'd be."

"But you're some tired. Right?"

"Some."

"Well," Scotty said, "I'd just as soon go home, now we've come this far, but you're the one better say. It's gonna be toughest on you."

Jake turned back to him. "How are you making it?"

"I'll be okay. I'm kinda used to it by now, and the foot ain't bothering me too much. You're leaving me a pretty good trail to get through. I'm doing okay."

Jake stretched his hands to heaven and dropped them to his side. He turned and began walking. "Let's go home," he said.

They kept going until Jake, resting and waiting as Scotty caught up with him, looked at the sun again. "It's about noon," he said. "Wanta eat?"

"If it's noon, I better," Scotty said. "I ain't never missed a meal yet."

Jake turned a slow circle, looking all around.

"Whatcha looking for?"

"A place to set."

"There ain't none out here," Scotty said.

Elaborately, raising his knees high, Jake began to tromp on the unbroken snow. He moved back and forth, crisscrossing, until he had pounded the snow down to a hard floor in a space about five feet square. He took off his coat and held it in one hand while he emptied food from the pockets with the other hand. He handed some of the food to Scotty, who let his stick drop so he would have both hands free. Still holding some apples in one hand, Jake used the other to spread his coat on the snow and arrange it. Then both sat on it. They wriggled and shifted, each seeking a dry and comfortable seat, and wound up sitting back to back, leaning against each other, biting off and chewing chunks of the meat they had cooked that morning, mixing it with bites of the apples they had brought with them.

"How far we come?" Scotty asked.

"Did you notice that fence corner back a ways?"

"I seen one to the east of us."

"When we passed that, we was one mile from the junction."

Scotty nodded his head and wrenched off another mouthful of the meat. He leaned forward and rubbed his foot through his shoe, kneading the foot in time with his chewing until he had swallowed. "I kinda wish we had some coffee," he said. "And maybe some aspirin."

"You getting a headache?"

"I just don't feel good. My foot hurts some. It don't hurt so bad when we're going."

Jake raised to his knees and looked around him, twisting as far as he could to the right and then to the left, then sat back down.

"Whatcha looking for?" Scotty asked.

"I was trying to see if there was some place we could put up for a while."

"There ain't no place out here. Just miles of sagebrush."

"And you can't even see none of that."

Scotty laughed.

"What's funny?"

"I was just thinking about my uncle. He was in the war and he went to France and come home on a boat. He says he was sick about half the time and wished he could get off the ocean. One day he says to a sailor, 'I ain't never seen so much ocean in all my life,' and the sailor said, 'You still ain't seen much of it. Just a little bit of what's on top.' I kinda feel like that. All you can see is just what's on top, and there's a awful lot of it."

Jake sat cross-legged, eating. He leaned over, grabbed a fistful of snow, packing it tight in his hand as he picked it up. He bit off a piece and chewed it slowly, allowing it to melt in his mouth. He finished the rest of it in another bite.

Scotty said, "Look over there." He nodded his head toward the west.

Beyond the western hills the sky had begun to cloud up. It was dark gray on the horizon and becoming darker. The gray lightened as it went higher into the sky. Above them, the sky was still blue.

"Looks like a storm's building up," Scotty said.

"Ya." Jake bit into an apple and sat watching the grayness as he chewed. He took another bite, and another, and a fourth, and threw the apple core away from him. He stood up. "I think we better get going," he said.

Scotty took another bite of meat and put the remainder back into his pocket. He extended a hand and Jake took it and pulled him to his feet. Jake bent over and picked up his own coat and Scotty's walking stick. He handed the stick to Scotty, shook the snow from his coat, and put on the coat. He looked once more to the clouds building in the west, buttoned his coat, and pulled on his gloves. "It won't hit for a while," he said. He plunged into the snow ahead of them.

Step by step, the landscape moved past them. A hump of ground off to the left. A fence post showing through the snow on the right. A distant haystack that made a white mound on the landscape. Jake pointed toward it and said, "That's that rotten old haystack of Dell's. It's twelve miles from there to our place."

A cut in the earth on their left, where snow had not covered the sliced-away dirt. The earth was a sandy yellow here. Jake stood looking at it, waiting for Scotty to come up.

Jake nodded toward the embankment. "It might pay to dig in here for the night and finish tomorrow."

"We'd run outta food before morning."

"We can go hungry for a while."

"I druther not." Scotty looked at the embankment. "Anyhow, she's probably froze, and if she ain't, she'd cave in on us. You can't dig in that kind of ground. Even if you got something to dig with, and we ain't."

The snow had piled extra deep on the road below the embankment, and it was another struggle to get through it. Jake stopped twice with snow above his waist to take a quick breather before he moved on, forcing snow out of the way with the weight of his body, trying to step high enough to get on top of it and only sinking down into its softness at every step. On the far side of the long deep drift he broke into a long quick stride as if trying to make up for lost time, but after thirty yards of this he stopped again to wait for Scotty, and after that he resumed his normal pace, or as normal a pace as he could manage in the drifts that rippled and billowed, rose to become soft barriers, then shallowed out to calf-deep easiness.

The road veered a little to the east, and the line of hills fell back a little to the west, and as they moved northward they moved out more and more toward the center of the flat white expanse of the valley floor. The snow became more erratic in its depth, sometimes now barely covering their shoe tops but often hip-deep, even waist-deep.

Jake pushed through the deepest drift so far and stood on its northern side, breathing deeply through his mouth, waiting for Scotty to catch up with him. Jake said, "Some of these is pretty good snowbanks."

"They get pretty deep out here on the flat," Scotty said. "There ain't nothing to stop the wind and she just blows through here like sixty once she gets started."

"How's your foot?"

"It don't hurt much in snow like that. I can almost dig my knee in some places and take the weight on my knee."

They moved on, encountering less than usual snow for some distance, then struggling through several more of the deep drifts, then finding easier going for a ways.

Jake said, "Don't that look like a road to you?"

"Sort of. I can't tell for sure with all that snow on it."

"I think that's the old road used to lead up to Lewis's place before he give it up and moved out. It's ten miles from that road to my place."

They looked along the path of the presumed road. The ground here sloped gently upward for more than a mile to the hills, which rose to the horizon. That horizon was black now, and the overcast extended from it toward them.

Scotty said, "Look," and pointed. Off in the distance they could see the edge of a shadow on the snow. The shadow was moving toward them steadily, sweeping down the long gentle slope in a straight line that extended as far to the north and south as they could see. It was the shadow of the clouds above. The sun was sliding behind the edge of the overcast, and as it did the shadow advanced relentlessly toward them, taking the sparkle and the whiteness from the snow and turning it a lifeless pale gray. They stood still, watching the shadow come closer and closer, its speed unchanging, until it swept across them and continued eastward over the sagebrush fields. Jake looked up. There was no more blue between the sun and the western horizon.

They turned to continue their journey. A chill that had not been there before suddenly gripped the air around them. Scotty's shoulders quivered in a sudden shiver.

"It's getting cold," he said.

"We'll keep warm if we keep walking."

They moved on another fifty yards, another hundred, a quarter of a mile, a half mile.

Then the wind began. At first it was gentle. All it did was pick up puffs and skiffs of snow and blow them skimming and whirling across the valley floor.

CHAPTER TWENTY-TWO

It was only a light wind, not yet enough to raise much snow or do more than ripple their pants legs as it blew across them. It was not a loud wind, although it broke the silence that had prevailed that day. It was just loud enough, perhaps, to delay a little bit the sound that Jake finally heard.

The sound began somewhere in the wind and rose above it, and finally he became aware that it was not the sound of the wind. He looked around him. He stopped to wait for Scotty and spent the time looking all around in a circle, then looking up into the sky. And then he saw it.

The airplane was flying low, well below the overcast, and to the east of them. It was flying northward.

Jake pointed to it. "Look."

Scotty stopped and looked until he, too, saw it. It would pass a half mile east of them, and was beginning to draw abreast of them now.

And then it turned. Scotty was up with Jake now, and Jake turned and walked again, but he kept glancing toward the airplane. It turned in their direction, flew toward them, flew over them. Jake looked up at it as it flew away.

But it did not fly away. It banked into another turn, curving toward the north and flying back toward them. And losing altitude now. Coming lower. Coming very, very low.

"Wave at it," Jake yelled, waving.

"I think he already seen us." But Scotty waved.

"We gotta make sure. Wave at him."

They waved. They jumped up and down, waving their arms, and because it seemed silly to jump up and down waving their arms in silence they jumped up and down and waved their arms and yelled. That seemed silly, too, but they yelled.

The plane banked in a semicircle around them, and they could see the pilot's head, encased in flying cap and goggles, as he peered at them from the cockpit. They saw him lift an arm and wave back. Then he turned the other way. The airplane banked and hid the pilot from view. The plane gained altitude and straightened out in a northeasterly direction, headed toward Malad.

They stood looking after it. Jake said, "He seen us."

"I know it."

"Maybe he'll help."

"How can he help?"

"Maybe he could come back and land."

"He can't land out here. He'd stick his wheels in a snowbank and go tail over teakettle."

"Maybe he'll go to Holbrook and send back help."

Scotty said, "He can't land at Holbrook, neither. There ain't no place without snow."

"Maybe they cleared one off."

"Why would they? He'll have to go to Malad to land."

Jake looked after the plane, now a speck they could no longer hear above the wind. "Maybe he'll send help from Malad."

"That's close to forty miles. How's anybody going to get to us from Malad?"

"I don't know," Jake said. "I wish they'd try."

The airplane was out of sight. They turned northward and walked. A handful of snow blew skimming and whirling across the roadway. It settled down and the wind was merely a mild noise in the ears. Another skiff of snow rose from the surface, hurried off into the fields. Through the crest of a wave of snow they worked, Jake pushing with his belly and swinging his arms a little like an awkward boxer throwing slow roundhouse punches; Scotty using stick and hands and knee and his good foot to follow in the channel Jake's body had dug. Then they crossed the trough of the wave, snow hiding their shoes and slipping inside their pants legs to brush against their shoe tops and their socks.

The only blue sky now was far off in the east, and they looked that way often. Above them, the clouds grew darker. The wind gusted up, once throwing an armload of snow at Jake, then calmed to a slight breeze again, still skimming the cream of snow from the road and fields about them.

As if from a distance, Jake heard Scotty call, "How far do you figure it is now?"

Jake looked around, tried to find a landmark. "Maybe nine miles," he shouted back. "Maybe less."

Another crest. Another trough. He waited for Scotty. Scotty came up to him, stopped to inhale big and exhale big and catch his breath. He gazed toward the retreating blue sky. He said, "Is that him coming back?"

"Who?"

"That airplane."

Jake stared into the eastern sky. He picked out the aircraft moving toward them, flying low.

"Why's he coming back?" Jake said "He can't land. He's just going to get caught in the wind."

"I don't know," Scotty said. "I ain't talked to him about it."

The plane came closer, closer, and was almost overhead before they could hear its engine above the wind. The plane circled, lost altitude, swung in a big arc to the south and again east, and passed over their heads a second time, this time very low.

"Look at him!" Jake shouted. "He's got skis on! He ain't got wheels this time!"

They watched as the plane made one more circle, then settled gently to the snow two or three hundred yards south of them and landed, losing speed, taxiing toward them. They had left the road now and were plunging through the deep snow in the borrow pit, feeling for the fence submerged in the snow, getting across it, floundering toward the airplane that now stood still, its propellers turning at idle, the pilot standing up in the cockpit to encourage them on. They came around a wing tip and could see the pilot. It was Quin!

"Hi ya, Quin! It sure is good to see you!"

"It's good to see you! Come on—climb on up here!" He was leaning over the side of the plane, showing them where to step on the lower wing, giving them each a hand so they could climb the fuselage.

"Squeeze right in that back seat together and I'll get you out of here," Quin said.

Jake and Scotty squeezed into the rear seat together. Quin sat down, adjusted his goggles. The engine revved up. The plane began to move. The wind buffeted them, blew snow across the fuselage. The plane picked up speed. Jake looked over the side and saw the snow whizzing past, faster and faster, then falling away below them. They were in the air, climbing! They turned, headed northeast.

Quin turned his head, shouted above the wind, "I can land in your pasture and let you out."

"Better stay there yourself and visit," Jake shouted back.

"I will," Quin answered.

In a few minutes, Jake was able to look off ahead of him and see the roof of his own house far below. Soon they would land and he would be safe at home.

That was the first of his fantasies.

CHAPTER TWENTY-THREE

Had there really been an airplane, there might have been enough time for it to fly from them to Malad and back between the time the wind began and the time it was blowing big clouds of snow across the road at ground level. Sometimes Jake could look down toward the ground and not be able to see his knees because of the thick snow blowing.

He was brought to reality from his daydream by Scotty's distant shout—"Hey! Jake! Wait up!"

He stopped and turned. He had been so absorbed in his imagination that he had built up another fifty-yard lead over his friend, who was now standing in a snowbank with his face turned away from a sudden wind flurry, holding himself steady with his stick and waiting for the wind to abate so he could continue.

Jake stood still for a minute. The cold crept in on him. He began walking backward, stamping the snow down as he went, moving vigorously but slowly, staying warm while waiting for Scotty to catch up.

Scotty, when he did catch up, shook his head in a gesture that could be translated "Wow!" and said, "We're gonna get us a blizzard."

"I think she's already here."

"What are we gonna do?"

"Keep going. There ain't nothing left for us to do. How's your foot?"

"It's like the rest of me. It's tired. Are you tired?"

"Some. I was just thinking how good it would be if Quin was to fly up here right now and give us a ride out of here in his airplane."

Scotty looked at the sky. It was gray now from horizon to horizon, and black over much of the western part. "I'd hate to see him try it right now. I don't think a airplane could take this much wind."

"Well, we better get going or there'll be more."

Jake turned his coat collar up against the wind and pulled the earflaps inside his cap down to protect his ears. He hunched his head down inside the protection of his left shoulder whenever the wind got particularly bad, or sometimes stopped altogether and turned his back to the wind until a burst of snow had blown past him and he could see to go again.

He stayed close to Scotty now, checking back frequently and not allowing himself more than a five-yard lead. It would not do to get separated in a blizzard much worse than this, and it could become worse at any time.

There was a faint jingle of sleigh bells above the wind. A faint jingle growing louder and louder. He turned and looked back, looked beyond Scotty. The wind blew a high, thick cloud of snow across the road, obscuring the view for several seconds. When the air cleared, Jake saw a team approaching, pulling a sleigh. The team seemed both light and strong. It trotted over snowbanks as if they were solid, hoofs sinking into the snow hardly at all. The horses pulled the sleigh up and down over the snowdrifts as if over a wavy road. Jake and Scotty stood aside to let the horses pass them. The sleigh came abreast of them and stopped. There were two people seated on the front seat. The driver looked down at them and Jake recognized Max Griffeth.

Griffeth said, "Where are you boys going?"

Jake said, "We're trying to get home."

Griffeth said, "You ain't gonna have too much luck the way you're doing it. Here. Get on."

As Scotty started to climb onto the sleigh, the other figure stood up and leaned across her father. She said, "Set in the back with me, Jake. Scotty can set up here with Dad." She crawled across the back of the seat. Scotty crawled across Griffeth and sat down, pulling the lap robe over him. Jake swung into the box of the sleigh. Maxine was sitting with her back to the front seat. She said, "We can cover ourselves with this straw and these blankets and keep warm. Here. Set close to keep warm."

Griffeth said, "I was just taking my girl over to Downey to catch the train. She's going to New York City to seek her fortune. It's a good thing we happened to come by just now. This is a pretty bad storm."

Scotty said, "Do you think we can make it? It's another five or six miles or better."

Griffeth said, "Oh, we'll make it. This is a good team for going through snow. They're a couple of high steppers."

In the back, Jake and Maxine arranged straw and blankets over themselves and inched closer together. He was aware of the fragrance of her soap or shampoo or toilet water, or whatever it was, mingling with the scent of the straw and the blankets. Snow blew across the sky just above the sleigh, but it didn't matter. Under the blanket, her fingers touched his and he gripped her hand in his own.

Scotty was yelling, "Don't just stand there! Let's go!"

Jake had paused to wait for him and had paused too long. He shook his head sharply and headed on up the road. The wind died down for several minutes and they were able to move rapidly. Then it hit them with a moving wall of snow, sent them reeling. They recovered themselves and tramped on, their shoulders to the wind, their heads down to protect their faces from stinging wind-blown snow.

Scotty yelled, "Do you think we can make it?"

"It's another five or six miles or so."

"But can we make it?"

"We'll make it. We're a couple of high steppers."

"You ain't funny."

"Come on."

The wind settled into a steady force, blowing an endless sea of snow that came down off the western hills and moved toward the eastern horizon, loose and flying, filling the space between the surface of the solid snow and the level of their chests. Sometimes the wind picked up a little force and the snow obstructed their view; sometimes it lost a little force and the level of the wind-blown snow was no more than hip-high. But for long long minutes, stretching into quarter-hour periods, an observer would have seen the heads and shoulders of two men struggling steadily, slowly, northward, their bodies below the shoulders hidden by thick blowing snow.

"Do you hear somebody yelling?" Jake asked, his voice raised to be heard above the wind.

"It's just the wind," Scotty called back.

But he heard it again, long-drawn and wailing, born on the howling wind: "J-a-a-a-a-a-a-k-e! S-c-o-o-o-o-o-o-t-t-e-e-e-e-e! J-a-a-a-a-a-a-k-e! S-c-o-o-o-o-o-o-t-t-e-e-e-e-e!"

He plowed on, trying to look around him for the source of the calls he was hearing.

"Ja-a-a-a-a-a-k-e!"

He looked back for Scotty, waited for his friend to close the gap of a few yards that had opened between them. It was bad to stop. He could feel his weariness when he stopped, feel the tiredness in his legs.

"S-c-o-o-o-o-o-o-t-t-e-e-e-e-e!"

Scotty caught up. Jake turned to the north, took a stinging cold slap of snow on his cheek before he could hunch up his shoulder for protection.

"J-a-a-a-a-a-a-k-e!"

He struggled through a deep drift, feeling it shifting in the wind even as he broke through it. He looked back. Scotty, braced against his stick, hopping once to keep the weight off his bad foot, pushed through along the path made by Jake.

"S-c-o-o-o-o-o-o-t-t-e-e-e-e-e!"

In two more steps, he saw who it was. Colin Baker, barely visible through the blowing snow, was standing beside the road.

"Jake! Scotty!"

"Colin! What you doing out here in this weather?"

"I been homesteading a new place. I got me a cabin built. It ain't far. Come on. Get out of the storm and keep warm."

He led the way and they followed close behind. In ten minutes they reached the door, burst through it, and shut it behind them against the gathering wind. A coal-oil lamp sat burning on a table, sending a warm glow through the cabin, and a fire was burning in the heater.

Scotty said, "Jake!" He had to stand close to Jake and raise his voice to be heard above the wind. "Jake, we gotta get out of this!"

"That's what we're trying to do."

"I mean, we ain't gonna make it to your place. We gotta find a haystack or a hole or something."

"There ain't none."

"I can't go much further, Jake. Ain't there a haystack around here?"

"I don't know of none."

"I thought somebody put up the hay in that old field of Lewis's. That shouldn't be much further."

"Maybe so. I don't remember."

"We gotta find a place, Jake. Maybe it's off that way. Let's go look."

"No. If we come to it, we'll see it."

"It's gonna get dark pretty quick."

"We can see yet for a while. Let's get as far as we can while we can see."

"Jake, we gotta find a place to keep out of the storm."

"We'll try, Scotty. We'll try. Come on."

"'Cause I ain't gonna be able to walk much further, Jake. If we don't find no place to stop, I just ain't gonna make it."

CHAPTER TWENTY-FOUR

It was getting dark. Some way or other, light from the hidden sun had been filtering through the black overcast and the blowing snow, and when the wind lapsed they could see the landscape. But the light was failing rapidly, and before long they would be blind.

"How far we got to go?" Scotty asked.

"I figure three miles to the turnoff. I ain't sure."

"It's gonna be dark by then."

"I know."

"We can't find our way in the dark."

"Maybe."

"Let's look for that haystack."

"I don't think there is one."

"Yes there is. Yes there is! Look!"

Jake stopped and turned back to Scotty. Scotty had stopped and was pointing his stick. "There!" he said.

"I don't see nothing."

"Wait till the wind dies down."

They stood in the snow, knee-deep at this point, and stared eastward. The snow swirled past them, large flakes and handfuls of powdery snow flying in arcs and playing tag in the wind. Then the wind paused to refresh itself, and over the momentarily calm landscape Jake could see a dark form rising up from the snowy fields.

"I told you there was a haystack," Scotty said. "Let's go! We can burrow in there and keep warm until the storm's over."

He headed for the haystack, pushing forward and breaking trail for a few yards until his foot forced him to slow down and let Jake move past him.

They waded through the soft snow in the borrow pit, sinking in farther than they had on the road.

"It's gonna be hard going," Jake said.

"That's okay, just so we get there."

Jake advanced cautiously, feeling for the barbed-wire fence he knew was somewhere under the snow. He found it by hitting it with his leg.

"Take it easy. Here's the fence. Let me borrow your stick."

Scotty came up beside him and let Jake take the stick. They both paused to duck their heads and ride out a fury of wind, and when it eased somewhat Jake planted the stick firmly into the snow and used it to help support him while he put one foot on the top wire and stepped across the fence. He sank down waist-deep into the snow and handed the stick back to Scotty. Scotty followed him across the fence, grimacing in pain when his bad foot took all his weight as he stepped off the fence. "Just a minute," Scotty said, and they waited until Scotty had recovered himself and had his stick ready to support himself again. Then they struck off across the field toward the haystack.

It was something like wading against a swift current on a soft muddy bottom. It was hard to force a passage, hard to keep moving, hard to muscle the snow aside and make a trail. Sometimes it was like swimming. Jake used his arms to push snow aside, to pull himself through the snow. He lunged forward, inclining so sharply he would have fallen except for the snow against his chest, holding him upright, impeding his passage.

The darkness deepened and became complete. Even when the wind subsided for a moment or a few moments, they could no longer see the haystack. They kept pushing forward.

"We should be there by now," Scotty yelled.

Jake turned to call back over his shoulder, "It's quite a ways."

"It ain't this far."

They plowed on, struggling in the snow. The trail behind them was lost to sight in a few yards or a few inches, depending on the ferocity of the wind.

Scotty yelled, "Just a minute."

Jake stopped, turned back. Scotty had both hands raised higher than his head and was gripping the stick with them, supporting himself on that stick as his head hung down and he gulped deep breaths. Jake waited until Scotty could speak.

"I can't go no further," he said.

"I don't think I can, either," Jake said.

"We gotta rest."

"Okay. Let's huddle down and try to keep warm."

Jake used his last strength to stamp and kick and push the snow to make a little hollow or hole. They sank to their knees in the hole, got into a sitting position. They scooted close to one another.

"I'm still cold."

"So am I."

They put their arms around each other, lay down, clung together for warmth.

Snow blowing down on top of them felt cold at first. Jake turned his face away from its coldness, felt it cold on the back of his neck as the wind worked it under his coat collar. Then more snow came down on them. Jake worked his head and shoulders and elbows and made a space to breathe in. He and Scotty stayed close together, drawing warmth from one another. More snow was piling on top of them. It no longer felt cold. It felt warm and good. Lying down felt good. They could close their eyes and rest.

Jake said, "You know what the worst of it is."

"What?"

"Them posts is worth a lotta money. Papa don't know where they are. He might not even think to look. It's half a winter's work gone to waste."

"Well, maybe we'll be able to go back."

"Maybe." Jake adjusted himself to be more comfortable. "It's bad this had to happen now. I was just getting old enough to help out."

The wind whipped across the valley most of the night. It planed the fields like a level. By morning, when the wind died down and the sun came out, there was not so much as a mound in the snow to mark their tomb.

That was the worst of his fantasies.

CHAPTER TWENTY-FIVE

Scotty said, "I can't see nothing."

Jake said, "I haven't saw nothing in a hour."

They had to shout to hear each other.

"It sure is dark."

"Sometimes when the wind ain't too bad I can see a little."

"The storm's getting worse."

Jake was advancing steadily now, and cautiously. He lifted each leg high, planted it gently, and if it did not find firm footing soon he withdrew the leg and tried a step in a different direction.

"We're off the road again, I think," he yelled at Scotty. "Let's go more to the left."

"How do you know we're anywheres near the road?"

"I think we're on it." He stepped, stepped again. "I think we're on it again. The snow ain't so deep on the road, and it's harder underneath. We get off in the ditch and it's just deep soft snow. We sink in too far."

"I'm sinking in too far now."

Scotty was using both hands on his stick, putting a lot of his weight on it. Once he yelled, "My arms is tired from holding me up."

"I'm tired all over."

The sun above the black overcast had long since gone down, and they were feeling their way through blackness. The storm was angry and intense and only rarely took sufficient respite to let the blowing snow settle around them. When it did, they found that somehow there was enough light to let them make out dim shapes—the eastern horizon sometimes, or a hill to the east, or each other, or a sagebrush left bare against the snow by the blowing wind. Then visibility would be obscured by another surge of that wind.

Jake said, "I wish we'd come to a hill."

"We're on one. Why do you want a hill?"

"I think we're on the level."

"We're on a hill," Scotty insisted. "Why do you want one?"

Jake did not answer at once. He stepped through the snow for almost a minute, twenty or thirty steps, before he said, "We have to go up a little hill and then partway down the other side to get to the turnoff to my place."

"We're going up a hill."

"It seems level to me."

"We're going up a hill."

They kept going, getting off the road again and picking their way back. Minutes went by. The wind roared. Once Scotty had to jerk the pole out of the snow to his left and jam it into the snow to his right to brace himself against a sudden increase in wind velocity and keep from being blown over. Jake simply stood in the snow, held upright by being wedged into it, and bowed to the right, letting the suddenly stronger wind blow over him. When it slackened he had to tuck his shirt back in on the left side. Wearing gloves, he made a sloppy job of it, and bits of snow blew under the shirt from time to time, the cold piercing his underwear to chill his sweaty skin.

Scotty said, "Now we're going downhill."

"How long?"

"We just started."

Jake moved on. Scotty said, "Is there only the one hill to go up and down? Is this the right one?"

Jake didn't answer. He continued walking. Scotty hurried, jabbing his stick into the snow and hopping to catch up. He said, "Did you hear me? Is there only the one hill?"

Jake shouted without turning around, "I'm counting."

He marched on, Scotty struggling to keep up. Jake was moving a little faster than he had before. He stopped and turned back.

"What did you say?"

"Is there only the one hill?"

"I don't know. It's the only one I ever noticed. If we're really going downhill, this should be it."

"Don't it feel like we're going downhill?"

"A little. I can't tell with that wind."

"What was you counting?"

"My steps. Come on. Let's get over to the side of the road."

Jake led the way. This time when he sank into the soft snow in the ditch he kept going. Scotty carefully followed him.

Jake said, "Let me have your stick."

He took the stick and jabbed it into the snow ahead of him, jabbed several times, moved forward three difficult steps and jabbed again.

"Whatcha looking for?"

"The fence." He took another step, continued to poke into the snow again and again. "There ain't no fence the other side of the turnoff. If there ain't no fence, we've gone too far."

He jabbed, paused, wiggled the stick, began digging with the end of the long stick. He withdrew it and turned back to Scotty—at the same time turning his face into the wind. He ducked his head and shut his eyes against the driving snow, then cautiously looked up. "I found the fence," he said. "We ain't to the turnoff yet. Let's go."

He gave Scotty's stick back to him and led him back to the road and along the road another hundred steps. "Let's take another look," he shouted to Scotty, and led him eastward again.

They moved cautiously, expecting to sink into deeper snow, but they did not. After twenty steps, Jake turned and shouted, "We ain't come to the ditch."

"What? I can't hear you for the wind."

Jake stepped into the teeth of the wind and came even with Scotty. He yelled close to his face, "I think we're on the cutoff to my place. It feels like there's still a road under us. We didn't get off the road into the ditch."

"How much further?" Scotty yelled.

"It's a mile from here if we're on the road."

"I don't feel like I can walk a mile."

"You got to."

Jake turned and started again. After four steps he stopped and turned back. Scotty hadn't moved. Jake beckoned to him. Scotty stayed where he was. Jake turned and walked back and grabbed Scotty by the shoulder. "Come on!" he said. "You can't stand around here!"

"I gotta rest. Let's find a place to rest."

"There ain't no place. Come on!"

After every few steps, Jake looked back to make certain Scotty was coming. He had to go back for him once.

"Come on, Scotty. It ain't so hard now. We got the wind behind us."

"Yeah, but the snow's deeper. Can't we rest?"

"We can rest when we get up to the house. It an't far. Come on."

The wind behind them made walking easier, but Jake could not turn around to check on Scotty without getting the wind's full force in the face. He would turn with his head bowed and slowly look up, blinking against the snow that was being blown furiously into his face.

And the snow was deeper. He could not lift his legs high enough to get his calves out of it. His walking was a form of floundering. He had to use his hands more and more to help clear a path for himself.

The wind suddenly died almost completely, and both men stopped in their tracks, breathing deeply in weariness and in relief at the moment of respite. Jake scanned the valley ahead of him, looking for a sign of buildings. He could see nothing except the snow lying all about and, far off in the east, a faint light differentiation that might indicate the horizon.

Scotty shouted, "Lookee there!"

Jake turned. "Where?"

Scotty was using his stick to point south, jabbing the air with the stick, excited. "There! Is that your house?"

Jake looked south and saw a shape in the darkness. Then the storm hit again and it was obscured.

Jake stood close to Scotty and shouted, "No, that ain't my house. That's a old broken-down cabin. That proves we're on the right path."

Scotty grabbed Jake by the lapel as Jake started to turn away. Scotty yelled, "Let's go over to that cabin and get warm."

"We ain't gonna get warm in that cabin. It ain't got no doors nor windows and it's full of holes. It's colder in there than it is out here walking."

"It's a place to rest."

"No it ain't. We only got three quarters of a mile to go to my house. And the first quarter mile of that is downhill all the way to the crick, just like it's been. And then there won't be so much snow."

"Why not?"

"'Cause they have to drive the cows down to the crick ever morning and ever night to let 'em drink. They'll have the snow tromped down. Come on!"

Jake turned, breaking Scotty's grip on his coat, and walked ahead four steps. He stopped and looked back. Scotty was following.

The snow hit Jake's face with stinging force whenever he looked back. The snow on the ground fought him at every step. But, step by step, he pushed through it, and every few steps he looked back. Scotty followed. Sometimes the driving snow all but hid them from each other when they were less than six feet apart, but there was always that shape.

The way became steeper. When they were close together Scotty yelled, "We're going downhill. Are you going to look for the turnoff?"

"We're past the turnoff."

"What?"

"Never mind."

"Jake!"

"What?"

"We got to go over to that house!"

"That ain't a house. Come on!"

Jake fell in one drift, it was so deep, and crawled through it, the snow rubbing along his shoulders. On the other side he pushed himself up, fell before he was upright, and scrambled to his feet again. He walked back through the drift to deepen the trail he had made.

He yelled to Scotty, "Be careful! Don't fall down! It's hard to get up again!"

He went back through the drift, looking back at Scotty at every step. He walked more slowly now, bracing himself against wind and soft snow and the possibility of falling.

His feet hit something slippery. He stopped, carefully advanced in tiny steps, then scraped around with his left foot.

"I'm on the ice!" he shouted to Scotty. "Here's the crick! It's another half a mile home!"

He took Scotty's elbow and helped steady both of them as they crossed the shallow, narrow creek. On the other side he plunged through drifts for several steps before Scotty's shout stopped him.

"Jake!"

Jake turned around. Scotty had barely crossed the creek. Jake said, "What?"

"There's a lot of snow over here."

"I know it."

"What?"

Jake lowered his head against the wind and walked back to Scotty. "I said I know there's a lot of snow."

"You said there wouldn't be none."

"I said there wouldn't be as much."

"But there's a lot."

"I thought the cows would tromp it down coming down to get water. I guess the wind blowed more snow here."

"The wind didn't blow that much snow. There ain't been no cows down here. The crick's froze over."

"Okay. There ain't been no cows. Come on."

"We ain't on the right road, Jake."

"Yes we are. Come on."

"Are you sure?"

"Yes, I'm sure."

Scotty looked at him. "I think we better go back to that cabin."

"No. We ain't got but half a mile to go. Come on."

Scotty looked around again. "Okay."

Jake turned and plunged forward, through the drift, up the hillside. He looked back. Scotty, looking over his shoulder once or twice, was following.

It was a struggle not to fall. Jake paused once, started to fall, caught himself, and moved on. The wind died abruptly. In the silence he yelled over his shoulder, "Don't stop walking! You might fall if you stop!" The wind hit again. He turned his back to it and kept going.

Jake was breathing heavily now, for the first prolonged time since they had begun. His chest and shoulders heaved. His breath came in great gulps and left in loud blowing puffs. He stumbled in a drift, caught himself, went on. His hands rested on his thighs as if pulling them up and pushing them down. In deep drifts his hands reached out to support him against the snow or to push it aside. In a trough where the snow was not deep he paused again, started to fall again, walked again.

The fury of the wind increased. Once the wind caught him off balance and threatened to knock him down, but he stayed on his feet. Even with the wind at his back he had to raise his hands sometimes to shield the sides of his face against blowing snow. When the wind suddenly stopped he jerked backward almost as if he would fall on his back.

The snow that had been whipped into the air by the wind settled in the sudden calm. And there, ahead of him, he saw a light. A square light—a light in a window.

His shout of joy mixed with a sob. "Scotty! There's a light! They ain't gone to bed yet! We're almost there!" Tears starting from his eyes, his fists clenched and raised face-high in joy, he turned to look at his companion.

But Scotty wasn't there.

CHAPTER TWENTY-SIX

"SCAW—TEEE!"

Jake roared the name once before the wind roared back, hitting him once again with its full force. It blew him backward, knocked him off balance. He jerked himself forward, still off balance and fighting to stay upright. He staggered in a circle, reeling as if drunk, fighting for headway in the drifted snow that was trying to trip him up. He looked back toward where he had seen the light. He could see no light. He turned the other way, braced himself, and yelled again, "SCAW—TEEE!"

Jake raised an arm to shield his face against the stinging snow being driven by the wind. Then, arm raised and head lowered, he headed back into the storm.

He could trace his own path through the drifts, although the wind had begun to fill it in with snow. By the time he reached the creek and crossed it, it was difficult to find his tracks. He had to break new trail back up the slope in the direction from which they had come. This time he was working into the teeth of the wind.

Twice he stopped and turned his back to the wind to get his breath. Both times he began to fall forward; both times he staggered, got his balance, turned and resumed his push.

"SCAW—TEEE!"

He repeated the forlorn bawling every few steps, turning his face in one direction or the other so he would not be yelling directly into the wind.

"SCAW—TEEE!"

The wind would not relent. The wind, or his weariness, kept him from following a straight course. He reeled into the chest-high wall of snow on his right, pushed through and away from it, tacked across toward the left, got straightened out for a few steps, and was off again on a crazy winding way.

"SCAW—TEEE!"

He swore through his teeth at the wind, and step by dragging step he struggled up the hill through the deepening snow against a wind that seemed to grow stronger by the minute.

"SCAW—TEEE!"

Jake looked often to the left, the south, but he could see no more in that direction than in any other. He tried pausing while facing into the wind, leaning against it, and again caught himself before he fell.

"SCAW—TEEE!"

His left hand, waving ahead of him in a floundering effort to move snow or keep balance or ward off wind, grazed across something hard. He lowered his hand, moved it again, and hit a post. He said out loud, "Fence," and turned to his right to get back on the road. But he stopped. He reached again for the post, found it, grabbed it with both hands, pulled.

It came free of the snow. He held it close to his face, turned in a little walking circle to put his back to the wind, felt the post and tried to see it.

"SCAW—TEEE! SCAAAWWW—TEEEEE!"

He was holding Scotty's walking stick.

He turned and put his right side to the wind and, using the stick to probe the snow and to support himself, he slowly began advancing south. The stick sank into deep snow, and he followed it, wallowing through the high soft drifts that had filled the ditch beside the road.

"SCAAAWWW—TEEEEE!"

It was progress made inches at a time. He stumbled, but the snow itself prevented a fall, and the stick helped.

"SCAW—TEEE!"

His foot came up slowly, dragged by snow and weariness; his knee pushed into the drift ahead; his toe dug in; the foot went down, found solidity beneath, supported him as he took another step.

"SCAAAWWW—TEEEEE!"

The stick was lifted out of the snow, poked ahead, pushed down into the snow at an angle. It hit something. Jake poked, probed, explored with the stick. It was finding the wires of a barbed-wire fence.

"SCAAAWWW—TEEEEE!"

He started to take another step.

"Jake?"

It sounded like a shout, but it sounded weak or far away.

"SCAW—tee!"

No response.

"SCAAAWWW—TEEEEE!"

"Jake!"

Jake turned to his left, his back to the wind again. He waved the stick slowly ahead of him. It encountered nothing but snow. He pushed forward two, three, difficult steps. He put the stick out ahead of him.

"Ouch! Hey!"

Jake withdrew the stick and tried, without success, to hurry the last few steps to Scotty. "Whatcha doing here?" he yelled.

"I'm caught in the fence."

"Let me see." Jake stuck the walking stick into the snow and grabbed Scotty by the shoulders. He ran his hands down Scotty's arms until Jake's right hand found the fence wire, just under the snow. He held it with his right hand and with his left followed Scotty's leg down until he found the second wire. Scotty's leg was between the wires.

Jake gripped the wires and pulled them apart.

"Ouch! You cut me!"

"I don't care. Pull your leg out of there. Watch yourself. Don't fall down."

He heard Scotty moving, felt Scotty's clothes brush against his face.

"Are you out?"

"I'm out."

Jake let go of the wires and reached for Scotty. He grabbed an arm and began pushing through the snow to get back to the road.

Scotty yelled, "We got to get to that cabin and keep warm."

"Forget that cabin. Come on!"

"We can't stay out in the storm."

"We was almost home and you turned around. We'd of been there by now if you'd stayed with me. Come on!"

Jake fought his way sideways through the deep snow of the borrow pit, hanging on to Scotty's arm and jerking him along behind.

"You're hurting my arm!"

"Come on!"

Jake worked himself out of the ditch and back onto the road. Three or four steps more and he turned sideways to the wind and began pulling Scotty down the road toward the creek.

"Don't pull on my arm!"

"Do you wanta walk beside me? Come on!"

Jake pulled Scotty up beside him. With his left hand, Jake reached across his own body and took a firm hold on Scotty's sleeve at the shoulder. He put his right arm around Scotty's back.

"You don't need to hang on to me."

"I'm gonna hang on to you until we get home. Come on!"

The wind was behind them again, pushing, for what good that did. Jake shifted his grip so he could help support Scotty's bad foot to some extent. Then they shifted again. Breaking a double trail was too much for them. Scotty dropped behind, and Jake walked now sideways, now backward, tugging on his arm.

"I need my stick."

"You should of thought of that when you throwed it away. Come on!"

"You tore my sleeve."

"I'll tear your arm if you don't keep moving. Come on!"

They gained the creek and, slipping a little on the ice, crossed it.

"I ain't sure I can make it up that hill."

"It ain't much of a hill. Come on!"

Jake let go with one hand, hanging on to Scotty's cuff with the other as he leaned into the slope and the snow and struggled to take step after step after step up from the creek. He lost his hold once and turned so fast he almost fell down; he grabbed Scotty's arm, fell against him, and they both staggered.

"Don't fall down!" Jake yelled. "Don't fall down! We can't get up again!" They balanced themselves, and Jake started walking backward, pulling on Scotty's arm. "Come on!"

The wind quieted once and Jake looked about him, but he saw no light. He paused a moment for breath, began to fall, started walking again. "Come on!"

The fresh onslaught of the snow stung his face, staggered Scotty, but they stayed upright. Jake turned his face away from the snow but walked sideways, always gripping Scotty's arm.

"Let's rest a minute."

"No! Come on!"

"I can't walk no more!"

"Well, I can't carry you! Come on!"

There was a trough and for a few steps the walking was almost easy. Then they were once again waist-deep in snow.

"My foot hurts, Jake! My foot hurts bad!"

"Good! I'm glad it hurts! I wish it hurt worse! Come on!"

An extra fury of wind tore up the snow around them violently. Scotty came to a complete stop. Jake yanked on him and lost his grip. In spite of the snow in which he was wedged, the force of the pull against no resistance made Jake stumble, and he staggered a few floundering steps in a circle, trying to stay upright and to get back to Scotty. The two collided, and Jake gripped Scotty in his arms. When he started going again he continued to hold Scotty in an embrace, pulling him along.

"Come on!"

Scotty was breathing heavily. Jake was breathing hard and crying a little.

"Come on, Scotty! Come on!"

"Jake, let me rest."

"Come on!"

Scotty kept moving his feet, but more and more he let his weight rest on Jake. Jake was moving backward now, struggling to carry his comrade, catching the wind full in the face when he forgot to duck away from it.

"Come on, Scotty."

He stopped crying. There was not enough energy left to cry. His shoulders slumped and his arms almost lost their hold, but he tightened his grip and pulled.

"Come on!" He was panting the words, not shouting them.

Scotty said something, mumbled it.

"What? Come on. What'd you say?"

Scotty mumbled, "There's a light."

Jake looked over his shoulder. Even through the blowing snow now he could see, faintly, a light.

"That's my house!" His voice rose in joy. "I told you we was almost there!" There was a tinge of hysteria to his shouting, and the tears had started again. "Ain't they gonna be surprised to see us! Come on!"

He tried to quicken his pace and was almost dragging Scotty with him. "The door's right over there. Come on!"

He had taken on almost all of Scotty's weight now. Scotty barely moved his legs, but Jake, staggering and straining, hugged him close and pulled.

"Ain't they gonna be surprised! I ain't gonna just walk in! I'm gonna knock on the door and when they open the door we'll just stand there and say, 'Howdy, folks. We thought we'd drop in and visit!' Come on!"

They broke through one last belly-high drift. It stopped them for a moment, but Jake regathered himself and threw his weight against it, dragged Scotty through it, broke free into knee-deep snow on the far side.

"I can see the house! Come on!"

A last few, straining, dragging, puffing steps, and Jake's foot found the doorstep. "Come on!" He mounted the step, dragged Scotty up, raised his left foot to the doorsill, and leaned against the door. He braced himself, lugged Scotty up to a standing position, and clung to him in a tight embrace.

"We're there," he puffed. He balanced on his right foot and, with his left, kicked the door as hard as he could four times.

Then the strength drained from him. He slumped against the door. Scotty sagged in his arms. Jake's shoulder began to slip down the door, inch by inch toward the stoop. When Jerry opened the door, they both collapsed toward it and through it and fell in a crumpled heap on the front-room floor.

CHAPTER TWENTY-SEVEN

Jerry and Jeff and Mama and Papa were still up. They dragged Jake and Scotty into the house and shut the door. They helped them get close to the fire, and they took off their coats. Their caps and trousers, like their coats, were white with the snow that had been plastered onto them by the wind. Mama got a towel and wiped the snow from Jake's face. Jeff built up the fire to roaring heat.

Mama still had soup simmering on the kitchen stove. They called it soup. A little meat, some potatoes and carrots and cabbage and turnips and water. Lots of water. They helped the young men spoon some of it down. Both emptied their bowls and about finished their second helpings.

But both needed help to sit up straight and to eat. Someone brought two sets of long underwear and Jerry and Jeff helped them take off their wet clothes and dry off with a towel and put on the clean underwear. By that time Mama had put extra covers on her own bed and moved the baby into the front room. Mama slept on the front-room couch and Papa went out to the lean-to to sleep with the boys. They let Jake and Scotty sleep in their bed, with the door to the front room open, and twice in the night someone came in to build up the fire.

When Jake awoke, he was alone in the bed and it was daylight. The door to the front room was closed. The bed was high and wide and very comfortable. He had both pillows under his head and shoulders, and he was covered with blankets and quilts. There was a fragrance of wood and powder and shoe leather in the air, overlaid with a faint odor of cooking. It was warm under the covers, but the sheets felt cool and good.

He lay quietly, looking for a long time at the ceiling, then around the room at the dresser, the mirror, the closet with his father's and mother's clothes hanging in it, the bedroom with the blind pulled down and the curtains closed, but the brown light shining through.

The door opened quietly, almost stealthily, and Scotty's head appeared. Scotty looked toward the bed.

Jake said, "Howdy."

Scotty came into the bedroom and quietly shut the door behind him. He walked to the bed and looked down at Jake. Scotty walked with a limp, and his injured foot was thickly wrapped in white sheeting. The wrapping was tied with strips of a torn white sheet. He stood on his good foot with a hand on the brass bedstead to help support him.

Scotty said, "How you feeling?"

"Wore out."

"You sure slept a long time."

"What time is it?"

"Three in the afternoon."

"I was up a couple times in the night to use the pot."

"Ya, I heard you," Scotty said, "but you sure slept."

"Looks like you got up in time for dinner."

Scotty grinned. "Heck, I got up in time for breakfast. I ain't never slept through a meal in my life. I slept some after breakfast, though." His face grew sober again and he studied Jake for a moment. "Are you sick or anything?"

"No, I'm just plumb tired."

"I guess you would be." Scotty heaved a deep sigh. "What you gonna do now?"

"Lay here a while. I ain't rested yet."

"I mean whatcha gonna do about them posts and such?"

"Oh." Now Jake looked up closely at his friend's face. "I guess I won't do nothing for a few days. Get rested up and figure out how to get new stuff for what we lost. Wait for them to start using the roads again. When they get the roads open for sleighs, I guess we might as well go back up and clean out that dugout and get back to work."

Scotty looked at his injured foot and said, "I ain't going back up."

"Oh?"

He looked at Jake. "It ain't cause you hit me nor nothing like that. We're still friends as far as I'm concerned. I guess I'm just a little scared. I was lucky to get out of there this time, I reckon, and I don't want to push my luck any by going back."

"Ya, I see." Jake looked at the ceiling for a time and Scotty shared the silence. Then Jake said, "Well, I have a pretty good count on the posts. I'll keep track of how many you cut, and when I sell them I'll give you your share of the money."

"I'll be glad to get it."

"I'll take out for your share of the groceries."

"Fine. I figured on that."

Jake twisted in bed, trying to see Scotty's foot. He asked, "How's your foot?"

"It hurts some. I sprained it pretty good. Your ma wrapped it up real good. It sure is swoll. I'll be settin' in the rocker for a few days while Ma chops the wood."

"It ain't broke or nothing, huh?"

"I don't think so. It don't feel broke and your folks couldn't find no sign it was broke. They're pretty good horse doctors, I figure, so I guess I'll be okay once I let her heal."

"That's good."

Scotty said, "I sure didn't think we was gonna make it all the way."

"Is that why you throwed away your stick?"

"Throwed away?"

"Your walking stick."

"I didn't know I did."

"You left it sticking in the snow."

Scotty shrugged. "I don't remember."

"Well, it's good you did. I wouldn't of found you."

Scotty licked his lips. "I want to thank you. I sure appreciate what you done."

"What was that?"

"You saved my life. Saved it a couple of times. Thanks."

"Well, don't spread it around none. I've got few enough friends as it is."

Scotty said, "Are you hungry or anything? Your ma made some real good chicken for dinner. I can bring you some of that if you want."

"Naw, I don't want to eat just now. I druther lie here and rest some more."

"Okay."

"Say, I'm glad you knowed we was on a hill last night. If you hadn't told me that, I wouldn't of knowed to turn off. I'd of kept on going clear to Holbrook. Or tried to. I wouldn't of made it."

Scotty laughed a little. "I don't remember that neither. I guess I was pretty much in a daze."

Jake said, "I might come ask you to help me haul them posts in the spring."

"Okay, if I ain't shearing sheep or nothing. Tell you what, though. I've got to go now."

"Go where?"

"Old man Smith come over to buy a heifer off your dad, and he says he'll give me a ride on his sleigh out to my place. So I better get out there before he decides to go."

"It'll be good you can see your folks again."

"Ya."

"I'll see you in the spring, then." Jake stuck his hand out toward Scotty.

Scotty shook hands with him and said, "If not sooner."

Scotty left. Jake lay quietly in the bed for another half hour, dozing a little, looking at the ceiling and the drawn window blinds.

When Jake came into the front room, Jimmy Junior was playing on the floor and Jeff was in the rocker, holding Julia in his lap and reading to her.

Jake had one blanket wrapped around him and carried another blanket and a pillow. He looked around the room. Jimmy didn't seem to notice him. Julia was absorbed in her book. Jeff looked up and gave a little nod of greeting but kept on reading.

Jake walked barefoot across the room, taking short, slow, stiff steps. He sat on the couch, arranged the pillow at one end, and shook out the blanket he was carrying to its full size. Lying on the couch and pulling one blanket over him, he wiggled around until he had loosened the blanket that was wrapped around him and could lie comfortably on the couch.

Jeff finished what he was reading and closed the book. He said, "How you feeling?"

"Tired."

"Scotty was telling us you had to do all the work of breaking trail."

"Ya."

Jeff said to Julia, "You get down now, honey. I got to go help Jerry do some shoveling."

Julia slid down off Jeff's lap and trotted over to Jake. "Did you bring us more stick candy like you did the last time?" she asked.

It made Jake laugh, although the laugh was barely audible. "No, honey, they don't sell stick candy out where we was. That's only in Malad and Holbrook."

"That's okay," she said. She leaned over him and put her arms around his neck and gave him a big hug and a damp kiss on the cheek. He gripped her shoulder gently in one hand and shook her affectionately. "I'm glad you're home," she said.

"Me too."

She disengaged herself and trotted into the kitchen, saying, "Jake's awake."

Jeff had already gone into the kitchen. Jake watched Jimmy Junior playing on the floor near the heater with the farm set Jeff and Jerry had made. He herded cows and rode horses and plowed ground, lost in the world of his imagination.

Jake heard the back door open and close as Jeff went out. Janet came into the front room from the kitchen. She said, "Hi, Jake."

"Howdy."

She walked through the room and went into the bedroom. Joe came in from the kitchen.

"Scotty said you almost got lost in the snow."

"Something like that."

"I wouldn't want to go out in the storm like that."

"Me neither."

Joe stood over him, looking down at him. "Want me to get you something?"

"No."

"If you need something, just holler."

"Thanks." Jake reached out to him, squeezed his forearm. Joe went back into the kitchen.

Jake heard the back door open and close again and heard Jerry's voice and the stamping of Jerry's feet as he got the snow off himself and tried to get warm after his work outside.

Janet came back into the front room from the bedroom. She carried a doll and a sheet of paper. She was aglow with a smile, and she looked at the doll all the way across the room until she was standing by Jake.

"Look what I got." She handed the doll to Jake.

He took it and held it in both hands while he examined it. "I think I seen her somewhere before," he said.

"Your friend sent her to me."

"What friend?"

"Maxine."

"How do you know her?"

"Read this," Janet said. She handed Jake the sheet of paper. He gave back the doll and took the paper.

"Dear Janet," said the letter. "I am getting ready to move away from the house where I have lived all my life (so far), so there are a lot of things to put away, throw away, or give away if I don't want to take them with me.

"My friend Amanda has been my favorite doll since I was a little girl. I can't take her with me, but I certainly don't want to throw her away. My friend Jake told me that he has a sister named Janet, and Amanda and I talked it over and decided to ask you if you could take care of Amanda from now on. If you don't want to, please send her back to me. I want her to have a *good home*. The way Jake talks about you makes me think you are a nice girl and will be kind to her.

"Amanda will be very good company. Many times, she and I have sat in the window seat of my bedroom, sharing our secrets and watching the world happen at our feet. I hope you will enjoy her.

"Say hello to Jake, and please take good care of Amanda.

"Your friend,
"Maxine Griffeth."

Jake read the letter a second time, then handed it back. "That's nice," he said.

"She's a beautiful doll."

"Yes, she is."

"Maxine must be a very nice lady."

"Yes, she is. You'd like her."

"Oh, I do like her. I just love my doll."

Jake put his hand on Janet's waist and squeezed her gently. "I'm glad you got the doll."

"Me too." Janet carried the letter and the doll to the rocker and sat down. She folded the letter and put it into an apron pocket and sat rocking her doll, singing to it under her breath, adjusting its clothing minutely with the tip of an index finger.

Julia scampered in and stood with her hands on her knees, watching Jimmy Junior play.

"Whatcha doing, Jimmy Junior?"

"I'm playing."

"Oh." Julia watched a little longer, then trotted over to watch Janet and to caress Amanda carefully.

Jerry came in. "How you feeling?"

"Some better."

"I opened the door last night and you fell on me. That don't seem like much of a way to say hello to your brother."

"I'll try to do better next time."

"Whatcha gonna do now?"

"You mean about the posts?"

"Ya."

"After I round up some clothes and blankets and dishes and one thing and another and somebody gets the road open, I guess I'll go back up and clean out that dugout and get back to work."

"I was figuring you would."

"Want to come help?"

"Oh, no. I ain't gonna get stuck out there in no snowbank. That's for tougher guys than me. Say, speaking of clothes—can I wear your dress pants tomorrow night?"

"They got burned up."

"Darn. I got a date for the dance and I wanted to look my best."

"If you want to look your best, stay home. The further you are from the dance floor, the better you look."

"Next time, I'll throw you back in the snow."

Jerry laughed and went back to the kitchen. Jake watched the three younger children and began to doze.

A noise awakened him. He opened his eyes and saw his father standing beside the couch looking down at him.

"You awake?" Papa asked.

"Ya."

Papa sat down carefully on the edge of the couch. "Scotty says you had a pretty hard trip yesterday."

"It about done me in."

"I'm glad you made it. I sure would hate to lose one of you kids." Papa put a hand on Jake's arm.

Jake said, "We thought when we crossed the crick we'd have it easier. I figured the cows would have the snow packed down better. It sure was deep."

"Oh. Jeff found a twin pinion over to Blaisdell's, and we fixed the windmill. We been watering the stock in the corral. We ain't took them to the crick in a couple of weeks."

"Oh."

Papa patted Jake's shoulder absently, then withdrew his hand. "I been thinking," he said, "that there warn't no good reason for me not to sign them papers for you. You might as well go ahead and buy that truck."

Jake's face did not change expression. He looked at his father for a long moment before replying. "That truck wouldn't of done me no good yesterday. In the first place, I wouldn't of even had it with me up to camp. I'd of left it home. In the second place, I couldn't of drove it through all that snow if I'd had it."

Papa shook his head. "Oh, it ain't got nothing to do with yesterday. I been thinking about this ever since you left. There's no reason for me to do all the worrying I do. You're dependable. You'll pay for the truck. You seem to do what you set out to do." He gripped his son's shoulder and shook him gently, and smiled a little. "So if you want to, you send over to Malad and get another set of them papers, and I'll sign them."

Jake said, "I never throwed away the old set. They're out in my dresser drawer."

"Well, when you feel up to it you go get them and I'll sign them."

"Thanks, Papa."

"Is there anything you need before I go outside? Are you hongry or anything?"

Jake stretched and yawned. "Ya, I guess I am some hungry. I wouldn't mind having a piece of that chicken."

"What chicken?"

"Scotty said Mama made some real good chicken for dinner."

"Oh, that warn't chicken. That was rabbit. I guess Scotty don't know the difference. I'll get you a piece of that."

Jake grinned. "I hope you give Scotty the gizzard."

"What? Rabbits don't have gizzards. You know that."

Jake said, "It's a kind of a joke. I'll tell you about it at supper."

Papa said, "Okay. While you're at it, you might tell us what happened yesterday. Scotty tried, but there was a lot he couldn't remember."

"Okay." Jake laughed a weak, two-syllable laugh. "Someday I'm gonna tell that story to my grandkids," he said, "and if they don't cry, I'm gonna lick 'em."

ABOUT THE AUTHOR

Dwight Jensen was born at Malad, Idaho, in 1934 and spent the first two and a half years of his life at Holbrook. His father had been born and raised at Holbrook; his grandfather, who was born in Denmark and came to the United States as a child, moved to the area early in the twentieth century and was a farmer there until he moved away in 1939.

Both father and grandfather wound up taking their families to Oxford, Idaho, just across the mountain from Malad, and Dwight spent most of his childhood there. He returned to Holbrook just after his high school graduation to work on one of the dry farm wheat ranches in the area.

As a fourth grader, he attended a one-room school of the type mentioned in this book, and his mother taught at several such schools in southeastern Idaho.

Dwight Jensen attended Idaho State College, taught school, served in the U. S. Army, and became a journalist, doing most of his work in Idaho. He was a columnist, reporter, editor, and television anchorman in Boise before beginning to concentrate on creative writing. This is his first novel.